Not For Small Minds

I0666991

Aaron Rosenberg

CRAZY 8 PRESS

Mary looks—well, worried. "This is Planet 4593 of the Virulga system," she informs me, and I know she's consulting the galactic database the Grays downloaded into her head when they first modified her to work for them. "Also known as Obscura Major by some races. And by the Grays"—she sighs, and it's full of fear and anxiety—"as Prime." She turns to face me. "This is their homeworld."

"This?" I frown and take a second look. Nope, still nothing but rock. "What, do they all live underground or something? And leave the surface for parking? Or the future site of the universe's largest food court?"

She shakes her head. "I have never been here before, but I have heard tales from other travelers of this world. Of its soaring towers, its majestic arches, its sweeping bridges, its long, sloping lanes." Her voice dips a little. "And of the Quantum Singularity, the wellspring of energy around which all of their technologies are based. In truth, I have always longed to behold that for myself, but had not yet been granted such an honor."

The problem is, there's nothing here to see. No towers, no arches, no bridges, no lanes, no singularity—and no Grays. They've up and left, closed up shop and taken the whole store with them.

It's like if we'd just found the *Mary Celeste*, only this time there's nothing but empty water, a scrap of old sail, and a dip in the water where the boat should be.

For Jenifer, Adara, and Arthur, who are my world—
and that's no small thing

With thanks to Bob, Mary, Russ, Dave, and Steve
for their feedback and their friendship

Chapter One
"Getting grilled" isn't just an expression!

"Mary, come on, we're gonna be late," I call out. But about as loud as you'd shout, "I'm a pharmaceuticals rep!" at a "We Hate Big Pharm!" demonstration. Which is to say, about as quietly as I can and still have the words emerge from my bill.

It's not that I don't want to go. I do. And I want Mary to go with me. Of course.

But I think I may be a masochist, so I can hardly trust my own judgment, can I?

Of course she hears me. Why is that when I'm trying to make myself heard, half the time it's like I'm wrapped in the Cone of Silence—which had better be a chocolate-covered waf-flecone, because otherwise what's the point?—but if I'm trying to be quiet I'm likely to wind up being broadcast on the news? So I can't say I'm totally surprised when the bedroom door opens and my ladylove calls out, "My apologies, my love. I was endeav-oring to attire myself in something appropriate for the gather-ing we are about to attend. Did I accomplish this successfully?"

The pose she strikes is classic "come-hither"—framed in the open doorway, one hand resting high up against the frame, the other at her hip, leaning her head against her upraised arm, those big sapphire-blue eyes batting at me like, "What, you like?" She's wearing one of my Mets jerseys, but tied just below her awe-inspiring chest, and a pair of my old jeans she's cut off at mid-thigh, cinched tight around her waist with a web belt. She's got on a pair of still-new hightops—her own, it's not like mine'd fit her unless she was in a car and parked inside one!— and her long, dark hair's pulled back in a simple braid, with a Mets cap perched atop it.

Baseball has never looked this good.

"You look amazing, babe," I tell her, and my reward is a big, beautiful smile. When we first met I thought maybe Mary's face had been sculpted from plastic, both because her features were so perfect and because she barely seemed to show emotion, but I later realized that was just because 1) she was focused on the task at hand (and yeah, maybe saving the universe was important enough to not giggle a bit), and 2) she's actually a bit shy at first and didn't know any of us from Adam (even she and Ned had only met once or twice, and only on the job). Now that we've been together for a bit, though, she's got no reserves from me, which means I get treated to things like smiles so sunny you might need lotion against 'em and pouts so deadly the last time I just handed her all my bank info and computer passwords so she wouldn't need to try getting anything else out of me.

"Your family will approve?" she asked, abandoning the doorway—which I'm pretty sure just sighed sadly as she left it!— and crossing to join me. The way she's biting her lower lip and tugging absently at her braid, I can tell she's nervous. Which is funny, seeing as how we've faced down all kinds of threats together and she's barely blinked. But I guess it's less stressful saving the universe than meeting your boyfriend's family.

"Yeah, they'll definitely approve," I promise her, scooping up my keys, wallet, and Metrocard from the little dish on the table by the front door. "Don't worry about that." I'm certainly not. I can't imagine they won't fall instantly in love with Mary.

It's their reaction to me I'm never quite sure about.

"Right, time to get a move on," I tell her, and tug the door open, gesturing her out into the hall. Still not totally used to having a pad here in Manhattan—I keep expecting to see the area around the Matrix when I do that. Not that most New Yorkers would look all that out of place at the center of the galaxy, or be that phased by what they saw there. Most of 'em would probably just ask about the rent, what kind of food was available for delivery, and how long the subway ride was to downtown.

That last one might be a bit of a deal breaker, though. At least, for your average Joe.

"I still do not understand why we do not simply teleport there," Mary is saying as she lets me usher her out and waits while I lock up behind us. "I could place us a block from your mother's house, to ensure no one saw us arrive in that fashion." She could, too—Mary's got a real knack for the Greys' teleportation system, pretty much pinpoint accuracy. Me, I've got a key fob that lets me go back and forth from the Matrix to my apartment—used to be to Grand Central but we changed that once I got this place—which is all I really need. She's always off on missions for the Grays, though, so she's got unlimited access to the system.

We're not using it, though. Not this time. "Can't take the risk," I remind her. "Low profile, remember?" None of my family know anything about the whole Matrix thing, and I'm not allowed to tell them. One of the Grays' rules, for security. "Besides, this way you get to see some of the city."

She smiles and pats my hand, then slides one arm around my waist. "That I am looking forward to," she admits, and we saunter down the hall together, arms around each other. That's one of the ways you know you've found the right person, if you can actually walk while holding each other. Not as easy as it looks, but Mary and I manage it perfectly, despite her having a few inches on me height-wise and my having feet the size of old Cadillacs and a head the size of the Hindenberg.

Ain't love grand?

Ninety minutes or so later, we're exiting the LIRR station at Little Neck. The family home is just up the street here, near the top of the hill. I lead the way.

Last time I was out here, Ma'd called because three wise-guys from Ned's homeworld had turned up to lean on her in order to get me to back off from investigating what was happening on their planet. Ha, saying it like that, it sounds like some cheeseball TV show from the Eighties, like the one with the kid and his grandpa in the old camper van or the one about the alien with the pendant and the three different colors and powers. Like *Tales of DuckBob* or some such.

Yeah, I'd watch that.

Anyway, I'm a little wary as a result, but don't see anything out of the ordinary on our uphill trek. There's old Mr. Baumgarten across the street, peering at us through a gap in his living room curtains, but that's to be expected. When I was a kid, if Ma needed to know when one of us has left or gotten home, all she had to do was go ask the neighbor—he kept better tabs on us than Homeland Security. I keep half-expecting him to set up some kind of sentry station at our front door and demand proof of identity before he'll let us into our own house.

Right now, though, we're not going in. Instead I lead Mary around the side to where a six-foot gate blocks access to the back. "You ready?" I ask her. "If you wanna turn around and hightail it out of here, you know I won't judge."

She gulps a little, but then straightens and gives me a firm nod. "I am ready."

I can't help but smile at that. Then I unlatch the gate and push it open, letting a wave of sound wash over us like the jetwash from a big commercial plane. "Okay, here we go," I declare, taking her hand and leading her down the path toward the backyard.

We don't even get all the way past the house before a small blonde bullet comes hurtling toward me. I swear, Lizzy's got me chipped. Either that or she conned Ned into giving her access to the GPS in my headset. I wouldn't put it past her. "Uncle Bob!" she shouts, wrapping both arms around me and squeezing so hard I'm glad I decided not to go for that last breath mint on the way. "You're here!" She's also mastered the art of ducking under my bill as she goes in for the hug, so I don't wind up braining her. Which is good, because I like my favorite niece just the way she is.

"I am?" I say, stopping and releasing Mary's hand long enough to wrap both arms around Lizzy in return. "Are you sure? I could have sworn I was in Boise."

She groans and lets go long enough to step back and turn toward Mary. "Hi, I'm Lizzy," she announces, holding out her hand. "I'm his favorite." She tells everybody that—it's true, of course, but I wish she wouldn't announce it. At least, not to her sister and the other relatives.

"I am Mary," my lady replies, accepting the hand and shaking firmly. "I am his girlfriend." She beams down at Lizzy—they've got maybe a foot difference in height—in a way that says, "I know you are his favorite, and I have no intention of trying to muscle in there, as long as you treat me with respect, too."

I'm guessing Lizzy reads it the same way I do—hey, we're family, we share enough genes and enough books that it makes sense—'cause she laughs. The next thing I know, she's hugging Mary, too. "I like you," she states. Then she glances over at me and gives me a big thumbs-up.

Cheesy, I know, but the fact that Lizzy approves has me all teary-eyed already. On the list of relatives I want to impress, she's right near the top.

Just below the woman now barreling toward us. The one who gave me birth—fortunately, long before the whole duckbill, or she probably wouldn't like me nearly as much.

"There you are, Robert!" Ma declares. She gives me a hug too, though a little more cautiously than Lizzy. Ma doesn't have quite the same hand-eye coordination, and the first time or two she got the concussions to prove it. "And you must be Mary," she says, turning to give my gal the hairy eyeball.

"Yes," Mary confirms. "It is a pleasure to meet you. Thank you so much for inviting me." She holds out the package she's been carrying. "I did not know what to bring, but I hope this is acceptable."

Ma takes the bag, reaches in, and pulls out a bakery box from Veniero's. No need to ask what's inside—they have the best cannoli in the city, which means by default the best outside Italy and maybe Chicago, though that's a tough call. And one I'd be happy to officiate. "Thank you," Ma says, beaming. "That's sweet of you. Come on back and meet everybody else." She doesn't say anything else, but pats me on the cheek as she passes, which is at least an "okay, she's got high marks so far, but jury's still out."

I'll take it.

The next person I see is Harold, who's manning the grill. He's wearing an apron that says "I'm not in charge but at least I get to play with fire," and truer words were never written. The happiest I've ever seen the man are when he's out hunting and when he's grilling. An attitude like that, it's a wonder he's not on some watchlist somewhere, but I'm pretty sure he's the one family member who isn't. Unlike Ma, who might've been fine if not for those letters she kept sending our local rep, warning him that, "she knew where he slept and where his wife shopped for fish every Wednesday." Which is also true, but not something you should really put into writing.

My view of Harold is eclipsed by a small mountain that's

suddenly lurched into my path, and I glance up—and up. "Hey, Andy," I tell him. He grins down at me and reaches around to pound me on the back, which is dangerous when you're as front-heavy as I am. "This is Mary," I gasp out, gesturing toward her while I struggle to remind my lungs that now would be a really good time to quit loafing about and start working again. "Mary, my nephew Andy."

Andy smiles at her—he looks a little smitten, which I totally understand—but then he frowns. "I know you," he says, his voice as quiet as his footsteps are loud, and those register on the Richter scale. "That mix-up a few months back."

Damn. Andy's so quiet, and so big, you forget sometimes that the kid's not dumb. Not by a longshot. I'm sure Lizzy remembered seeing Mary before too, but chose not to say anything about it. They'd all met her, in fact, back when I dragged them to Ned's world to help stop the invaders from taking over our reality again. But we had to wipe everybody's memories afterward—the Grays let them remember there'd been some kind of fight, and that I'd been crucial to its success, but that was about it.

"We did meet then, yes," Mary agrees. "It is nice to see you again."

We're rescued from any awkward questions about what exactly happened by the arrival of Andy's dad, Grant, who throws an arm around my shoulders in one of those effortless cool-guy hugs he's always been good at and I struggled for years to master but never managed. More often than not I'd wind up just dislocating people's necks, which is why I stopped. Grant's wife, Reynata, is right behind him, as is Bonnie. "Hey, little bro," he tells me, tugging affectionately. "'Bout time you showed up! And brought your girl out to meet us!" He offers his hand. "I'm Grant."

"Mary," she replies. "A pleasure." She hits him with a half-power smile, which is still enough to blind most people. "DuckBob speaks often of you, and fondly." Her glance goes to the blonde Valkyrie now sidling up on my other side. "And you must be Bonnie."

"Caught in the act," Bonnie agrees easily, linking her arm with mine. "Nice to finally meet you. The kid here hasn't said much—which, for him, is pretty significant—but what he has speaks volumes." Somehow Bonnie pivots so that she's perpendicular to me, and loops her other arm through Mary's, easy as you please. "Now, what say we get you some grub, a drink or two, and give you a chance to eat before you have to face the rest of the crowd?"

Mary laughs. "This seems sound strategic advice," she confirms, her smile widening to three-quarters strength. "Thank you." And she lets herself be led out into the backyard and toward the trestle table that's already groaning a bit under the weight of all the food piled onto it.

Or that could be my stomach, making its own interests known at the sight of all that food. In which case my digestion has learned how to throw its voice. That could be fun at restaurants, though I foresee problems the next time I'm doing a late-night snack run. Especially if it learns to form coherent sentences: "I want Ring Dings!" "Jasper, did you say something?"

"And tacos! And chocolate-covered pretzels! Post-haste!" "But, Jasper, you hate chocolate, and you're allergic to corn!"

I could be a big hit at dinner parties, though. Or at least I'll be able to provide my own distraction while I scarf down all the tiramisu.

Chapter Two
A little on the slow side

An hour later, we've had some food—okay, a lot of food, my family has always been a big believer in stuffing its collective face—and some drinks and Mary's met just about everybody. Which means that she's:

- Been hit on by Ed, and none too subtly;
- Been glared at by Caitlyn, Ed's wife, as if it was Mary's fault;
- Been hit on my cousin Sue Louise, so blatantly it almost made Ed look subtle;
- Been propositioned by Frank and Jimmy, also not subtly but about money for one of their get-rich-quick schemes rather than for sex, though I'm sure they'd have gotten around to that one too if I hadn't rescued her in time;
- Been addressed cattily by Tina, Lizzy's old sister, who doesn't do well with not being the brightest and prettiest around. Of course, that's made her life a bit difficult, since Lizzy's been outshining her since she was born, but Tina's unpleasant enough that it's tough to feel sorry for her;

- Been ogled but discretely and chatted up a little by Joe, Matt, and Marty—yes, Marty, too;
- Been spoken to by Harold, in his usual mild, inoffensive way;
- Been used as a pillow by Aunt Arlene, who passed out while standing there chatting—fortunately Uncle Joe saw it coming and snatched her tankard and plate as she dropped, or things would have been a whole lot messier;
- Been entertained by Grant, Bonnie, Lizzy, and even Andy;

Now, however, she's facing the toughest gauntlet of all—Ma.

"So, what exactly do you do for a living, Mary? Ma asks, plopping herself down in the chair she just dragged over directly in front of where Mary, Grant, Bonnie, Lizzy, and I are all sitting. "You work at the same call center as Robert?"

Mary frowns ever so slightly and shakes her head, causing the braid to whip about. "I am employed by the same parent company," she answers slowly, "but not in the same capacity. My work activities involve negotiating with clients and assisting to overcome any operational difficulties." Which is more or less true—the Grays use Mary as a scout, a translator, a diplomat, and a troubleshooter. All rolled together into one lovely package.

"Sounds like you travel a lot," Ma says next. "No plans to settle down?" The words "and start a family" are hovering so clearly on the tip of her tongue it's a wonder they don't clink up against her front teeth.

Mary just shrugs. I love it when she shrugs. Or sighs. Or takes a deep breath. Or... "I do travel a great deal," she agrees.

"It is one of the reasons I accepted this career, so that I might see many places I could not visit on my own." Yeah, like the Horsehead Nebula. "I have no desire to give it up at present, or to curtail my mobility." She smiles at me and links her hand with mine. "But I return as frequently as I am able. I have an excellent reason to do so."

The sight of Mary's obvious affection for me softens Ma up a bit. She's just looking out for her little boy, after all. Still, that doesn't stop her from asking, "And you don't have a problem with…" she gestures at my face.

There's a subtle collective intake of breath all around us. After my "change," Ma did her best to pretend it had never happened. Most of the time she won't even mention it, and she still insists upon calling me "Robert" rather than "DuckBob." But yeah, obviously my looks are the thousand-pound duck in the room, and there's no getting around the question of why any girl, much less one as brainy and gorgeous as Mary, would want to settle for a feathered shmoe like me.

Mary only smiles more, though. "What would I possibly object to?" she asks. "Your son is one of the kindest people I know, and, in his particular style, one of the cleverest. He is loyal and brave and funny and sweet, and…"—her voice dips an octave or two, sending a delightful little shiver up my spine and into certain other areas as well—"…he is a delight to all of my senses."

I think Ma's eyes are about to pop out of her head. For a woman who birthed practically a whole litter—though spread out over a dozen years—and has something on the order of two dozen kids and grandkids, she's still awfully prudish when it comes to talking about certain things.

Then Grant laughs—not meanly, just in that "that's awesome!" way he has. And Bonnie joins in. So does Lizzy. You know how sometimes you can tell when someone's laughing at you, and sometimes it's just as clear they're laughing with you? This has the latter hung all about it in light-up letters ten miles high, and I'm getting teary again. This is my family, the best of them, and they couldn't have shown their approval of Mary more if they'd offered her their house keys or the last slice of pie.

Not that they'd do the latter. In my family, you've gotta earn that one.

Finally, Ma smiles too, though hers is a little more strained. "Well, I'm glad to hear that," she says carefully. "I always tell my kids it's important to find someone who appreciates you for you." What she actually says is "it's important to find someone who appreciates you enough to give you a good alibi, or at least post bail, because Lord knows I can't keep doing that," but I guess it's close enough.

I lean back a little, really relaxing for the first time since even before we arrived—

—which is right when a stuffed mushroom comes flying out of nowhere and bonks me on the bill.

Oh, goody, I think. Here we go again.

But, I catch and swallow the mushroom, of course. No sense letting good food go to waste.

Then there's a small, wire-taut figure marching toward me across the lawn, as other relatives scramble to get out of the way.

Lila was always good at carving her own path. Usually through the flesh of those foolish enough to oppose her.

"I thought I'd find you here," she states, coming to a halt between Ma and me and glaring down at me with both hands on her hips. She's got a big black messenger bag slung across her, and I eye it warily. The last time I saw that bag she was pulling her trademark pink baseballs out of it and using them to clock attacking mooks. I'm worried that this time I get to be the target dummy.

"Hey, Lila," I tell her. "Lila, this is my girlfriend, Mary. Mary, this is my favorite little sister, Lila."

Mary stands and offers her hand. "I am very happy to make your acquaintance," she states. "I remember you and your formidable skill with the baseball."

"Yeah?" That distracts Lila a second, which is a feat unto itself, since she's got laser focus most of the time. I should know—I've got the burn scars to prove it. "Thanks." She accepts Mary's hand. "I remember you, too. You held your own." Coming from Lila, that's high praise.

The distraction only lasts a second, though, before her dark eyes are targeting me again. "I want to talk to you," she says at last. One hand slips into that bag, and I tense. "About—this!"

What she pulls out isn't a baseball, though. Not unless it was flattened by a steamroller and then wrapped by a blind man. It's a package, messily done in brown paper that's now tattered and torn and in some places even blackened, the whole thing sealed inside a large Ziploc. There's a piece of paper in there, too, with writing on it, but I can't tell from here what it says.

"Uh, okay," I tell her, leaning forward but keeping my hands free in case I need to defend myself. "That's seen better days."

"I'd imagine so," she snaps back, but there's something funny in her voice, and with her face. It doesn't look as hard as usual as she adds, "It's apparently been bouncing around from post office to post office for the last ten years."

Oh.

Wow.

Now that I look at it, the bedraggled package does look familiar. As does the handwriting still barely visible on the front.

And I can guess what the scrap of paper says. Something along the lines of: "We apologize for the state of this package, and for any delay in its arrival. Though we are constantly improving the speed and accuracy of our deliveries, no system is perfect. We regret any inconvenience this may have caused. Sincerely, the U.S. Post Office."

Yeah, thanks for that one, guys.

For once, I'm not sure what to say. "I told you I sent it" would be too on-the-nose, and too confrontational—even with her guard down Lila could still take me out without even trying, and might out of pure reflex. "Guess you owe me an apology, huh?" is right out, too. So instead I opt for something hopefully a little safer, offered with a shrug and a smile and a "what can you do?" look:

"Happy Birthday?"

Lila's face contorts, and I think she's gonna bite my head off—possibly literally, which would be something considering the relative size of our noggins, but I wouldn't put it past her to try or be completely shocked if her mouth unhinged like a boa constrictor's and elongated like an Anime girl getting ready to cry. Then she just nods and turns away, the package now clutched to her chest.

But as she turns to go, she slugs me.

On the shoulder.

Hard.

But it isn't the pain that brings tears to my eyes. I know Lila way too well not to recognize that this is the closest she can come to "I'm sorry" and "I forgive you."

I'll still take it. Happily.

Mary is glancing my way, one eyebrow up as if to inquire whether she should go after Lila and put a beatdown on her. Now that's a fight I wouldn't want to have to bet on! Fortunately, I can just shake my head and motion her that I'm okay. And she believes me, because she knows me pretty well, too.

This is shaping up to be the best family picnic ever.

Lila doesn't stick around—or, if she does, she stays out of my line of sight—but that's okay. Now that the dam's burst it's only a matter of time before we manage to reconnect. It'll probably take a while, and it'll be awkward at first—hard to get past a decade of not speaking to each other or one side hating the other all at once—but we'll get there. I can wait.

The sun goes down, and the tiki torches get lit all around the edge of the yard, giving the place a nice festive feel. And conveniently hiding all the divots and pits and holes and other dangerous spots in the lawn, so everybody's a good deal more careful walking around after that. Ma moves on to check on some of the others, and to make sure everybody's eating, and to send people off with leftovers when they eventually start to drift away in ones and twos and small groups. Finally I turn to Mary and smile.

"You ready to go?"

She nods, but not eagerly, not "oh God yes, I was about to chew off my own arm in order to necessitate the 911 call and the ambulance out of here, it'd be a small price to pay!"—and aren't I glad *that* girl didn't stick around, even after she healed up! Mary's is more like "sure, that's cool, it is getting late." She's comfortable here, I can tell.

And that's got me flying so high I could probably just flap my wings all the way back to my apartment.

If I had wings.

But you know what I mean.

"We're gonna get going, Ma," I say as we get to our feet. "Got the whole train back and all." Most of the others still live in town or a town or two over, so they've got a lot shorter distance to go, and most of 'em that aren't close enough to walk drove. Easier to make a fast getaway if you've got your own wheels— that was another thing Ma taught us early on. Right around the time Uncle Pete showed us how to hotwire a car "in case your wheels aren't quite close enough." Good old Uncle Pete. Shame about him, but we all told him hotwiring that police cruiser was a bad idea. Especially since he didn't bother to make sure both cops were out of the car first.

"Already?" Ma replies, but she's just giving me a hard time.

"Here, take this," she says, passing me a bag that weighs as much as a small child. I check to make sure Lizzy hasn't snuck into it—wouldn't be the first time. Ma's already turned to Mary and is giving her a hug. "I'm so glad we finally got to meet you," she says, "and shame on Robert for taking so long! I expect you back soon!" Which is Ma's way of saying "welcome to the family." Unless you're the plumber.

"Thank you," Mary replies. "This has been truly lovely. Thank you so much for inviting me." She beams. "You have a lovely family."

Lizzy says good-bye but can't manage her usual "don't go without me!" death-grip hug because she's already more than half-asleep in her chair. Bonnie and Grant say good-bye, too, and Harold waves from the grill. That man isn't going to give up his post without a fight, not as long as there's a single thing left to cook. I hope they've got the dog hidden well away.

As a result, it takes us a lot less time than usual to extricate ourselves and actually get clear. We don't say anything as we stroll down the hill, both nice and full and comfortably tired from a long day of hanging out with my family. Which is the kind of thing most people would give you medals for.

It's not until we're back on the train, curled up together on one of the benches, that Mary says, "I truly did have a lovely time."

"I'm glad," I tell her. "Me too. And my family adores you. Of course."

She smiles but is honest enough not to deny it. Instead, after another minute, she says, "May I ask you something?"

"Of course." I give her a careful peck on the cheek. "You

can ask me anything, you know that. And if I don't know the answer, I'll just make something up." Hey, I may not be the best person at Trivial Pursuit, but I'm one of the most entertaining!

"There is something I have been meaning to discuss with you," she says, looking down at her hands. Which are twisting around each other like a pair of curious dogs meeting for the first time. Uh-oh. "It is a matter of some import, and I have been loath to raise it, but now I feel perhaps I can. And indeed I must, for there is some urgency to it."

Wait, hold on. I grab both her hands. "Mary—are you pregnant?" I blurt out. "Are we gonna have a little duckling?"

"What?" For an instant she freezes, caught totally off-guard. Then she laughs. Whew! Not that I don't want kids some day—duck or human or hybrid—but I don't think either of us is quite ready for that yet! "No!" she manages after she's recovered. "Oh, no." She pats me fondly on the cheek. "Not that the possibility dismays me. But no, this is something different." She's back to the hand-twisting again. "DuckBob," she says, and it only just now occurs to me how carefully she avoided calling me by name the whole time we were at my family's. I vaguely remember telling her once how most of them won't, but clearly she remembered, and avoided it just to make things as easy as possible for me. With that in mind, I'm ready to hear whatever she has to say, no matter how painful. Which is good as she continues, "DuckBob, would you, perhaps, if it is not too arduous... accompany me to my college reunion?"

Who the what now?

Chapter Three
Alma mater are belong to us

I shake my head to make sure I heard her right—I'd clean out my ears if I still had 'em! "Did you say your college reunion?" I ask.

Mary nods, and I can't say she looks too happy about it. "Indeed. Francis Arnold Radcliffe Trumbull College for Advanced Personages."

There are some things it takes me a while to get. Others, not so much. When it comes to off-color acronyms? I'm faster than a supercomputer. Which is why I just blink at her for a second. "You went to a school called Fartcap? Seriously?" I'd grin if my bill worked that way. "That. Is. AWESOME! Man! I couldn't come up with that if I tried!"

She doesn't seem as thrilled about this as I am, but I guess that's the difference between finding a ridiculous acronym and attending a school that has one. Wouldn't that make her—and all her fellow alums—Fartcaps? "I confess, I had not realized its initials spelled such a colorful euphemism," she says, and I know it must be true because Mary's painfully honest. Which is great when you need to know which tie works better or what she wants for her birthday, not so hot when you try to impress her with a home cooked meal and she warns that eating it could leave us both radioactive. But hey, no pain, no gain!

"Uh, okay." I scratch my head. Four years there—or however long, since with Mary's brains I wouldn't be surprised if she breezed through a full degree in a long weekend!—and she never noticed that? I'd have been howling over it from the first time I saw the brochures. And, knowing me, I might've gone there just for that. But Mary's looking a wee bit upset, and I worry that I might be the reason. I'm working on the whole sensitivity thing, but it's still a bit of an uphill battle for me. Both ways. In the snow. With driving winds. And grease on the slopes.

"Sorry," I tell her, taking her hands in mind. "Of course I'll go with you. I'd be happy to."

That brings a smile to her face. "Truly? You would not mind?" She squeezes my fingers with hers. "I did not wish to burden you with such a chore, but it would vastly improve my own experience if you were there with me."

"Hey, no worries," I say. "Even if I didn't want to for myself, you know I'm here for you, whatever you need." Unless it involves laundry. Or differential calculus. Or apparently Beef Wellington. "You want me to go to this shindig with you, I'm there with bells on."

She gets an impish look on her face, which brings out her dimples. I can already feel myself melting. "I do not know that bells will be required," she says, squeezing a little tighter. "But perhaps you should model them for me nonetheless. Just to be certain."

That's my girl—looks like a Playmate, talks like a librarian, thinks like a supercomputer, fights like a Marine, and, underneath it all? Can be as naughty as a Catholic schoolgirl.

To say I'm a lucky guy is like saying the Himalayas have a little altitude and a few rocks.

It's a few hours before the topic resurfaces—turns out bells are a lot of fun if they're attached and then jangled in just the right way. Who knew? I'll never think of Mozart's Piano Sonata Number 11 the same way again.

But as we're laying in bed, relaxing and recovering—and untying knots that got a bit tighter from vigorous motion—my mind drifts back to that earlier conversation. "So," I say, keeping my tone light as a feather, "where is the old stomping grounds, anyway?"

Mary's look says she's not entirely sure what I'm asking, which I'm guessing is partially from being lulled into near-sleep but also because sometimes even her DuckBob translator doesn't cover everything, so I clarify: "Your old school. Where is it, exactly?"

"Oh." She nods, but fortunately stays relaxed and smiley, nestled against my chest. Hey, who doesn't love a down body-pillow? "It is in Vermont. The school sits upon the edge of Stratton, near to the Green Mountain and Finger Lakes National Forests."

"Huh." I stretch, careful not to dislodge her. "Vermont, eh? Never been. That's cool, though." I stop to think about it. "Vermont's not all that far from here, right? Still New England and all that? So, what, driving distance?" Not that I have a car, and I haven't had to drive in a while, but I'm sure I could pick it back up again. Long as it was a convertible. Or something with a huge dome on top. Like the Popemobile.

Mary sighs, though not unhappily. "It is perhaps two hundred miles from here," she admits, "and roughly four hours by car. But we need not take a vehicle—I can transport us there far more easily."

"Well, easily, sure," I agree. "But maybe not as much fun." I hug her to me. "Come on—me, you, the open road, the wind in your hair and in my feathers, the radio blasting? Sounds like a lot more fun than the usual 'close your eyes and try not to puke' teleport."

That makes her giggle, which sends pleasant, tingly little ripples through my chest feathers. "A road trip with you would be lovely," she says, "and yes, certainly moreso than the teleport, though I do not suffer your gastric or sensory distress from it. But perhaps some other time. We will have little enough time to arrive for the reunion as it stands."

"Wait, what?" I lever myself up a little so I can look at her—otherwise my bill's totally in the way, since it's capable of blotting out whole mountain ranges—and she does her best not to meet my eyes. "When is this reunion, exactly?"

I almost don't hear her reply, muffled into my chest as it is: "It begins tomorrow."

"Tomorrow?" Okay, so much for being all relaxed. "Babe, why didn't you say anything about it before?"

Mary wraps both arms around me. "I was unsure whether I even wished to attend," she answers quietly, "and then I worried over whether to trouble you with the suggestion that you escort me there. Even now I am tempted to send my regrets instead." She hugs me more tightly. "We could simply stay here instead," she offers, freeing one hand to tap one of the bells still tied around my upper arm.

For once, though, I'm not so easily distracted. "Hey," I tell her. "Hey, look at me." She does finally, lifting her head up so I can see her properly. "You're not troubling me or upsetting me," I promise. "And you know I'm happy to hole up here with you at the drop of a hat. But this is your college reunion! How often do you get one of those? I think you should go, and I'm happy to go with you."

If I'm being honest, I'm actually really excited about it—a lot more than Mary is, evidently. In all the time we've been together, I don't actually know that much about her. Well, that's not entirely true. I know a lot about her, from how she takes her tea (a splash of half-and-half—before the water, thank you very much!—scalding-hot water filled nearly to the brim, and then a teabag—preferably Irish or Scottish Breakfast—left to steep until the mug is, as I read in a book once, "the color of old teak.") to her favorite lounging-about-the-house clothes (plaid flannel pajama pants, one of my T-shirts so old it's super-soft, and fuzzy bunny slippers) to the best way to scrub her back (no, I'm not telling you that one!). I know how crazy smart she is, and how incredibly calm under pressure, and how fiercely loyal, and how wickedly funny she can be when it's just us and maybe Tall and Ned and she can really unwind.

What I don't know is where she came from, and what she

was like before. Mary never talks about her past—I know there isn't any family still in the picture, but whether that's because they're all dead now or because they won't speak to her or she won't speak to them or just because they're in some commune Upstate and aren't allowed to make outside calls I have no idea. Heck, I don't even know how old she is, and that's not something you can ask. Is this her five-year reunion? Ten? Fifty? Mind you, I don't care if she'd older than me—even a lot older—or younger or the same age. It'd just be nice to know.

So the idea of getting to see where she went to school, getting to meet her old classmates, getting to see her old school photo and hear stories about what she was like back then—that's awesome to me. It's like a little glimpse into the person she once was, the person who grew up to be my Mary. And, nosy as I am, I would never snoop on her—I respect her way too much to violate her privacy like that. But if she's the one inviting me to go to her reunion with her? I am so totally there it hurts.

Except that it looks like it might hurt—her. And that's not something I ever want to do. So I add, "We don't have to go. Not if you don't want to. You just tell me what you'd like and we'll do it. I promise. Though we might need more whipped cream first."

She smiles and kisses me on the tip of my bill. "Thank you," she says. "I am, as always, grateful for your support, and delighted in the affection I know it springs from." Yeah, love you too, babe. But her brow furrows as she continues, "I am still of two minds about attending. On the one hand, I do not know that it will be the most pleasant of experiences. But on the other,

I feel I may owe it to myself and others to at least put in an appearance." The smile steals back in. "And I am aware of your eagerness to see something of my past."

Darn! And here I thought I was being all subtle! Then again, Mary's always been able to read me like a book. One with big pictures and simple words.

"I'd love to see the place," I admit. "But if going's gonna make you miserable, I say we skip it."

"Not miserable, perhaps," she answers slowly, clearly considering. "And it has been some time since I attended there. I believe we shall attempt it."

I squeeze her tight. "Cool! And if it turns out to be a drag, we'll just pop back here." I raise my arm so that last bell jingles again, and her smile turns slightly wicked.

Then there's a whole lot of jingling and jangling and a whole lot bells being rung. You can paint your own picture here, 'cause I'm a little too busy to paint one for you.

Chapter Four
They're like kneecaps, only higher?

"Wow." I look around us and shiver a little, tugging my coat a little tighter. I wish I'd thought to bring a hat, but honestly unless we're talking a laundry bag there's not much that's gonna fit over my noggin. "I didn't think it'd be cold here." We were wearing shorts back home, but even though Mary warned me to switch to jeans and a sweater I'm still close to shivering.

"We are nestled at the base of Stratton Mountain," Mary points out. She's looking very chic in her own jeans, black turtleneck, and deep blue ski jacket. With matching boots. All she needs are the skis and the goggles and she'd look like a model for hitting the slopes.

And maybe getting in some skiing, too.

"Yeah, sure," I agree, glancing around. "It's real pretty. But the snow's supposed to be up on top of the mountain, isn't it? Not down here with us poor shivery folk?" I hold out one hand. "You can't tell under the feathers, but I'm turning blue here!"

She shakes her head and takes a little disc out of one pocket. "Hold still while I affix this," she warns, then proceeds to plaster it to the back of my neck, maybe with a little more force than was strictly necessary. I don't mind, though, because all of a sudden I'm warm again!

"That's awesome!" I resist the urge to try twisting my neck to peek at it—I'm a duck, not a crane, and I've no desire to look like the top-heavy version of the dog spinning around trying to catch its own tail. "What is it?"

"A portable microenvironment," she explains, taking my hand. "It will keep the air just around you at a comfortable temperature, regardless of external factors."

"Neat!" I frown at her. "Wait, if you have this thing, why're you wearing a ski jacket?"

Spots of red appear on her cheeks. "I enjoyed the look of such attire," she admits quietly, ducking her head. Which is freaking adorable.

"You look amazing, like always," I promise her. "But if you need this thing back, let me know." Then I swing our hands. "Now let's go check out this reunion!"

Together we stroll across the campus—Mary said she was 'porting us in near the dorms rather than by the Great Hall where they're holding the reunion proper, so that we'd be less likely to draw attention:

Though how she thinks the hottest chick in the world and a mallard on two legs aren't going to draw attention, I've got no idea.

It is a pretty campus, I'll give it that. The trees are still covered in leaves of russet and gold, the lawn is trim and green, the mountain is rising up right behind us, and the buildings are arranged in what looks like almost an eye shape, with a single road looping around between them and creating a neat little park right at the center. The buildings are big and clean and white-washed and have that old Colonial look about them, but I can see they're fully modernized, too.

The other thing is, it's quiet out here. Really quiet. Back at the Matrix, the darn thing is always humming—when it's not whistling show tunes. I keep asking it to stop, or at least to pick something newer than *Bye, Bye Birdie* and *Finian's Rainbow*. You can only listen to "How Are Things in Glockamora" so many times! But there's always some noise there, plus there's the sound of the nearby businesses, people walking around outside, any arriving or departing spacecraft. Heck, the stars themselves make noise, a lot like the buzz of electronics mixed with wind chimes. And then of course Manhattan is never quiet, even at 3 am. But here? There's the breeze rustling the leaves, and the distant sound of people walking and chatting, plus a stray bird or two, but that's it.

It's eerie.

The building Mary steers us toward isn't the biggest on campus, but the others all clearly have multiple floors. This one looks like it's just one big, white-sided shell, though there's a clock tower atop the front end of the steep roof. Columns hold up a small portico, flanking big French doors, and if Washington and Jefferson and Franklin came pouring out of there, arguing wording and mocking poor Monroe for his cravat, I wouldn't have been surprised. "Are you ready?" Mary asks me, clutching my hand almost tight enough to cut off the circulation.

"Sure," I tell her. "You? Last chance to turn around and head home instead."

I think she actually considers that, but Mary's made of

tougher stuff than that. "No," she decides, lifting her chin. "We are here to attend my reunion, and we shall do so."

"Okay then." I glance at the doors. "Shall we?"

Together we stride toward the doors, tug them open, and step inside.

If I was expecting more Old World charm, I'm a little disappointed. Instead, I find myself standing in a gleaming auditorium or lecture hall, the kind you'd see at, well, a top-rate university. The back wall is a soft taupe with just a hint of texture, the ceiling has rows of inset spots for a gentle, even lighting, the seats are clean and cushy and blue and arrayed in neat rows radiating out from the space in front of the wide podium with its back to the stretch of smart boards covering that long wall. The two side walls have alternating wood and recessed white, the latter looking like fabric and probably good for blocking any noise from outside. There's an upper floor, too, a balcony forming a gentle curve above the back half of the room, and in back is what looks like an entire AV section. I wonder if NASA rents the space for its annual presentations.

Of course, right now the purely academic vibe is broken by the "Welcome Back, Class of '08!" banner that's hanging from the front of the balcony.

Though I can't help but notice that the background is made entirely of fractals.

There's a long table near the front, manned by two women and a guy, and although she slows a bit, Mary does finally take us in that direction. "Welcome back!" One of the women declares as we approach. She studies me for a second, her eyes widening like she's trying to place the face before finally admitting that there's just no way unless it's from the nearest duck pond, then shifts to Mary and breaks into a big smile. "Well, hello there!" This lady's got to be in her fifties, heavyset with graying blonde hair pulled back in a severe bun, so I'm guessing she's a teacher rather than a former classmate. Unless she got held back even more times than I did!

"Good day, Ms. Fontaine," Mary replies, nodding politely as we stop right in front of the table. "It is a pleasure to see you again. You look well." She's taken on that polite, slightly formal—even for her—tone you get when you're in one of those situations where you have to be polite even if you really don't want to be. At least, I've heard about situations like that. From people with self-control.

"You too, dear," Ms. Fontaine says, sounding a bit more genuinely pleased than Mary does. "You look as lovely as ever!" There's an array of badges laid out in neat rows in front of her, and she frowns for a second, searching the names, before selecting one. "Ah, here you are!" And hands Mary a badge—

—that says "Mirabella Rosalind Jost."

My lady love has the good grace to blush a little as she unzips her jacket and affixes the badge to her sweater, since she knows as well as I do that this is the first time I've ever seen or heard her birth name. Not that I'm one to talk about name changes, but it might have been nice to know!

"And you are?" The lady behind the desk is asking me pointedly. She already has a blank badge in one hand and a Sharpie in the other.

"DuckBob Spinowitz," I tell her proudly. "I'm with her."

I'll assume that the "harrumph" is because she's trying to figure out how to spell my last name, rather than commentary on our love match. Though she all but throws the badge at me after. Maybe she's hoping to put an eye out with the pin. No such luck, lady! I'm tempted to toss it back at her, sneer, and declare, "Mad scientists do not wear the 'hello, my name is' badge!" But I've got the feeling that, in this crowd, all they'd do is ask for my bona fides!

"Enjoy!" she tells Mary, handing her a brochure and shooing us away. The other two at the table, who also look like professors, nod hello but are too busy arguing about something to spare us more than a quick glance.

"I am sorry," Mary tells me softly as we wander toward the podium, where it looks like most of the other attendees are gathered. There are tables set against the wall behind it, bearing food and drinks. "I should have informed you of my former name before now."

I shrug it off as best I can. "Hey, it's cool," I promise. "I didn't figure you were born with 'MR3971XJKA.'" That's the name she gave the first time we met, and it's not only what the Grays call her but what she uses for official encounters. I'm the one who started calling her "Mary," and it stuck. Guess I wasn't too far off from the truth, and honestly I can't see her as a "Mirabella." "Mary" suits her a whole lot better. Maybe it's one of those knacks, like guessing somebody's star sign, knowing what their real name is?

"Mirabella!" someone calls out, and we both turn to see a

guy detach himself from the punch bowl and head toward us. He's a little shorter than me but just as rounded, with thinning light brown hair and a chubby face. He's got on tan slacks and a gray V-neck sweater over a blue button-down shirt, and looks like your average accountant. "It's me, Charles Anthony Bordeaux III," he declares when he reaches us, and—holds out his hand.

Which Mary shakes.

Clearly best buds. Or tempestuous lovers. Or maybe hateful rivals—apparently I'm not as good at deciphering handshakes as I am at names.

"Hello, Charles," Mary tells him. "You are looking well. Allow me to introduce my boyfriend, DuckBob."

Charles—I relabel him "Cab" in my head—turns to me. "Delighted," he states with all the warmth of a small polar ice-cap, offering me his hand now that Mary's released it. It's cold and clammy and his grip's about as limp as an overcooked noodle. "Are you an astrophysicist as well?"

"Oh, yeah, I'm all about the stars," I reply. Which is true, I guess, whether because I live out among the stars or because I love celebrity gossip. Especially the stuff that comes out of the Tri-Gamma Quadrant, where the quickest way to become famous is to climb over somebody else. Literally. It's like Jersey Shore meets mountain climbing, complete with designer spiked boots. It's all fun until the pitons come out.

"I had hoped you might attend," Cab admits, sweat already starting to plaster his remaining hair to his head. "I have often thought of you when I reminisce about this place."

Well, this is awkward! I'm not surprised that some of Mary's former classmates would have pined over her, of course, but I guess I'd expected them to look more like, well, my old classmates. And to have more emotion than canned tuna. If this guy gets any more passionate he might freeze to death!

"Hey, so you guys took classes together, huh?" I interject, forcing his attention toward me. "That's cool. What was it like, back in the day? Got any good stories?" I elbow him in the side. "Must've been some fun pranks going on around here, huh?"

"Pranks?" Poor Cab looks like he's trying to parse the word, but then he brightens and manages a weak smile. "Oh, yes. We were regular pranksters, weren't we, Mirabella? There was the time we refused to recite the periodic table unless we could be allowed to do so in Greek instead of Latin! Or the time we all sat in reverse order to torment poor Professor Arminglade! Or what about—"

"Foolish juvenility," a voice interrupts, and Cab's attempts at bragging dry up faster than tears on the subway. We all turn to study the newcomer, who's a little taller than Mary and beanpole thin, with a long face, long nose, long chin, long fingers— long everything except his dark brown hair, which is buzzed short. And his mustache, which looks like it might've been penciled on. "Those of us who cared about our studies had no time for such pointless frivolity." He studies Mary from behind thin rectangular glasses in matte black metal frames. "Mirabella."

"Jerome." With each new encounter Mary's voice reaches new levels of cold. I'm surprised we don't all get frostbite from this one. "Jerome, may I present my boyfriend, DuckBob. DuckBob, my former classmate Jerome Hansen."

"Doctor Jerome Hansen," he corrects. "There's little point to having five PhDs if one does not avail oneself of the accompanying title, hm?" He peers down his nose at me. "And how many doctorates do you have?"

"Eh, I'm not much of a doctor," I tell him. "I make a mean vet, though. Or maybe that's just that I make vets mean." I wait for it, but he doesn't even raise an eyebrow. Tough room!

Instead Doctor-doctor-doctor-doctor-doctor Jerome turns back toward Mary. "I see you continue to keep company with inferior minds," he sneers. "Such a waste of potential."

I want to tell him, "Hey, this mind keeps the Galactic Matrix running, bud! Bet you can't even operate a can opener with yours!" But of course I don't. Stupid secrecy!

Mary looks about ready to give him a piece of her mind, too, but she's prevented by the sound of someone tapping on a mic. We all glance over at the podium—and for a second I think I'm not the only alien-altered face in the crowd.

Otherwise, who let the Yorkie in, and why is it standing at the podium wearing Harris tweed?

Chapter Four
Is this thing on?

"Greetings, Class of Aught-Eight," the Yorkie declares in a thin, reedy voice perfectly suited to those whiskers and that tweed, and I revise my assessment. No way a dog's throat is making those well-modulated words! Besides, nobody's staring at him like, "Hey, what's up with the talking dog?" the way they're gawking sidelong at me, so either they're all really used to him— and particularly narrow-minded, like it's okay for dogs to wear suits and give speeches but Heaven forfend a duck should go around in a coat and ask for a proper rum-and-coke!—or it's just a spindly old man with almost Muppet-level bushy eyebrows, sideburns, and mustache. Or maybe it *is* a Muppet? We had a puppet show at my class reunion, but that was kindergarten. Much lower bar, entertainment-wise. Though we did have really good snacks.

"It is lovely to see all of you again," Whiskers continues, clutching both sides of the podium like it's the only thing holding him up. "We are very glad you could all make the effort to attend the weekend's festivities, and look forward to hearing about your latest ventures. I am pleased to inform you that only three of your classmates were unable to attend. Sidney

Rappaport is currently in the middle of clinical trials for his new anti-pneumonia treatment, and his entire lab is on full quarantine to avoid contaminating the results. Douglas LeMarque was injured in a freak collider accident and is currently confined to full bedrest, though he continues to study antimatter equations from his chamber. And of course Andrew Lorimer"— and I swear behind those little old glasses his dark, beady eyes seek Mary out of the crowd and a smirk shows beneath that mustache—"is only midway through his latest rotation on the International Space Station and could not leave high-Earth orbit at this time."

Mary's hand found mine when Dog-boy started talking, and at that last bit she squeezes so tight I think I hear a few finger bones pop. Clearly there's a story here.

I'm not going to get it right away, though, because before I can ask someone coughs pointedly behind us. Mary and I both turn—and peer down, since the person fake-coughing is at about belly-button level.

"Hello, Mirabella," Little Miss Cougher says, though it'd be more accurate to say she fires those two words at Mary like bullets from a gun, with just as much velocity and twice as much anger. If this was a gathering of Gray-altered folk, I'd say that, with her sharp features, big, glittery eyes, tight bun (maybe Ms. Fontaine helped her do her hair?), almost ebony skin, and tiny frame practically quivering with rage, I was looking at a wasp-human hybrid.

Ech!

"Hello, Theresa," Mary replies. Such warmth to this place!

Even with the microenvironment I'm tempted to ask for a parka! "It is good to see you again. You look well."

It's then that I notice something. Or, really, that something I already noticed but hadn't really caught onto finally pops into focus. You know, like when you hear something in passing and later go, "Wait, what?" as the meaning hits. Sometimes days later, though maybe that's just me.

Anyway, I realize that Mary and I are about the only couple in the room. Everyone else we've met so far has been here alone, and with their winning personalities I'm hardly surprised. But the rest of the crowd looks the same way. None of Mary's former classmates brought significant others, or domestic partners, or even siblings or friends.

And Mary and now Madame Hornet are, aside from the two ladies at the registration desk, the only women here.

Apparently for all its boasting about brains this place buys into the whole "women aren't good at math and science" baloney. Forward thinkers stuck in a mindset from the Dark Ages. Great.

You'd think, as the only two girls evidently allowed into the Old Boys' Club, Mary and this Theresa would have been close. Solidarity and all that.

Then again, I've seen the opposite before, too. The whole "if I throw you under the bus, maybe they'll leave me alone" mentality. You get that a lot in bully groups, there's usually the one little kid who'd be their punching bag except that he helps them find real targets.

Plus there's the whole "Mary looks like Miss Universe

and Theresa's more like the Wicked Witch." That can't have helped any.

Sure enough, "You look the same as ever," the Walking Yellowjacket snaps, which I'm guessing is meant as an insult though I know plenty of people—women and even a few men— who'd gladly kill whole busloads to look like my sweetie. I can see where it'd be a sore spot, though. Meanwhile, Wasp Lady's eyes are raking across me. "And you are?" Man, she makes the ladies at the DMV look like kindly old aunts, the type who smother you in hugs and cookies!

"DuckBob Spinowitz, pleased ta meetcha." I offer my hand, which she stares at as if *it* were the venomous insect in this equation.

"Such . . . interesting company you keep, Mirabella," is the next barb to be fired at us. Though it's a pretty weak one, as insults go. Interesting company? Really? And yeah, I'd say me and Tall and Ned are pretty interesting. I'd hate to think we were boring!

Mary seems to feel the same way, as a small smirk settles across her face. "Thank you" is all she says, but with enough obvious pride to make Lady Sting flush and almost grind her teeth. Ha! Amateur! I should get Tall to give her a few lessons!

Just then my cell phone goes off. Only, it's my left pocket that starts vibrating, and I keep my phone in my right. Confused, I reach down and pull out—my key fob. Which is shaking in my hand, and glowing.

That can't be good.

At the same time, I realize Mary's stiffened like somebody

just grabbed her butt. In this crowd, though, that hardly seems likely, and besides, most of them are still watching the Dog That Quotes Shakespeare go on at length about this institution's venerable history or some such.

I study the fob. The Grays gave it to me after the whole thing on Ned's world, as both a perk of the job and a show of thanks. It's got three buttons—the one that transports me instantly to the Matrix, the one that takes me to my apartment, and the third one, which is my Emergency call button. If I push that, the Grays are supposed to come a-running.

Only, that's the one that's glowing.

Oh, so not good. Like, double-plus-ultra-not good.

Mary looks over at me. "We must depart at once," she says, and I know she just got whatever alert lit up my fob. But direct to her cerebellum.

"Really?" Theresa sneers. "Leaving so soon? But Dean Pickens has not yet finished his opening remarks. And I was so looking forward to hearing what you've been up to lately." She says it in the same tone as somebody who's just realized the couple across the street are about to fight again, only this time with power tools and handguns, and is debating if there's time to break out the popcorn.

"Yeah, sorry, would love to stay and chat but we've got some urgent business to take care of," I tell her. "Maybe next reunion, huh? We can trade poison rings. Mine'll be the one made out of Sweet-Tarts." I want to pat her on the head but I'm afraid there's razor wire coiled in there, so I settle for a quick nod as Mary and I push through the crowd and head for the door.

"What's going on?" I ask as quietly as I can and still have her hear me over the Doggy Dean and the general shuffling of the crowd. Though there isn't much of the latter. For a roomful of people being forced to listen to a boring old guy drone on about nothing, they're all amazingly attentive. Guess all those years in Mensa was good for something!

"It is a distress call," Mary answers without stopping. She's leading the way, which should really be my job—I'm the one with the built-in cattle-pusher!—but it must be clear she means business because most of the people in our path hastily step aside to let her through.

"From the Grays?"

She nods. "Indeed. And that is unprecedented."

I'm pretty sure this is nothing like the time I decided to see if I could eat three slices of Mile-High Pie and was told that doing so without going into a dairy-induced coma was unprecedented. Sometimes, a little voice inside me warns, breaking precedent is a bad thing.

Old Judge Warner, who presided over our local court when I was growing up and so saw an awful lot of me and various siblings over the years, would be so proud.

Especially if I also returned his gavel.

As soon as we're outside, Mary stops and I see her concentrate. The world goes a little misty—

—and then, before I can shut my eyes, solidifies again.

In exactly the same place as before.

Ruh-roh, Raggy.

A line forms between her perfect eyebrows. "The

teleportation array is not responding."

Great. "Anything I can do to help?" I hold up my fob. Yeah, because my rinky-dink three-button gizmo is going to do a better job than the full-access wiring in Mary's head. That's like pulling up beside a Ferrari on a Segway and saying, "Hey, need to get there in a hurry?"

Except that Mary is considering my offer. "Yes, that might be exactly what we need," she agrees, smiling and holding out her hand. I give her the fob, of course, though I'm a little confused. Apparently I've outsmarted myself again. I do that a lot.

"My link to the array is through one channel," she explains, cracking open the fob's back panel and tugging a wire free with her fingernails, then jabbing it back in millimeters from its original position. "This device, since it has only preprogrammed responses, connects through a different protocol. By combining the two—"

"You can basically double-team it into working," I guess. The way her smile widens, I know I got it right. I feel like the little kid who tries spelling a word way above his reading level to impress his favorite teacher, and somehow manages it. Who needs a gold star and a smiley-face sticker now?

Well, okay, I'd still really like one of those, actually. But Mary's smile is nearly as good.

She concentrates again, jabbing the call button on the fob at the same time. There's that misting effect again—

—and this time it continues, everything around us blurring and fading until we're lost in a sea of color like a watercolor left out in the rain.

I remember to close my eyes just in time. Teleporting with them open is like trying to watch while you're stuck in an industrial washer on spin cycle.

Trust me, you don't want to try it. Though it does do wonders for cleaning your contact lenses!

"Open your eyes." That's either the first line in a really bad infomercial, the end of a cheeseball horror movie, the Hugh Hefner version of an alarm clock—or Mary, telling me we're here.

I open my eyes—and immediately wonder if she's decided now would be a good time for one of those pranks.

"Um . . ." I peer around. "Did we pause for a pee break? Because I'm not seeing much that looks like it's in distress—or a whole lot of anything else."

"No," Mary replies, also studying our surroundings. "We have arrived."

"Really? To where?" I ask her. "Land of the Awfully Boring Rocks?"

Because that's all I can see around us. Rocks, all either dusty brown or rusty red. And rocky ground the same shades. And a pale reddish sky.

I feel like somebody took a really boring stretch of someplace like Nevada and tried to make it more enticing by adding a rose filter over the whole scene, except they weren't looking and got "burnt sienna" instead. Then tried to put it back and replace it with rose after all, but some of the burnt bits stuck.

Mary looks—well, worried. "This is Planet 4593 of the Virulga system," she informs me, and I know she's consulting the galactic database the Grays downloaded into her head when they first modified her to work for them. "Also known as Obscura Major by some races. And by the Grays"—she sighs, and it's full of fear and anxiety—"as Prime." She turns to face me. "This is their homeworld."

"This?" I frown and take a second look. Nope, still deadly dull. "What, do they all live underground or something? And leave the surface for parking? Or the future site of the universe's largest food court?" Which I'd totally be down with, especially if they've got proper Bourbon Chicken like that one place in Milwaukee.

But she's shaking her head. "They do not. I have never been here before, but I have heard tales from other travelers of this world. Of its soaring towers, its majestic arches, its sweeping bridges, its long, sloping lanes." Her voice dips a little. "And of the Quantum Singularity, the wellspring of energy around which all of their technologies are based. In truth, I have always longed to behold that for myself, but had not yet been granted such an honor."

Now we're both looking, staring hard in the hopes that there's just some kind of jamming field up or something, like the curtains've been drawn over this whole stunning landscape she's just mentioned. After all, if this Quantum Singularity is such a big deal, they might very well have it locked away for safekeeping.

But if that's the case, that lockbox is still shut tight. And now it's expanded to include the entire rest of the planet. Which makes no sense, even to me. Besides which, both of us were modified by the Grays. If anybody was going to be equipped to see through their little "do not disturb" sign, it'd be us. Especially since they called us, not the other way around.

The problem is, there's nothing here to see. No towers, no arches, no bridges, no lanes, no singularity—and no Grays. They've up and left, closed up shop and taken the whole store with them.

It's like if we'd just found the *Mary Celeste*, only this time there's nothing but empty water, a scrap of old sail, and a dip in the water where the boat should be.

Chapter Five
No forwarding address, and no backwards one, either

"Okay, now what?" I ask after a minute. "Do we just start wandering around, calling 'olly olly, oxen-free' and see if they come a-running? Like maybe this wasn't a plea for help it was an invite to the biggest hide-and-seek game ever, and they're taking over-competitive to a whole new level?"

Mary shakes her head. "I am not detecting any transmissions here at all," she reports. "This world should be alight with activity on all levels. Instead there is nothing. Searching further would be a waste of time, and I suspect time is of the essence."

I'm scratching my bill. It helps me think, and besides, it itches sometimes. Though I suspect that might be like Phantom Limb Syndrome, only for my original nose. Anyway, I tell her, "Maybe it's a waste of time for you and me to search, but what about somebody with a few extra tricks up his salad-bowl sleeve?"

She brightens. "Ned! Of course!" The revelation earns me a quick peck on the cheek. "I will summon him to us posthaste."

"Cool." I whip out my cell. "I'll call Tall. Heidi's good at picking stuff up too—he actually did a better job pinpointing that second wormhole than Ned did, though don't remind Ned of that—and Tall's always good to have around in a pinch."

"Indeed." Mary is frowning slightly. "Especially since the teleportation array is still not performing within normal operating parameters. I suspect I will be able to return us home without difficulty, but although I have made contact with Ned I am unable to relocate him to us."

"Ah. Maybe Tall and Heidi can pick him up on the way?" I tilt my head and squint up at the stars, none of which look remotely familiar to me. Though, to be fair, I don't recognize most stars on sight anyway. Unless they're in pavement, with somebody's name on them. But that might be considered cheating. I call it "being observant enough to look down, and sharp enough to be able to read while walking." "Where are we, anyway? In relation to the Matrix, I mean. Or to Artelusia IX." That's Ned's homeworld, which as far as I know is where he is right now. Last I saw him, he'd decided to take some time off to spend with his family.

"A significant distance," Mary admits. "Even at maximum speed, it would take Tall and Heidi roughly nineteen hours to reach us from there."

"Ouch! Yeah, way too long." I seat myself on a nearby rock. Hey, standing on rocky ground is tough on the feet, and mine are surprisingly sensitive for being the size of moon landers. "Can Ned do something like what you did to overcome whatever interference there is?"

Mary shakes her head. "I used your fob and my own internal array because both had the coordinates for this location already installed, but different pathways for any communications—including teleportation—to follow. Ned has a pathway similar to mine, and no secondary route to overlay." She taps her cheek in thought. "Although, it might be possible for him to build a device such as your fob and then combine the two."

"Yeah, too bad we can't just send him mine," I offer, lounging back on my forearms. This rock wasn't exactly made for reclining! Or sitting in general. This is like the world's worst estate sale—"I'll take that rock, no, that rock over there!" The least they could've done was leave behind a Barcalounger! I don't say any of that, though—I really am starting to get the hang of this whole "inner monologue" thing!—but instead just point out that, "Then he wouldn't need to waste time making one, he'd have this one already in hand."

It's a good thing I'm practically laying down already, because otherwise my gal's shout might have bowled me over completely. "Of course!" she declares. "You are, as ever, a genius, my love!"

"I am? Cool. Be sure to let Mensa know—serves 'em right for booting me. All I did was ask when we'd get to actually do stuff, and point out that in the Boy Scouts I'd already learned ten useful things, including how to tie a proper slipknot and how to pee on a boat in the middle of storm." I study her closely, which is one of my favorite things to do anyway, before adding, "but just so I know, what did I do that was so genius-y this time?"

"We do not need to send Ned your fob," Mary explains, though she has that distracted look that tells me she's also carrying on a conversation with our techie pal at the same time. "Our difficulty lay in reaching this location, as something is interfering with the coordinates. But Ned has access to the information from your headpiece, including its location. And he has just confirmed that there is no interference there." She's still speaking when a patch of air a few feet to my left starts to shimmer. There's a warping effect as that space twists and darkens, a shape starting to form there like when you zoom in on a distant spot and the picture takes a second to resolve. Then there's a short, stocky dude in overalls and a T-shirt standing there, his skin emerald green and his head covered with what looks at first like tight little curls but what're actually tiny buds.

"Ned!" I'm up off the boulder and shaking our buddy's hand in a flash. "Man, it's good to see you! How're you doing, man? How're Nessa and the sprouts?"

"They're good," Ned replies, grinning ear to ear, his eyes glowing brightly. "Really good. I seriously didn't know what I was missing." Until recently Ned was pretty much an absentee—or maybe that should be absen-TREE?—husband and dad. He'd call every week but only actually visit maybe once a year. The whole thing on his world made him reconsider his priorities, though, and decide to spend some time at home for a while. Looks like that's really working out for him. I'm glad—his wife and kids seemed nice, and I'm a big believer in family. Especially since mine seem to be there whenever I look around.

"It is good to see you, Ned," Mary tells him, giving him a quick hug, and the difference between that and those same words to her former classmates is like night and day, if night is deep in the Marianas Trench and day is standing on a beach in the Bahamas. "Thank you for setting aside your family time in order to assist us."

"Yeah, of course," he says. "You know I'm here for you guys. So what's the problem?" Then he looks around for the first time. "Whoa!"

"That about sums it up." I study him. "Wait, have you been here before?"

He shakes his head, which is good—if he had, I think both Mary and I might be a little miffed. After all, we're full-time employees and he's just a contractor. Though I've had jobs like that before—the wage-slaves toiling away in our little cubicles for peanuts while the contractors roll in, get put up in fancy hotels, stationed in corner offices, treated like royalty.

"Naw, but I've heard about it," Ned's saying, which pulls me out of my reminiscences. And not a moment too soon! "And this?" He gestures around us. "This is not what it's supposed to look like."

"Yeah, we didn't think so either," I agree. "We're coming up empty here, but we thought maybe you'd have better luck." I glance up at the sky. "I sure wish Tall were here already."

Ned's already got one of his little gizmos out of his tool belt and is fiddling with it—and stroking it. I've still never figured out if his gadgets are alive or just funky, and I've never asked. Not sure I should, either. That feels a little rude to just suddenly blurt out, "Hey, do you and your sensor need some alone time?" Even for me.

"Sorry," he says without looking up from whatever the hell

he's doing. "I did check in with them, but they're already on the move, and trying to lasso them at those speeds is pretty risky. Especially since they were talking about slingshotting around a sun to really push the envelope. Once they're in the clear I can probably teleport them over."

"Cool." I know Tall's not going to be any more help with the techie stuff than I am, but he's my best bud and the guy you want backing you up in a firefight. Or actually the guy you want in front of you, guns blazing, while you stay safely in his shadow and hold the drinks. Look, it's an important job—nobody wants to come out of a tough shootout and find out they've spilled their beer!

After that Mary and I find ourselves standing around—or, in my case, trying yet again to find a comfortable way to sit on one of these rocks. Hey, hope springs eternal, especially if that spring includes some nice form-fitting pillows!—twiddling our thumbs for a few minutes while Ned paces here and there, taking readings. Or maybe snapping selfies. Or just taking his gizmo for a quick walk. I don't see him feed it anything, which would be a bit of a giveaway, but that doesn't mean he didn't slip it a quick cracker or two when I wasn't looking.

"Okay," he says finally, stowing the device back in his belt and rejoining us. "I've done about everything I can here."

"That doesn't sound good," I tell him. "In fact, that's what TV doctors usually say, right before 'now it's up to him' or 'but he's never going to pole-vault again.'"

Mary shushes me. "What have you learned?" she asks instead. Which I suppose is more helpful.

"Well, my first question was whether something had corrupted the array somehow, or messed up the Galactic Positioning System," Ned explains. "So I double-checked that against a few other locations, just to be sure." He sighs. "This is definitely Obscura Major, though."

"Crap." I'd had that idea too, that somebody had simply pulled a fast one, basically switching the nameplates on the rooms and letting us think we'd walking into the sauna when in fact we were in the glass elevator. What, it was funny at the time!

"Yeah." Ned's got his thumbs hooked on the straps of his overalls, and is rocking back and forth on his feet a little. He looks like a farmer breaking the news about a really bad harvest, which is ironic since he also looks a bit like the harvest. "Then I checked the array to see why we were having so much trouble getting here. I'm still not sure what's up with that, I need to run a few more tests, but I think it's because the system used the Quantum Singularity as its anchor point." We all turn and look out over the decidedly singularity-less landscape. I guess this is one of those times that being singular would actually be a good thing.

"What's really weird," Ned adds, "is that there should at least be traces of the singularity. Even if it was moved some-how—and I have no idea how you'd even do that—it should've left marks behind. But there's nothing. Like it's never been here. Only it definitely has."

"Right, so this is the right world," I summarize, "only the Grays aren't here, their cities aren't here, and their singularity is missing. Anything else?" I'm kinda itching to get the hell away from here. Something about this place definitely isn't sitting well with me, even aside from the whole "this is supposed to be a thriving world and instead it's a wasteland and the world's most boring rock garden" issue.

The way Ned stares down at his feet, I've got a sudden sinking feeling that we haven't even gotten to the really bad news yet.

"So," he starts slowly, "after I confirmed that this was Obscura Major, the obvious question was, 'where is everybody?' And what exactly happened to 'em?"

Mary and I both nod. "Where" and "why/how" were high on our list of pressing questions, too. "When" might be interesting, but probably wasn't as critical unless we were trying to figure out when to re-up the cable bill.

"Then I did a general scan of the area," Ned continues. "Just to see if I found anything out of place. There's barely anything here to find, of course, but what there was . . . stood out a bit." He trails off again, still not meeting our eyes.

"And?" I prompt. "Come on, man, spit it out!"

"There's some energy traces that don't belong here," he answers, finally looking up, and his eyes look…haunted is the only way I can describe it. "Some traces I've seen before. That we've all seen before."

Mary and I share a look. "The invaders," we both say. I'd be thrilled by our perfect harmony if I wasn't simultaneously furious and scared stiff. Why is it always the invaders? Why can't it be something else for a change, like fluffy bunnies or polka-dotted space walruses or animate toasters? But no, it's always these creeps from the neighboring reality with their plan to invade our universe and reshape it into something that works for them.

I'd say they really need to get a life, but they keep trying. The problem is, they apparently want mine!

Chapter Six
My security code is so tricky, even I can't guess it!

"Oh, crap," I blurt out, lurching to my feet. I think every inch of me is going to be protesting the whole "hey, let's try sitting on a rock!" idea for a while to come, but I don't have time to worry about that right now. Because if it really is the invaders who're back again—and I know Ned wouldn't have said it was if he wasn't totally sure—then we already know exactly where they're going to hit first:

The Matrix.

Mary is already holding a hand out to me and one out to Ned. "I have already dialed in the location," she promises. "We must go at once."

Neither of us argues, we just take her hands and close our eyes. I know Mary can do the whole teleport-with-her-eyes-open thing, but I think that's because the Grays modified her mind so she can comprehend the whole of space-time at once or something like that. For most of us, trying to watch as your body's disassembled into its component atoms and then digitized and beamed across like the world's weirdest YouTube video? Not only physically nauseating but also unsettling on a metaphysical level.

Especially since I don't even have my own channel!

Something else occurs to me, though, even as I start feeling that weird tremor in my body that means I'm about to become a high-speed transmission like the world's most oddly shaped email packet. "We need to call—" is all I manage to get out before Rocks R Us fades away, along with any physical sensation and all sensory input. For what feels like half a second, max, I'm nothing but thought, arrowing along across the cosmos. I just wish I could enjoy the view.

And maybe snag a pizza or two along the way.

I feel my feet first, which is probably just because, after my bill, they're the single biggest, heaviest part of me. Then I get all the rest in a rush—the ground beneath my feet, the air on my face, my clothing rustling against my feathers, the feel of Mary's hand in mine.

"—Tall," I finish in what feels like the same breath. But it can't be, can it? I mean, I was just transported halfway across the galaxy. Even if it's the same atoms as before—and why would it be, when it makes a lot more sense to disintegrate those old atoms and then build all-new ones here, rather than trying to transport the old ones across that distance? When you send someone a picture you just snapped on your phone, you're not sending the actual picture you took, much less the object you photographed, you're sending them the information to assemble a copy of that image on their end. Same thing here, I think— I've never actually asked, but that would seem to make sense. In which case my old body just died and my new one was just born. Hey, Happy Birthday to me! But that also means this is the first breath of this new body, even though I'm ending a sentence I started on another world, in a whole other me.

See what I mean about metaphysically unsettling? Next thing you know I'll be double-sleeving and one of me'll have purple hair and then all hell will break loose!

With all that going on in my head, I still manage to blurt out the rest of what I was trying to say as we left. "He and Heidi are en route to Stoneworld, but they need to turn around and get their butts here instead. Double-time."

Ned nods. "On it." He pulls a little tube from his belt, clicks it, and instantly a swarm of tiny, glittering motes is surrounding his head. His idea of a cell phone is still crazy-looking, though I bet if he could get those things to form the shape of an apple he'd have it sold in a heartbeat.

Meanwhile, I'm looking around. Sparkly pink walls that curve overhead, a clutter of strange and possibly useless devices strewn about the large chamber we're in, half-empty boxes and cartons and packets of food and drink in a few dozen different languages mixed in as well, a large screen straight ahead that looks to be formed out of solid ice, a shape behind us that's currently altering itself from something like a mix between an Iron Maiden and a Bowflex—which aren't that far apart, when you think about it—into a wide, cushy couch, a skylight above showing an insane number of stars sparking and strobing and flashing past.

Ah, it's good to be home.

Though I may have to have words with my couch later. It knows that it's supposed to clean up before it does its exercise routine, not after!

"I'm gonna check the Matrix," I tell Mary and Ned, heading for the archway connecting this room to the next. "I know we should've had an alert if there was something wrong with it and all that, but better safe than sorry."

They both follow me from the room, down the hall, and then through another archway out into the Matrix chamber that takes up the center of the building. It wasn't until I realized this whole place was actually some kind of crazily old giant skull that I understood that the Matrix sat where the creature's brain would have been.

Which is pretty much perfect placement, seeing as how the Matrix is part of what keeps our whole universe running smoothly.

Even after all this time, I'm still blown away a little every time I see it. Which isn't all that surprising—after all, how often do you run across something that looks like the most beautiful silver and gold ribbons ever made, woven and braided and twisted into an intricate rope that mixes with computer cables and fluted glass tubes and filigreed brass pipes and silken cords, occasionally wrapping cocoon-like around monitors and phials and beaded drums and circuit boards and jade carvings, all of it gliding by at slow, stately pace like somebody's art project doing a parade circuit. Or maybe the world's most abstract Mardi Gras float—"Thoughts in Hue."

It looks fine, exactly the way it should look. And, as always, it seems to brighten when I walk in the room. Yes, actually get brighter, the glow coming off it increasing from "hey, there are those flip-flops I was looking for!" to "um, I might like a few

less after-images when I blink, thanks." Even with my nictitating membranes automatically sliding down over my eyeballs,
that flare-up always blinds me for a second. Then it settles back
down again.

I think it's happy to see me.

"Hey, buddy!" I call out, walking over to the Matrix and
running my hand over one of the brassy sections. It chimes
softly at my touch. "You all good here?" It doesn't answer that
one directly—I'm honestly not sure how intelligent it is, or how
self-aware, or how capable of communicating, which makes
it like every toddler I've ever met and about half the girls I've
dated—but everything looks right.

Ned's got some of his gadgets out and is waving them over
the Matrix like he's trying to conduct Beethoven's Ninth—or like
it's a giant salad and he's sprinkling on a little more rosemary
and oregano, just to be safe. "Everything's running smooth," he
reports a minute later, tapping the two gizmos together before
tucking them back away. "No sign of any problem, and no record
of anyone trying to force entry, either."

"We must have returned before they could access it," Mary
suggests. "Or at least before they could find a way to bypass the
security measures we have enacted since their last incursion."
It's true, we did beef up the security since then—sometimes
when I get up in the middle of the night to grab a glass of lo-
pei berry juice (it tastes like you took the most beautiful pearl
you've ever seen—and ground it up, sprinkled it with carda-
mom and cloves and ginger—and mixed it into a glass of sweet
tea. Amazing stuff, though I have to steer clear of the jewelry

portion of those home shopping shows for a while afterward) it actually demands to know who I am and what I'm doing here!—but she's frowning as she says it.

I can guess why. The invaders aren't just creepy, with their penchant for lurking around invisibly (for a while after the first time I was swinging a pole around me every time I got ready to take a shower, just to be sure!) and their weird, hissing way of speaking, and not just pushy with their whole "we want your universe and we don't care that you were here first" mentality, they're also really darn clever. Every time we think we've gotten rid of them for good, they find a way to come back and poke at us again.

It's hard to imagine any security system is going to keep them out for long.

Speaking of which, the lights all around the place suddenly cut out, replaced by flashing red strobes from every corner and accompanied by blaring sirens. "Intruder incoming!" a voice declares loud enough to be heard over the sirens. "Intruder incoming!" The voice is deep, commanding, and gravely, and I recognize it instantly.

It's Tall.

I know he helped Ned set up the whole system, but I didn't realize they used his voice for the alerts! Talk about personal protection!

"They're here!" I shout, dropping into a crouch. Of course, I'm still standing next to the Matrix, which would be a big, shiny target even if it wasn't the actual, you know, target, so probably not all that inconspicuous. But it's the thought that counts. Especially when you're dealing with telepaths who're also Chinese vampires. Just think about grains of rice over and over. Makes 'em nuts.

Ned and Mary are looking around too, and I know we're all thinking the same thing—if the invaders really are here, why haven't they attacked already? What are they waiting for? What's their plan this time? And did anyone think to grab a sub or a pizza or some noodles?

Okay, that last one might just be me. They say an army fights on its stomach. Guess that makes me a one-man army.

But then the sirens stop—they just vanish mid-blare—and the strobes go dark, and the regular lights come back on. The silence is nearly deafening, so I fill it with, "Crap, they've cut the alarms!"

"Thump!" goes something down the hall.

"They're breaking down the door!" I shout.

"Thump!"

"They're . . . still breaking down the door!" I update.

"Thump! Thump!"

"Um . . ." I straighten up and scratch my bill. "They're knocking aggressively at the door?"

I'm distracted from the puzzle of the invaders' sudden and inexplicable new politeness by my phone. It's playing "Never Gonna Give You Up," which I assigned Tall both because his voice is as deep as Rick Astley's and because of the way it makes him grind his teeth every time he has to hear that song.

"Hey, where are you?" I say as soon as I accept the call. "We're at the Matrix, you gotta hurry, the invaders are right outside the door! Though for some reason they're just knocking, but that can't last."

You wouldn't think you could hear teeth grinding over the phone, would you? Amazing what they can do with digital sound these days. "That's me, you idiot!" he snaps. "Let us in!"

"Oh." I head for the door fast as I can, which isn't exactly all that fast. "Why didn't you say so? And why didn't you just come straight in like the rest of us?"

"Because I don't have a teleport key for the Matrix, numskull!" he replies. I finally reach the door, panting, and yank it open, to find a towering figure on the far side, with a floating bowling ball just behind his right shoulder.

"Hey, Tall," I say. "Hey, Heidi."

"Hey," Heidi replies. He's the bowling ball. Well, not really, but that's what he looks like—a floating glass sphere filled with some kind of strange, swirling gas that changes color with his moods. And has something small and dark darting around within it. For all that, he's a pretty cool dude, and he's Tall's partner in their interstellar trucking business.

Tall doesn't say hello, he just shoves past me. Or tries to—the front hall isn't all that wide, and my bill is, so we wind up just wedged in together as he attempts to muscle me out of the way. Which might work if my bill wasn't stronger than most concrete. Don't ask how I know that—let's just say I'm really glad I'm bill-heavy, otherwise I'd have broken some bones with some of those falls.

"Hey, slow your roll there, hoss!" I warn him. "Let me back up, 'kay? And nice to see you too, by the way."

Tall turns and locks eyes with me. "I'm right here," he growls softly.

"Yeah, I know. That's why I said hello." Sheesh!

More tooth-grinding ensues. "You can stop talking into your phone now," he explains finally, clipping each word short like the sentence is a bouquet and he's snipping the stems to make them all fit into the world's shortest vase.

Oh. Right. I end the call and pocket the phone. "Great reception, though, right?" I ask him. "It sounded like you were right here!"

Yes, sometimes I do this to him deliberately. He just makes it so damn easy, and I'm still trying to see if I can get steam to literally come out of his ears.

That one time doesn't count. We'd both just had Erlasi Vapor-flakes, and those make steam come out *everywhere*! Which looks a little weird, and can get you banned in certain restaurants. But hey, dry-cleaning without even having to disrobe first!

I can see Tall's not in a funning mood, though, so I back up a few paces, far enough to reach the door of the coatroom, and step back into it so he can bull on by. Heidi's floated in behind us, and shut the door again. Considerate little cuss, even if I'm not sure how he managed that with no actual appendages.

We both trail Tall into the Matrix chamber, where we find Ned and Mary still. "What happened?" Tall demands as soon as he enters.

"Short version?" I offer from behind him. "The Grays are gone, their whole world and everything, just some rocks in its place. The invaders did it, Ned found traces of 'em there. We high-tailed it back here, but it looks like they haven't hit us yet. Though the alarms—" My brain does work, if a little slowly and often on some parallel track involving a disco soundtrack and a buffet lunch, and now it catches up on that last bit. "Never mind, that was you, wasn't it?"

Tall doesn't have an answer to that, but Ned nods. "Yeah, the security logs show the system picked up their ship coming in hot," he explains. "It sounded the alarm, then cut off when they got close enough for it to confirm they were registered in its files."

Ha, so Tall warned us that there were intruders, but it was really Tall, only he didn't recognize himself at first? And I thought *I* had an identity crisis sometimes!

Chapter Seven
You can come play
but you can't bring any toys

"All right, slow down," Tall instructs, taking charge in that take-charge way of his. "The Grays are gone?" He turns to Ned and Mary for confirmation, which I'd be offended by if I hadn't pulled a few too many "hey, no, really" pranks on him. Including the time I had him convinced that all of this—me, the Matrix, all our adventures, Heidi, the whole bit—was just a prolonged hallucination and that he was really just an insurance adjuster in Boise, Idaho, who was part of the local bowling league (with a 93 average!) and was dating a veterinary assistant named Janice.

Yes, it's usually a bad idea to leave me to my own devices for too long. In my defense, I didn't expect him to take me seriously when he asked, "Why is this my life?" and I answered, "It's not, you're hallucinating," but once I did I had no choice but to run with it.

Anyway, they both nod, and Tall frowns, which is like watching tectonic plates move. And explains all that grinding. "When did this happen?" he demands. "How did you find out? What have you done to locate them?" Wow, that's three of the big questions rapid-fire. He really is good at this!

"We do not know the precise timing," Mary answers. "DuckBob and I both received an urgent plea for help from them, but by the time we were able to reach Obscura Major there was no sign of them."

"That's their homeworld?" Tall asks. I wonder how he knows that. Is it in the MiB dossier on the Grays, who they've worked with off and on for years? Have any of the MiBs been there? Or did Tall pick up the name from scuttlebutt on the space-trucker circuit, like there's a toilet stall out there somewhere with "Wanna party Gray-style? Visit Obscura Major for a good time"? "And what do you mean, there was no sign of them?" He turns back to me. "You said there was nothing left but some rocks. Someone blew up their planet?" Leave it to Tall to go for the most violent option first!

"Naw," I tell him, "planet's still there, just been stripped bare. Not even any ground cover, just rock as far as the eye can see."

Tall turns his laser-eye stare on Ned, who isn't fazed, probably because his eyes can actually glow on command. Or just when he's excited, which has got to be awkward at the grocery or in a crowded elevator but a useful indicator on first dates. "You found traces of the invaders there?"

Ned nods. "Yeah, their energy trail's definitely there, and definitely recent," he confirms. "Doesn't prove it was them that took the Grays, 'course, but if two and two equal four who'm I to argue?"

Tall's frown has reached monolithic proportions. "This makes little sense," he states, though he isn't looking at any of us when he says it so we know he isn't calling us liars or any-thing. If he was, he'd do so nice and direct. I can attest to that from frequent experience. "If it is the invaders, they know that the Matrix is the single biggest threat to their incursions," he continues. "Why wouldn't they come here first and try to shut it down again? Maybe nabbing the Grays was a diversionary tactic to get you out of here"—that's directed at me, or at least in my general vicinity—"but if that's the case, why didn't they use that window for a new attack on this place?"

"Yeah," I contribute, "and how'd they get back in, anyway? The Matrix is running fine; we plugged that wormhole on Ned's world, so they shouldn't have had any more doors or windows in. Unless they found a Port-key."

That earns me a fleeting "fair enough, good point" nod, so I know I'm at least out of the doghouse again. For now. "Right," Tall agrees. "We need to know how they got in again—or if this is just an isolated invader who somehow evaded capture the first time around. Then we need to know why they went after the Grays instead of coming here. Then we need to know exactly what they did to the Grays, in order to figure out if it's reversible." He straightens, and the look he shoots me this time is almost apologetic. I don't know why until he adds, "I need to call this in."

"What?" I wave my hands in protest. "Oh, come on! We can handle this! We always handle it! We don't need . . . them . . . involved!"

But Tall's adamant, and that's practically literal—I always think that, once he's set his mind and body to something, it'd take an atom bomb just to shift him an inch or two. I look to Mary for support, but she bites her lip and slowly, sadly, shakes her head.

"I am sorry, my love," she tells me, "but I must concur with Tall. With a situation of this magnitude, they must be informed. Both because we may require their assistance and because if we do not inform them and they hear of it later, they will use that fact as proof that you are not cooperating with them fully."

Sigh. Every so often I hate it when she's right—usually in situations like this, or when we're playing Scrabble and she insists that "gu" is a word. "Fine," I grumble. "Come on, Tall, let's go make the call."

We all trudge back into the living room, leaving the Matrix humming merrily to itself—something from Gershwin, I think, which is a nice change from its recent goth-pop fixation—and head for the computer. I warm it up—not literally, since it'd just melt—and tap an icon on the bottom of the screen. Instantly a window opens and, after a second, clears to show a narrow figure with razor-sharp features and equally sharp dark clothes.

"Heya, Smith," I tell the senior MiB, Tall's former boss and my ostensible contact in their organization. "How's it hanging?"

As usual, the look Smith gives me is about the same you'd give something you just collected on the bottom of your shoe, like you're trying to decide whether to scrape it off or just toss the whole shoe rather than risk any chance of direct contact. I've never really understood why he dislikes me so much. Unless it's my complete and utter disregard for authority. And my inability to follow even the simplest instructions. Or my constant need to speak, even when I'm not actually making any sense. Or the fact that he roped me into all this, and then I showed him up and got the girl and saved the universe while he was sitting around trying to decide if he should file in triplicate from back to front for a change, just to be daring.

Okay, maybe I do know why.

"Mr. Spinowitz," he replies. "Agent Thomas." He still calls Tall that, even though Tall's not officially a MiB anymore. "To what do I owe this pleasure?" It's funny how some people can use a word and make it clear they mean the exact opposite. Like when Southerners say, "Bless your heart" and what they really mean is "die in a trash fire."

"Oh, you know, just calling to say hi," I tell him. "See how the office is going—still that lovely shade of penitentiary gray? It really brings out your pallor—compare notes on the latest Mets games—poor guys, one of these days they might actually realize they're playing baseball, that'd help—let you know the Grays got abducted, you know. The usual."

Now, see, this is what I'm talking about. Most of the time, people like Smith are so used to my verbal spillage they don't even pay attention other than to make sure I'm still breathing, and then only as a common courtesy. I could blather on all day long and afterward they wouldn't remember a word of it. But now, when I'm trying to slip one by him, Smith sits bolt upright—he was already at something like three-quarters bolt anyway, I swear he's got a golf club or a piece of rebar in place of a spine—and leans in toward the screen. Which is terrifying, as his head is suddenly huge. I half expect him to say, "I know everything you are thinking, everything you will do, you cannot defeat me, now strike!"

"What did you just say?" he asks instead, and his voice has that deadly calm of a snake about to spring. "The Grays have been abducted?"

"Um, yeah, about that." I rub the back of my neck. "Looks like. They're all gone, Obscura Major's got a big 'for rent cheap' sign out front, they didn't even bother with the rummage sale first." I sigh and plunge on ahead with the worst of it. "Looks like the invaders again."

"The invaders are back?" Smith frowns, which just means his mouth compresses into an even narrower line and his eyes get thinner as well. It's bad enough you could normally cut yourself on the guy's cheekbones and chin, now every part of his face has edges! And all I can hear is, "even his eyebrow is a killing word!" which makes no less sense than anything else in a Lynch movie, really. "Have they made another attempt at the Matrix?"

"Not yet, no," Tall cuts in. "But we expect they will. It's the only logical course of action."

Smith nods once, sharp enough I'm surprised it doesn't pierce the screen. "I will dispatch agents at once," he informs us. "We will lock down the Matrix until the Grays' safe return." There's something in the way he says it that smacks of a sleazy landlord saying, "I'm gonna need to up the rent a little soon, but don't worry, it won't be too bad," or a soon-to-be ex-girlfriend swearing, "it didn't mean anything, honest, but maybe we should start seeing other people."

"Uh uh," I respond right away. "No way. We don't need your goons stomping around here, tracking dirt everywhere. We'll call if we need you."

"Unacceptable," Smith snaps back. He's always had this proprietary notion about the Matrix, like somehow he's entitled to part-ownership just because I'm from Earth and he's the one who first put me in touch with the Grays. Which is a lot like if some guy from Shebogyan became President and suddenly the town elders—all five of 'em—showed up at the White House and started walking around it saying things like, "Yeah, we'll knock down this wall here to make room for the pool" and "I'm thinking knotty pine for the exterior, give the place a more homey feel" and then got confused when they got forcibly shown off the property. "The Matrix is far too important a portion of this universe's defenses to be wholly entrusted to—"

"Yeah?" I lean in too, and maybe my bill isn't as sharp as his chin but it's a whole helluva lot bigger. "To what?"

"To whom," Mary corrects quietly behind me. Then she edges past me somehow and gets right in Smith's face. "I believe the answer to that question," she states firmly, "is that it be entrusted to the individual who has already restored it to full functionality once and protected it from control by these invaders twice. The same individual whom the Grays themselves have chosen to serve as its Guardian, and whom you have pledged to assist as needed, that last to be determined by that individual. Not by you." Damn! I've seen her get all science-y before, and that's hot, but watching her go all corporate-lawyer on Smith's bony ass? Freaking amazing!

It's clear he doesn't know what to do about this sudden barrage, either. Especially since he's been pretty much smitten since the first time he saw her. Which is one of the only things ol' Smith and I agree on.

"Yes, well, of course we have complete trust in the Grays' decision," he offers hastily, looking exactly like a little kid who's just tried bullying some even littler kids, only to have Mom show up mid-threat and give him that look that says "if there weren't laws in this country, I'd lock you up in the henhouse for a week—after rolling you in chicken feed." "But in their absence—"

"—in their absence DuckBob will continue to protect the Matrix, as intended," Tall cuts in. "The four of us'll be here to back him up. We'll keep you posted if anything changes, and we'll let you know the minute we need your help." His tone, like Mary's, makes it clear that this is not open for debate.

Ned and Heidi don't say anything, but their presence behind us offers a clear nonverbal, "Yeah, what he said!" Hey, I recognize that you don't always have to talk to make your point. I don't fully understand it, and I certainly don't know how to do it myself, but I recognize it!

Smith blusters a little more, but it's clear he's beat and he knows it. Finally, he harrumphs a bit, demands that we keep him apprised—which we already said we would—and signs off. Sheesh, I bet he flips the board when he's losing at checkers, too!

We all breathe a little easier once he's gone. Man, even having him on the screen feels like that dream where you're in the Army and it's Parade Inspection but you thought it was Pajama

Day and you're standing at full attention in front of everybody in your footie PJs with the butt flap hanging loose.

Or maybe that one's just me. Especially after a double-feature of *Stripes* and *Private Benjamin* and a few too many hot wings.

Chapter Eight
Why do I have to be Macaulay Culkin?

"**I still don't** get it," Tall insists. It's an hour later, and he's pacing back and forth so much he's starting to wear a path in the rug. Though that could just be because it keeps moving out of the way of his feet, which aren't as big or as heavy as mine but still can't be fun to have walk all over you. I think my couch may've eaten my rug at some point and just spread itself out across the floor in its place, hoping I wouldn't notice. Which has me worried, because what if it decides to start gobbling up and replacing more furniture? Or other occupants? Mary could wake up one morning beside me, except I'd be an odd greenish color and only able to say things like "I am DuckBob."

Is it asking too much to hope she'd be able to tell the difference?

"What's bugging you, tough guy?" I ask. I'm sprawled on said couch, which maybe I should be a little more worried about after the whole "consuming other items" revelation but right now I'm too keyed up to care. "You worried Smith backed off way too easy? 'Cause I sure am! I'm not gonna be even the least bit surprised if he and his goon squad show up at the front door, weapons hot, and say, 'Yeah, we changed our minds, we're moving in.' I'm thinking maybe we should change the locks, just to be safe."

But Tall shakes his head. "No, Smith will stick to the agreement," he insists. "What's bothering me is the invaders and their recent actions. They got back into our reality somehow, but instead of coming here straight off, they went for the Grays. Why?"

Nestled up against me, Mary shrugs. "Clearly they have devised a new strategy," she offers. "Which is sensible, considering that their last two attempts have met with failure. Whatever they have done to the Grays is no doubt only the opening move in their current gambit."

"Yeah," Tall says, stomping over and perching on the edge of the couch arm. It obligingly reshapes itself into a barstool. Suck-up. "But I don't know what that gambit is, which means I can't see what they're going to do next." He smacks one hand into the other, which is totally macho posturing except that he's not even aware he's doing it and it actually works for him. "And it's driving me nuts!"

"If it makes you feel any better," I offer, "I bet it's killing Smith, too." I chuckle a little at the thought of him pacing exactly like Tall, only with smaller steps and fancier shoes. "Dude's probably like a little kid who's been left alone in the house for the first time. He clearly wants to raid the fridge and the cookie jar and go check out the den for Dad's old *Playboy*s, but he's afraid the second he tries the 'rents are gonna pop back in and say, 'aha, gotcha!'"

You know how sometimes you're just letting the words spill

out of your mouth without really paying them too much attention because there's always more so why worry about it, and then all of a sudden you realize that everybody else is staring at you? But not with that "what the hell are you even saying?" look, which you're totally used to and barely even notice anymore even if it does occasionally sting just a little, but instead with that much rarer but far cooler, "Okay, wait, say that again, because I think you just made sense!" look?

Or is that just me?

Mary reacts first, hugging me close and kissing me on the cheek. See, her praise is totally the best! "Of course!" she cheers. "You have, as always, discerned the exact truth of the matter, my love."

I did? Cool. Wonder what it was. I glance at Tall for confirmation, and he nods slowly.

"She's right," he says. "That's got to be it." I've just earned Stare Number Eight, "Okay, that's actually really impressive but your head's already the size of Jupiter so I'm going to downplay my admiration and settle for a raised eyebrow and a comradely nod." Which is probably my favorite, except when I'm in the mood to torment him, in which case I gun for Two—"Remind me why I don't just shoot you and incinerate the body?"—or Seven—"I feel like you know more about something than I do, and it's making me crazy."

Fortunately, Ned's just as confused about my apparent brilliance as I am. "Sorry, I'm not following," he says. "The invaders are after cookies and *Playboys*?" Well, and who wouldn't be?

But Tall corrects him—and without sighing or rolling his

eyes, which I think is totally unfair. "They're trying to undercut our defenses," he explains. "And they're worried we'll call in the Grays for help—so they've taken the Grays out of the equation first."

"Leaving us weakened," Mary adds. "Especially since the Grays created the Matrix and established it here. They know its inner workings better than anyone else—"

"—so if the invaders can break it, that leaves us without the Grays to help fix it," Ned finishes for her. "Got it." He whistles. "Damn, that's actually pretty smart. Underhanded, but smart."

I'm thinking the same thing. I mean, it really does make total sense now that I've had my own thoughts explained to me. If you're trying to break into a house, you're a lot better off doing it when the owners aren't at home. So you wait until they leave—or, if you're impatient, you come up with something that gets them out of the house for you.

Once that's done, all that's left to worry about is the security system itself, and maybe the family dog.

Evidently in this scenario I'm the dog.

"No!" I shout, unsettling Mary as I leap to my feet. The couch makes this a lot easier by basically springboarding me upright. Thanks, bud. I guess I'll forgive the whole rug thing. For now. "I am not the family dog!" I shake my fist up at the sky. "I'm the pesky kid; the one they forgot or figured could fend for himself while they ran to the store! I'm the one who foils the burglars, using only some old paint cans and a few other household goods!"

Tall's staring at me like I've lost it, Ned's looking confused, but Mary's nodding. By now we've spent enough time together—and watched enough movies from my formative years—that about half the time she can figure out what I really mean by what I'm saying. She's like my own personal, really hot, translator.

"You are correct," she agrees, rising to stand beside me and slipping an arm around my waist. "The invaders may believe they have rendered us helpless by removing the Grays, but they will find we are far more resourceful tenacious, and durable than they expect."

"I'm on board with that," Tall states, straightening beside us. "If they think they're just gonna waltz on in here, they've got another thing coming." He crosses his arms over his chest, looking like he's just gonna bar them from entry by sheer bicep size, stony glare, and willpower alone. Which, knowing Tall, might actually work. He's like a cross between a bodybuilder, a bouncer, and a really tough school crossing guard. All he needs is the black muscle tee and the yellow vest.

Heidi's been hovering nearby, not adding much to the conversation but then he's only run into the invaders once before, since he wasn't around us the first time. Plus, I've noticed he tends to let others do the talking whenever possible, which is fine with me since I'll do pretty much anybody's talking for them. With or without their consent or sometimes even awareness. Now, though, he floats over in front of us, the colors of his sphere shifting to orange and red. Which is bad, 'cause I know him well enough by now to recognize that those are signs of alarm.

"Um, that all sounds nice and defiant and all," he starts,

those colors flickering faster and faster until he's practically strobing, "but I hope you're all ready to put your money where your collective mouth is." He dips, wobbles, then rises back up again, ascending until he's just above our heads. "Because if those energy readings I was getting near that wormhole on Artelusia IX are from these invaders?" The red is mixed with flashes of pure white, which I know are fear. "Then they're somewhere nearby, and they're closing in. Fast."

"Damn! Battlestations!" I shout, racing from the room. I'm back a second later. "I forget," I say, already panting a little. "Where are our battlestations?"

Fortunately, Tall takes charge. This is exactly the kind of stuff he's really good at. "Ned, check the security systems, make sure everything is online!" he orders. "Heidi, check the front door, make sure it's secure! Mary, get up top, holler when you can see them coming. I've got a few things stashed here from last time, just in case—guess I'd better break them out now." The others all scatter, off to their individual tasks. We can all feel the Doomsday Clock hanging over our heads, its minute hand almost to the twelve, the first of the gongs beginning to vibrate through the air.

There's only one problem. "Hey, what about me?" I demand. "What'm I supposed to do?"

For a second I think Tall forgot about me—which, believe me, is no easy feat, a lot of people have tried! I think there's actually clauses in most psychotherapy program's contracts now—but then he grabs me by the shoulders. "You need to get back to the Matrix," he says, and I can see he's being completely serious.

"I know you've got the wireless connection and all, but it's going to be a lot stronger and more secure if you're actually right there with it, and right now we need all the strength and security we can get."

Okay, that does actually make sense. It's like connecting via wi-fi versus actually plugging directly into the router—the first one works, but the second one's a lot stronger and faster, and doesn't have to worry about interference from the annoying neighbor's network that's called "Krazy Karaoke" or "The StanCave."

"I'm on it," I promise, and high-tail it out of the room, heading straight for the Matrix chamber. I'll plug myself back into the circuit directly, and stay jacked in until the threat is past.

Or until I need to hit the head.

Or I get peckish and have to nip off to the kitchen for a quick bite.

Or one of my favorite shows comes on.

But otherwise? There's nothing that could make me budge. I'm like a big, duck-headed rock. A dock. Or maybe the Matrix is the dock, because I'm the ship coming into the harbor?

Great, now I've got visions of me as a boat, with a duck head prow and a sail made from one of my favorite, loudest shirts, and my bill as the deck.

I've gotta stop eating those flash-frozen Rigelean laser-pepper poppers between meals. I already knew they were messing with my stomach, but I think they're starting to set fire to my head, too.

Chapter Nine
Stop confusing my FitBit!

There's just one problem—I can't seem to reach the Matrix.

I mean that in the most literal sense. After Tall's instructions, I take off out of the room, running full-out for the Matrix chamber.

Now, I've been the Matrix's Guardian almost a year already—hey, wonder if I get a certificate for that? Or a medal? Or a nice lunch out? Anyway, that also means I've been living here at the Matrix for almost a year, too. And up until a few months ago, I couldn't go out except for short breaks, and never farther than a few blocks.

Which means I've spent a lot of time in this place.

A lot of time.

You know how, when you really stop and think about it, you spend more of your life at work than you do awake at home? Depressing, but true—you work nine to five, so a solid eight hours out of the day, and then you might spend another hour or two commuting, and another hour or three out socializing, and then another six to eight asleep, so your "at home awake" time? Maybe four hours a day. Half the time you spend at work.

Except if you work at home. Then your "at home" time is

pretty much tripled, maybe even quadrupled since you don't have to deal with a commute.

So, yeah, lots of time rattling around in this wacky place. With not a lot to do, since my job basically consists of "be plugged into the Matrix and stay alive." Always good to know the job requirements up front.

But that means I've had way too much time on my hands. And one of things a lot of people do if they've got the time and they're constrained to a certain physical space? They measure it out. Ask any ex-con and he can probably still tell you the number of paces within his cell. Hell, I can tell you how many it was in my first dorm room—exactly ten by ten, because it was a ten-foot square cinderblock room and, pre-alteration, my feet were exactly a foot long.

Come to think of it, if you'd replaced the door with bars that room basically was a prison cell. We had a lights-out and everything. Though I can't entirely blame the dorm managers for that, not after the first two times we broke things. Like the fire exit door. And the elevator.

Point is, I know exactly how many steps it takes to get from my living room to the Matrix chamber. If you're curious, it's ninety-three. Of course, my feet are a hell of a lot bigger now, but my legs are still the same length so my stride hasn't really changed, which means it's about ninety-three feet from here to there. Why ninety-three? I have no idea. This place is actually an ancient skull, after all, so it's not like some architects got together and said, "hey, let's put the main room here and have a hall run off it and have the next door be ninety-three feet away!"

But that's how far it is. Ninety-three feet.

And yeah, I'm not exactly in the best shape ever, but I have been getting more fit recently, thanks to Tall and his psychotic need to whip everyone around him into shape. When I'm just strolling, it takes me about as long to get to the Matrix and back—if, say, I forgot I'd left my Madralusian comet-shake ("made from real comet ice! You can taste the exotic minerals! Comes in strawberry, mint, tamarind, and dedranut flavors! For a real taste blast, order them all at once!") by the Matrix and waited until a commercial break in "Real Laserbrides of Techzilicone 7-B" to go retrieve it—as it does to sing the whole of that show's theme song ("I am a silicate computing organism that did not realize it suffered from isolationism until I discovered the beauty of binary pairing, so I crafted myself a match from spare circuit boards and a digitized construct based upon Lindsay Lohan and now I cannot imagine existence without the deadly creature-device at my side," to a tune that's awfully similar to the Gilligan's Island theme song). That's maybe three minutes, tops.

But three minutes later, I slow down to catch my breath. And I'm still in the hall. In fact, it barely looks like I've gotten anyway—the archway leading to the Matrix is still at least sixty feet away.

Maybe, in my haste, I started running backward by mistake? I hate it when I do that!

So, gulping some air, I take off again like a bullet. Well, maybe a cannonball. Or one of those things where it was two cannonballs connected by a chain, only in this case the chain is more like an inflatable raft. Whatever, I'm running fast as I can—and after a minute I'm sure of it.

That archway still isn't any closer.

"Tall!" I shout. Though it comes out more like a wheeze at this point.

He's standing next to me a minute later. "What's wrong?" he asks, though it's more like a demand. "Why aren't you at the Matrix already?" He's got a big huge gun cradled in his arms, all gleaming metal tubes and barrels and clips. I think I see a nozzle clipped to its side, and a temperature gauge. Reassuring.

"I'm trying!" I tell him. I wave at the archway. "It's not cooperating!"

With a scowl he pushes past me—I take up a lot of room, and this hallway's not all that wide—and stomps toward the Matrix.

Only, he doesn't get anywhere. I'm watching him, and though I can see his legs working and his feet lifting and lowering, he's not advancing at all. It's like he's marching in place.

After a minute of this, he stops and turns to study me. We're only a few feet apart. "Something is wrong," he says.

I cross my arms over my chest and glare at him. "Gee, ya think? I figured that part out already, thanks!"

His nod is a grudging acknowledgment and an apology. Tall's actually willing to admit when he's wrong—once you pound it into his head. With a sledgehammer. Made from a white dwarf star. And propelled from orbit.

We're a lot alike that way.

Just then we hear a soft whine behind us, and then Heidi

floats into view. "Guys, something's going on here," he reports. "I can't seem to get to the front door. I'm moving forward, but the distance to it remains constant."

Tall and I exchange a glance. So it's not just this hallway, it's the whole building.

Ned and Mary rejoin us a minute later. "I cannot access the upper levels," Mary declares with a frown. I try not to get distracted, but it's awfully close to her pout and I can already feel my willpower fading. "There is some sort of distortion to local space-time, and no matter how quickly I move, the distance to my destination remains unchanged."

"Yeah, we've got the same thing here," I tell her. "Can't get to the Matrix. Heidi can't get to the front door." We all turn to Ned, who shrugs.

"I was fine," he reports. "But I was only going to your computer, which is right there." That's true, he didn't actually have to leave the living room.

Until now.

"Crap," I tell him. "Get back to the computer! Now!"

Ned's eyes widen—it's a little alarming when they do that, since it's a lot like searchlights suddenly clicking on—and, turning on his heel, sprints back for the door.

Only he's not getting any closer to it.

"Damn!" He shakes his head. "Sorry, guys. I heard all the commotion and figured I'd better see what was up."

"What's up," I reply, "is that those guys are clearly messing with my head. And by my head, I don't mean this big noggin"— tapping my bill. "I mean this one." And I press a hand against the wall. "They've figured out a way to screw with its dimensions or something, and they're keeping us trapped here, well away from anything useful."

"I was able to grab one of the guns I'd stashed here," Tall points out. After a second's thought, though, he nods. "It was in the locker room. Not what anyone'd normally consider a key strategic location."

Unlike the door, the balcony, my computer, and the Matrix itself. Check.

"How're they doing this?" I demand. "Ned, Heidi, you guys got anything on your scanners?" I turn to Mary. "Is this screwing up your teleport, or can you maybe pop us out to the living room from here?" Tall's next. "And is it just us because we're inside? Because if so, much as I hate to say it, we might need to call Smith in after all."

This nod is tied to Stare Number Six: "So your brain does sometimes work after all!" "I'll call him now," Tall promises, hauling out his phone. "They've got an emergency teleport for just outside the front door, he can scramble some agents and have them here in minutes."

Mary closed her eyes but now opens them again, looks at me, and shakes her head. "I am unable to access the array," she informs me, looking apologetic. "Whatever they have done to alter space and time around us, it is interfering with that network." Great, so we're stuck here.

Ned is fiddling with some of his little doohickeys, and Heidi's humming and flashing shades of gray, which I think mean's he's cogitating. Ned looks up first. "Yeah, there's some pretty heavy distortion going on here," he reports. "I'm getting crazy breaches to local physics. It's like they took the natural laws and just twisted 'em all into a knot."

"Same here," Heidi agrees. "Energy fluctuations all over the place, weird gravitational readings, unstable geometrics. They've warped us into a little box."

Mary frowns. "Are you capable of projecting your readings for the rest of us to see?"

Heidi brightens, the gray shading to blue. "Sure!" A second later, a beam of light emerges from his front—at least, the side of the sphere facing us—and projects onto the nearest wall. It's a whole bunch of charts and displays and I have absolutely no idea what I'm looking at, but Mary steps closer and studies them intently, tracing a finger along one or two graphs.

"I understand," she says finally. "Thank you." The image winks out. I wonder if he can get Netflix on that thing? "They have indeed altered reality around us," she states. "But where before they have simply modified surroundings to give themselves a tactical advantage by creating desired items or removing potential threats, this is a more subtle approach. They have modified the underpinnings of space-time itself, but only in this location. Effectively they have unmoored us from the rest of reality, trapping us, as Heidi said, within a little box."

"Great." I stare at the wall—those images are gone now, of course, but at least it gives me something to glare at besides my friends, who're just as stuck as I am. "So we're in a little lifeboat floating on an ocean, cut off from the ocean liner that's the rest of reality?"

It's Heidi who replies. "Not exactly," he says. "More like we're in the lifeboat and it's tethered to the bigger ship but the water's rough so we keep bobbing about and those lines keep us connected but sometimes we're close, sometimes we're far, and even when we're bumping right up against it there's too much turbulence for us to jump back across."

"Ah, okay, got it." This is what I like about Heidi—for a floating, swirling bowling ball, he makes a lot of sense. "So, anyway we can fire a grappling hook, yank ourselves right up to the hull, and then lash ourselves in place so we can climb back onboard?"

Tall starts to reply, his scowl clearly warning that he's going to say something like "don't be an idiot," but Mary cuts him off. "In point of fact," she says slowly, a smile beginning to form on her lovely face, "that may indeed be the solution." Now she's got everyone's full attention. "If we can create an Einstein-Rosen bridge, we might be able to anchor our surroundings back onto the rest of reality. Essentially we would be overwriting the changes they have introduced, which are preventing us from crossing, and synching this box back with normal space-time."

"Great!" I rub my hands together. "How do we do that?"

Her smile fades. "Unfortunately," she answers, "that may be beyond our current capabilities. We would need a way to introduce the necessary changes to our surroundings, which would require an immense amount of power and computing capability."

"I can help with the power," Heidi offers. "If I max out my motors and totally redline all my systems, I can produce maybe—" He spouts a number, and I have no idea what it means because it's got weird integers in it and I'm suddenly flashing back to Mr. Barbosa's high school algebra class, but Tall blanches, Ned blinks, and even Mary looks a bit taken aback.

"Is that a lot?" I ask Ned quietly as I can. Both so as not to distract the others and so Tall doesn't mock me for not knowing.

"Yeah," he answers softly. It's about on par with a small nuke."

Oh.

"That would be more than sufficient to generate the bridge," Mary confirms. "The computing capability would still be an issue, however." She's frowning, not really looking at anyone or anything, and I know her mind's racing through computations. "I am capable of shouldering perhaps half the burden," she declares after a minute. "But I would need either another with my intellectual capacity or several others of at least super-genius level IQ working in tandem. The calculations are exceedingly complex." She's looking apologetic again, and I wrap an arm around her in support.

"Right, so we're gonna need a bunch of geniuses," I say. "No problem." And, as I say it, I realize maybe it isn't. Because I know exactly where to find a group like that. "Hey," I tell Tall. "You talked to Smith?"

"He should have agents here in the next few minutes," Tall confirms.

"Call him back," I instruct. "Tell him we're gonna need them to make a quick detour." I grin at Mary. "There's a certain school out in Vermont they need to stop off at on the way."

Mary gets my meaning right off, as usual. But instead of

looking pleased she frowns and shakes her head. "I do not know if this is wise," she warns, looking down at her hands. "The individuals in question can be . . . difficult."

"Difficult like they'd be tough to manage, or difficult like they can't or won't be able to do what we need?" Ned asks.

I'm guessing it's more the former than the latter, and sure enough after a minute Mary sighs. "I can provide a list of names," she states. "Between those, we should have more than sufficient brainpower to complete this task." She doesn't look thrilled about it but this isn't exactly an ideal situation we're in and the sooner we can get out of it, the better.

Tall passes Mary his phone and she types in that list, plus some coordinates. Hey, if you can't make it back to the reunion, bring the reunion to you! And what good's a whole school of eggheads if you can't drag them across the galaxy to fix a little glitch in the space-time continuum every now and then?

Let's see what's-his-butt up on the International Space Station top that!

Chapter Ten
Like connect-the-dots
meets a high-speed car chase

In all the excitement of being out of step with regular reality—which you'd think wouldn't be anything new to me, but it's not usually quite this literal!—I almost forget about our other, bigger problem. "Hey, what about the invaders?" I ask, and two heads and a bowling ball swivel my way. Tall's still giving Smith his new marching orders. "We were going into battle mode before their attack, and then we got stuck here. But they are still attacking, right?" I answer my own question. "No, wait, that was the attack, wasn't it? Damn!"

"It was," Tall agrees slowly, "and unfortunately it worked like a charm. They've got us boxed in where we can't stop them." He glances at the impossible-to-reach archway. "And the Matrix is completely undefended."

The hallway brightens as Ned's eyes light up, along with his smile. That darn ladybug is still there, and it winks at me again. Cheeky little bugger! "I don't know that I'd say 'completely,'" he corrects. "They might find a little more than they bargained for if they get too close."

I step in close enough to crowd him. "What do you mean?"

I demand. "Damn it, Ned, have you been messing with wires again? We talked about this! I have to live here, man! And I sleep-walk!" Also apparently sleep-jog, and at a pretty good clip—one time I woke up to find I'd apparently completed a marathon. Fifty-third place, which has got to be pretty good for somebody who can't even see where he's going! Though I've always wondered if they just took pity on me and gave me that medal to make me feel better. Or to confuse me, in which case it totally worked.

Ned's managing to look both guilty and gleeful at the same time, kinda like a Keebler elf. "There's no wires this time," he promises. "And it wouldn't effect you anyway. Or any of us. I think. I haven't really tested that part yet."

"What did you do?" Tall asks, cutting through the excuses. "Exactly?" He's got that "I'm not in the mood look on his face, and I don't blame Ned for gulping.

"Yeah, so I rigged up a low-intensity warp field around the Matrix," he explains. "It's actually not all that different from what they've done to us here, just in a much more constrained setting and of course a completely fixed field."

"Which means what, exactly?" I query. A warp field? Does that mean the next time I walk up to the Matrix I could find myself suddenly floating in the Beta Quadrant without a space-suit? Or back on Earth and in line at Second Avenue Deli? Okay, that last one might actually be a good thing. Except when I actually need to reach the Matrix to fix something, because I don't think this time a pastrami on rye is gonna do the trick.

Though you never know. Their pastrami is pretty amazing.

"There's a thin layer of space around the Matrix that doesn't line up with the rest right now," Ned answers. "Kinda like—you know how, if you watch a movie that had subtitles but someone blurred those out there's that thin band at the bottom of the screen that doesn't perfectly match the rest, but it's close enough that you can ignore it most of the time?" I actually know exactly what that's like, courtesy of a misspent youth, a love of bootlegs, and a buddy who can find you pretty much any movie you like, including ones still in the theaters, as long as you don't mind all the title cards and any pop-up text being in Korean or Swahili. "So that's what that field does," he continues. "It shouldn't affect any of us beyond maybe a chill down our spine, and DuckBob won't be affected at all 'cause he's already tied into the Matrix." The smile's back. "But for somebody from another reality, who's already altering space-time just to be here?" He's full-on grinning now. "It's gonna be like blowing up a balloon nice and big—and then having another balloon bump up against yours. Only this one's covered in sharp, spiky things. One spike connects and—pop!"

I'm not exactly sure who's gonna want a balloon covered in sharp spikes. Maybe it's for Shredder's birthday party? Or Edward Scissorhands' wedding anniversary? But I get the gist. "So they can't touch it?" I confirm, and Ned shakes his head. "Nice!"

"It won't hold 'em off forever," he warns. "But it'll definitely slow 'em down."

Eh, right now we'll take it. Though it sounds like we're basically in a race, then, to see whether we can get back before they can get through, and I have this bad feeling that I won't be able to do here what I always used to do in races.

Which is trip the other guy or distract him by shouting, "Hey, look, Elvis!" and then tying his shoes together and taking off before the gun while he isn't looking.

Then again, who knows? Maybe the invaders are fans, too. I'm pretty sure "Jailhouse Rock" and "Love Me Tender" translate anywhere. "Don't Be Cruel" unfortunately turns into an exhortation to do battle in certain tongues, though. Which I learned, much to my dismay, the last time the delivery guy showed up and I had the music blasting behind me. At first I thought he was only attacking because he wasn't happy with his tip!

Twenty minutes later—at least, it feels like twenty minutes, and that's what my watch says, but who knows if it's really that long? It could be five for all I know. Or ninety. This is like that whole "tree falls in a forest" thing, but with time. If it's twenty minutes for us but five out in the real world, which is right? I'd love to see the ghosts of Einstein arguing that with a Zen monk. And maybe a lumberjack—Tall's phone buzzes. Guess we still get service in here, which is pretty impressive but I'm not surprised. The Matrix is like the mother of all wi-fi networks.

"Yeah?" he answers, in his usual MiB way—no identification, no information offered, giving nothing away. "Very good," is his next reply. Then he turns and offers the phone to Mary, adding, "They're here."

At first I think he means the Grays, since that's what people usually say about them arriving, at least in cheesy movies and old comic books. But when Mary starts talking to someone named Professor Kimura, I realize it's her old classmates. And apparently at least one of the faculty.

Unfortunately, it doesn't sound like it's going well. Mary's trying to explain to this Kimura exactly what they have to do, but she keeps having to stop and apologize for their being "forcibly kidnapped and taken to a strange location via unknown conveyance to do who knows what at the hands of armed men in sunglasses."

This Kimura's pretty loud, and Mary's getting more and more flustered with each interruption. Which isn't like her at all, and that fact's probably just adding to all the flustering that's going on.

Finally I can't take it anymore and I tap her on the shoulder. "Let me cut in a sec," I whisper, holding out my hand, and Mary hands over the phone with undisguised relief. Tall, meanwhile, quirks an eyebrow, like, "What, you think you can speak brainiac-ese all of a sudden?" Thing is? I may not know much about eggheads, but belligerent loudmouths are speaking my language. You just have to know how to speak it back at them. Or how to undercut them completely.

"Professor Kimura?" I say once I have the phone. "Yes, hello, this is Director Spinowitz of the Quantum Fluctuation Academy. So glad you and the others were willing to accept our little theoretical…challenge…heh, though I have to tell you, in all honesty, no one would have faulted you for saying no. There's no shame in admitting when you're outclassed and outsmarted, am I right?"

I stop speaking, and there's an audible pause from the other end. Then, after a second, I hear, "Of course, it's our pleasure. I'm sorry, can you describe this challenge again? It was unclear the first time."

"Not a problem," I reply, winking at Mary. "It's quite simple, really. Ma—Mirabella and I, that is, Miss Jost"—it takes me a second to remember her old name—"were having a disagreement about Einstein-Rosen bridges. Specifically, whether it would be possible to construct one with one end anchored in normal reality but the other tethered to a more...unmoored position. I have to admit, I did not believe her when she suggested that it would be possible, and even less when she claimed that her former classmates and professors would be capable of working out the calculations for such a miraculous feat."

Yeah, I'm good at spouting believable BS when I want to be. I had a job back in college, selling stuff to people over the phone, and I'm convinced that half of 'em never knew what the hell they were actually buying off me but I still had the highest sales rate on the floor.

"Well," this professor responds, "we certainly appreciate Mirabella's confidence in our abilities. It does sound like an . . . entertaining little mind-puzzle. If you give me the specifics, I'm sure I can get everyone working on it right away."

"Excellent!" Yes, I fake "encouraging and enthusiastic" really well. I once thought I might have a career as a Lamaze coach, until I figured out they weren't really just cheering women on with their breathing. "Allow me to pass the phone back to Miss Jost, and she can provide all the necessary details." I lower my voice a little. "Of course, there's a case of Scotch in it for me if you lot can't deliver, so don't feel that you have to try your hardest, if you take my meaning."

And then, having properly insulted not only his intelligence and his school but his work ethic, I give Mary back the phone.

It's amazing what people will do when you dare them and even moreso when you make it clear you don't expect them to succeed. After a few seconds Mary's looking a lot more chipper and spouting all sorts of high-level math talk, and I can tell from the murmuring on the other end that this Kimura is copying it all down without a single argument. Finally, Mary hangs up and returns the phone to Tall.

"They are beginning their calculations," she reports. "Thanks to DuckBob's excellent motivational techniques." Yeah, she smirks a little as she says this. "Now I must calculate my half of the problem. They will develop the math necessary to build the bridge, but I must supply the formulae for linking it to our present location, otherwise the bridge will simply slide off the surface of our bubble and affix itself to the next patch of stable reality beyond."

"Great, so they're spinning the thread but you've got to figure out how to get it through the eye of a moving needle?" I peck her on the forehead as she slides down the wall to sit cross-legged against it. "Well, you can do it, babe. We'll be here if there's any way we can help."

She smiles, but I can tell by the glazed look in her eyes that her thoughts are already fully engaged in the problem at hand. Rather than bother her further I step over to Ned and Tall, the three of us retreating as far down the hall as the invaders' little trick will allow. Heidi remains hovering near Mary's head like a helium-filled watchdog.

"Any idea how long this'll take?" I ask Ned quietly. "And how long your little defense field'll hold 'em off?"

But he shakes his head. "The math she's doing is way beyond me," he admits, "so no, I couldn't even guess. As far as the warp field? I'd say we had maybe an hour, total, from the time they first ran into it."

And of course we don't know how much of that hour has passed out there. Great. Well, nothing we can do about it now. I just wish I'd known we were going to be stuck here with nothing to do but wait. I'd have brought a deck of cards.

If we do make it back, I may set up little "emergency diversion" stations all around the building. A couple beers, a bag of chips, a box of cookies, a book, a deck of cards. A finger puppet or two. That way, if anyone ever gets trapped in a corridor again, at least they'll have something to keep them occupied for a bit.

Though, knowing myself, the first time that happened I'd find a note in my own handwriting saying, "Sorry" and all the chips and cookies and beer would be gone, a random card used as a bookmark halfway through, and one of the finger puppets would now be sporting a little drawn on mustache and eyepatch.

But at least that would prove I'd been entertained!

Eventually Mary stirs and opens her eyes. "I have finished," she declares. "I require your phone again, please." She holds out her hand, and Tall hands it to her without comment or protest. We all watch as she calls Agent Smith, who connects her to Kimura, and then stare as she spouts what sounds like utter gibberish. But when she disconnects she's smiling.

"He states that they have finished their share of the computations as well," she reports, accepting my hand and rising to her feet with that sensual grace that has Tall blinking, Ned's eyes flashing, and even Heidi doing an impromptu lightshow. "Now we will see if they have done so correctly."

"Wait, I thought we needed Heidi to power it?" I ask. "How's that gonna work if he's in here with us?"

But Mary shakes her head. "Building the bridge from within this space and using it to cross the gap would have been the more logical approach," she agrees, "since in that scenario we would be calculating toward a known space rather than from one. But there is neither enough room here nor the raw materials for us to fabricate the machines necessary to fashion the bridge. Professor Kimura understands what is necessary, however, and Agent Smith is providing the necessary tools, as well as the required energy output. We have only to wait, and to hope they performed their portion of this task." She doesn't for a second wonder if she did her share right, and neither do I.

Though maybe we should have. Because a few minutes later, her phone rings. She answers it, and, well, I don't think I've ever seen her face fall like that before. It's unnerving, and my first impulse is to punch whoever's making her feel that bad, but all she says is, "Yes, I understand. I will."

"What was that all about?" I ask, but I'm doing my best to

keep from shouting, both because we're in an enclosed space and because she already looks close to tears. "What's wrong, babe?"

"The bridge failed to connect," she answers, lifting her chin but not meeting anybody's eyes. "It appears I made an error in my calculations."

Well, crap. I don't say that, though. Instead I put my arm around her. "Hey, nobody's right all the time," I remind her. "It happens. Can you run the numbers again?"

She nods. "They are gathering resources to recharge the machinery for a second attempt. I must find the error in my first solution and correct it." She gives me a quick peck on the cheek, which I know is a thank-you for the attempt at moral support, then she's lost in her own headspace again. I exchange quick glances and shrugs with Tall and Ned. We're all so used to relying on Mary's smarts, but of course she can make mistakes too. Anybody can. And I'm betting dealing with her old classmates has her more rattled than she wants to admit.

We are running out of time, though, and I don't know how many more attempts they can make if this one doesn't work either.

It feels like forever but it's probably only twenty minutes before Mary blinks and focuses on the world around her again. "I have discovered the error," she states. She flushes. "It was a foolish miscalculation on my part, but a costly one." Taking her phone, she calls and relays a new string of gibberish. Then she takes my hand and squeezes it tight. We all know there's a lot riding on this.

A minute later there's a strange buzzing sound like a million tiny bees are eating away at the walls from the outside. Then there's a shimmer in the air at either end of the hall, like the heat mirage of a jet engine. That subsides, and Tall immediately stomps toward the living room—and, reaching the door in a handful of long strides, disappears through it. "We're back in business!" he shouts, and that's my cue to disengage from Mary and take off running.

Charge the Matrix, Take Two!

Chapter Eleven
It's labeled "Mine" for a reason

I don't know that I beat any landspeed records—my feet are as big as landspeeders, after all, but without the nifty hover effect—but I do know I probably cover the distance to the Matrix chamber in less time than ever before. Funny how getting Ziploced in a corner of your own house for a while as someone tries to break down the very device it's your job to protect, which in turn protects all reality, can motivate you.

Plus, I really need to use the bathroom and I just know nobody's gonna take it well if I stop to go *before* we save the day. "Our reality—dead for a pee break" doesn't exactly have a compelling ring to it.

I sail through the archway like the Devil himself's behind me offering his version of a free spa treatment—"come for the heat, stay for the torture!"—and leap into the Matrix chamber. There's the Matrix right in front of me, as always—

—but the sparks coming off it every now and again at irregular intervals? That's new.

It reminds me of nothing so much as a giant bug-zapper, and I know right away this's gotta be Ned's warp field. And those sparks are invaders trying to breach it.

Looks like they haven't managed that, yet. Which means time's up, invisible baddies!

I haul my big feathery butt forward, straight toward the Matrix itself. I think something gets in my way, something whispery and shadowy like a stained-glass reflection on the wind, but I charge through it without stopping. I remember too late what Ned said about me and the warp field—"DuckBob won't be affected at all," but with all the sincerity of a used-car salesman promising, "Oh, this one was barely driven at all, only on Sundays and only two miles to church and back, it's practically still new" when in fact it'd been used for cross-border drug runs for years and the back seat cushions were pretty much stuffed with old bits of coke and weed—but it doesn't matter because I'm moving too fast to brake in time anyway.

Which is why I wind up throwing my arms out and slamming into the Matrix in a full body hug.

There is a brief zing as I pass through the field, but it feels like a quick static shock, nothing more. And there's another one when I connect to the Matrix, but that one's both less painful and more drawn out. It's like I've plugged myself into the middle of a live circuit, only it's not really hurting me, more like gently finger-massaging me from the inside out.

Over the hum I'm pretty sure I hear screeches of rage, only they're all thin and whispery too. Talking to the invaders is a lot like talking to your dottering old uncle who's been breathing through one of those neck thingies for the past decade and can barely manage to be heard in a dead-silent room. Only creepier, especially since you can't see them and their voices are coming from all around you and often several feet over your head. This time at least it's not words, just screams of frustration.

Then they're gone.

It's funny, but for creatures I can't even see and can barely hear, I can always tell when they're gone. There's an absence in the air, like when you smell something bad for so long you eventually stop noticing it but then it goes away and you totally notice that. Suddenly the air around me is decidedly invader-free.

"All good in here!" I shout, though I'm not sure anyone can hear me because my voice is swallowed up a bit by the Matrix's hum. It's a lot like talking through a fan, only with everyone else ten feet behind you.

A few minutes later, though, Tall marches in, massive gun at the ready. "All clear?" he asks, stomping over to stand beside me in full-on guard mode.

"Yep, they took off the second I plugged back in," I confirm. I let go of the Matrix, pat it once on the side, then step away. Whew! It's a good thing I don't have molars anymore, or they'd be sizzling!

"Good." He gives a sharp nod, eyes still roving the area just in case. "Ned and Heidi aren't picking up any traces now either. Looks like we got back just in time." Got back—to a place we never left. But couldn't reach.

Physics makes my head hurt.

Speaking of which, a small troop of people come parading in through the archway. Mary's in the lead, with Ned and Heidi, but right behind them are a whole bunch of others, only a few of whom I know.

But all of whom clearly go to the same tailor. And the same optometrist.

"Is the Matrix secure?" Agent Smith demands, getting enough in our faces that I can see the muscle in Tall's jaw jump as he has to shove down the fight-or-flight reflex. Though in his case I'm pretty sure it's just fight.

"Yeah, we're all good," I tell him. "Thanks."

Smith nods, but he's not looking at me anymore. Even with those sunglasses on I can tell he's eyeing the Matrix instead, with all the avarice of a comic collector who's just spotted a copy of *Sandman,* issue eight, the Berger variant, in a ten cent box at a garage sale.

"It seems this building may no longer be operationally secure," he says slowly, like a panther stalking its prey. "Now that we're here, I believe it may be necessary for us to assist in policing it properly. To prevent any further incidents."

"Nuh-uh, Charlie," I tell him, crossing my arms and positioning myself so I'm right in his line of sight. And there's a lot of me to block the view—I could be a portable barrier if this Guardian gig ever dries up. Even a sound wall, especially since I can provide my own sound. "We told you we'd call if we needed you. We needed you, though really just as a convenient taxi service. Now we're all good again, time for you to go. Veni, vidi, arrivederci."

Smith's a lot easier to cow through the phone, though, and he stands his ground now, in his slick black suit—the rest of the MiBs clearly shop at Mooks in Suits but he's all Savile Row, always has been. I've sometimes wondered if he only started dressing top-shelf after he made management, or if it was his snazzy suits that got him there—like "hey, that guy looks good, let's promote him so he's the one out there in people's faces!" Now he lifts his chin and gives me his best shark smile. "That hardly seems prudent," he replies, smooth as butter and twice as oily. "What if they return again, and in force? We should at the very least stay long enough to reconnoiter, make sure everything is safe and secure. Otherwise we might not be able to get back quickly enough to lend aid if there is a second attack."

Yeah, and somehow his "we're just doing a quick check to see that the windows are all locked tight before we go" will turn into "Ooh, this curtain doesn't look good and this door's got a crack under the one corner, we'd better stay to make sure everything's all right!" Next thing you know, they'll be using my towels and rearranging my closet!

Fortunately, I'm not alone here. "We appreciate the offer," Tall states, towering over his former superior, "but we've got this covered." He hefts the huge gun in his hands like he might turn it on Smith, and I've got to give the slippery MiB credit, he doesn't take even a single step back. Most people would be at least two states away by now.

Mary and Ned reach us and move to either side of me, in classic flanking position. "Tall is correct," Mary declares. "We are grateful for your timely arrival, but we are more than capable of handling the rest from here." Ned just nods.

Smith still isn't buying it, though—with the Matrix practically in arm's reach, even Mary's considerable charms aren't enough to distract him. "Be that as it may," he answers smoothly,

"I'm afraid I'm going to have to insist. For the sake and safety of our entire reality, of course. But don't worry, we'll stay out of the way. You'll barely even know we're here." Which translates roughly to, "if you're lucky, we might clear you for bathroom access once a day, and let you have a cracker or two."

Right, time for Plan B.

"You know what?" I say, clapping my hands together. "That's cool. You guys can set up here in the Matrix chamber, so you'll be on hand at a moment's notice." I grin, and Smith can't help himself, he grins back. He looks like he can't believe his ears, but he's smart enough not to argue when he's finally getting what he wants. "Oh, hey," I add just as he's turning to one of the other MiBs, no doubt to tell him, "set up all our gear—oh, and change the locks while you're at it." "You guys brought rad counters, right? If not, no worries, you can borrow one of Ned's."

That stops Smith in his tracks, mid-instruction, and he turns back toward me, one eyebrow rising just over the edge of his shades. "Rad counter?" he asks, then scoffs. "I hardly think that necessary. The Matrix does not produce any traces of radiation!"

But already he's sounding like he's not one hundred percent sure of that.

"'Course it does," I counter. "What'd you think, the quantum fluctuation didn't have any bleed to it? This thing leaks like a sieve!" I slap my chest. "Can't affect me any, that's why the Grays chose me—the mods they did on me run off the same radiation, my body soaks the stuff up like it's Vitamin D. Same for Mary, and Ned's got an anti-rad field rigged around himself.

He made one for Tall too, once we established that he'd be dropping by regularly, and Heidi can convert any wavelength to usable energy." I glance at Smith and frown. "You guys did come prepared, right?"

Smith is glaring at me, and I can see he's torn. His MiBs are backing away slowly, though, just like you do when you're sneaking into somebody's house, open the pantry door, and find yourself face to face with a very large, very hungry, very angry pit bull.

The Grays did me a favor when they replaced my old face, scars and all.

"There is no radiation!" Smith snaps, but Mary shakes her head.

"DuckBob is correct," she explains, and his eyes dart to her like homing beacons. "This entire structure is inundated with exotic particles thrown off from the Matrix. They are harmless for short periods, but can have severely debilitating effects over an extended time."

Smith frowns. He's still trying to figure out if I'm bluffing or not. The fact that Mary's backing me is a pretty big push in the "not" direction, though.

"Best to get back now, while you're still mostly clean," Tall warns, glancing at his watch. "Another ten minutes and it's the decontamination shower for you. Full hose down." He glances pointedly at Smith's immaculate black suit.

That does the trick. Smith might be willing to risk his own hide, but his precious clothes? Not a chance. "I will expect immediate notification if anything here changes," he demands, and then turns on his heel and marches away. A drill sergeant would be proud. His MiBs do their best to maintain ranks, but they're scared enough they break and run pell-mell for the exit after only a few paces. So much for fearless federal agents!

"I'm gonna go make sure they really leave," Tall says, and takes off after them like a cat who's just realized his favorite ball of yarn has rolled past. Better him than me—I always want to smack Smith at the same time that I feel like I should be apologizing and explaining why I didn't have his daughter home before curfew.

"Do I need to plug back in again?" I ask Ned next. He considers that a second before shaking his head.

"You upping the connection helped knock 'em out of here again," he tells me. "The Matrix's defenses should've held 'em off in the first place, but I think that little reality-warping trick of theirs is what let 'em slip through somehow. Now that they're back on the outside somewhere, those defenses are back up, and I'm gonna make sure they're airtight. So as long as you maintain your usual connection to it, it's all good." He wanders off, presumably to check those same defenses. He's already got one of his toys out, and I think he's crooning to it. I don't want to know.

That leaves just me and Mary, which is never a bad thing. Unless we're trying to field a basketball team. "You handled that well, my love," she tells me, slipping an arm around my waist and sidling in close.

"Thanks. You too." I return the favor, snugging her in tight. She smiles, seemingly recovered from her earlier embarrassment, and shifts to face me better. I lean in. So does she. Her eyes drift closed. So do mine. I lean in a little further—

Cough.

A sharp, bitter rasp sounds from just off to our side. It sounds a lot like an old Jewish man's "but why care about me, I'm dead soon anyway!" mixed with the angry buzz of a wasp about to strike.

Oh, joy.

Chapter Twelve
The shoe's on the other foot—
and ten sizes too small

I glance down and, sure enough, there's the Bee Queen standing there glaring at us like we've just tortured all the puppies and she's peeved because she didn't get a turn. "Hi, nice to see you again," I tell her, "but you'd better hurry or you'll miss your ride."

She sniffs, the kind of sniff you get from the head librarian when you ask if there's a maximum amount for library fines and what exactly qualifies as a misdemeanor versus a felony. "If you mean those odious men in dark suits," she snaps, crossing her arms over her decidedly uninspiring chest, "they just left. They shooed us in here and said something about how getting us back was your problem, not theirs."

Seriously? Thanks a lot, Smith! Talk about petty, foisting the eggheads off on us. That's like handing the poopy kid to the babysitter as you run for the door, screaming, "back by midnight, Haz-mat suits on the hook by the door, have fun!" But I do my best to muster a smile.

"Okay, no problem," I tell Little Miss Sunshine. "I'm sure we can arrange transport back. Give me a sec." I look around for Tall. Or Heidi. Or Ned. Or the Stay-PuftMarshmallow Man. Right now I'm not picky.

I don't see any of them, though. What I do see are a few other nerd-geeks I recognize from Mary's reunion, and a few I don't. And they're all approaching us—which means they're also approaching the Matrix.

Oh, crap.

"Mirabella!" Cab calls out as he waddles over. Yeah, I said "waddles." I know I do it too, but I've got good reason for having an awkward gait—my feet are flotation devices and my head's a parade float! What's this guy's excuse? "Where exactly are we?"

"Don't be dense, Charles," Jerome snaps, stalking along beside him. It's like watching a praying mantis pacing a dung beetle. "Look at the horizon. The overabundance of stars indicates that we must be at or near the Galactic Core." His eyes snap to the Matrix. "Hello, what have we here? Some sort of harmonic field equalizer?" His hand lifts of its own accord, drifting toward a gleaming golden-ribbon section.

"Don't touch that!" I snap, leaping forward and shoving him away before he can make contact. "It'll fry you to a crisp!" Well, maybe, maybe not—most unattuned minds can withstand direct contact for only a minute or two before the sheer magnitude overwhelms them and they start to melt. But there's also Ned's warp field to consider, and I have no idea what that'd do to someone not already aligned. Better safe than sorry.

Jerome straightens and glares at me, rubbing the hand I swatted aside. "You're touching it," he accuses, sounding exactly like a little kid watching his dad eat the ice cream he was just told not to touch.

"Yeah, and I've been modded to be able to do exactly that," I retort. I pat my bill. "You thought this was just to get the girls?" I see him dart a quick glance at Mary, as does Cab, and both of them flush. I knew they had a thing for her!

"You're saying you were modified in order to survive contact with that device," Killer Queen pipes in. "Why?"

"It needs a live operator," I tell her after a peek at Mary, who shrugs. Normally the Grays would brain-wipe anybody unauthorized who got anywhere near the Matrix, much less got inside and saw it firsthand. But they're not here, and these guys did just help us save it, so in a way I figure they're entitled to a straight answer or two. "Somebody who's been altered enough to function as part of the closed circuit. That's me."

They're all looking around now, their expressions ranging from distrust to careful calculation to total awe. "This really is the Galactic Core?" Cab asks. "Not just some elaborate VR scenario?"

"Real deal," I assure him. "The MiBs brought you out here by teleport to help pull us out of a little trap so we could protect the Matrix. Which you did. So thanks for that." I reach over and swat another guy's hand as it's reaching for the Matrix. "Seriously, dude, you'll be pulling back nothing but a blackened stump, assuming you don't go all end-of-*Time-Bandits* on me." He quickly retreats a step or two.

Someone else clears their throat, but not in the same way as Wasp Woman. This is more like "it is time for class to begin, please take your seats and open your textbook." It takes me a second to locate the source, but finally I spot the beefy-looking guy standing near the unfamiliar eggheads. He's got the same high forehead as half of 'em, but his is partially covered by big bushy eyebrows, just like his lips and part of his chin are hidden under a big, bushy, droopy mustache. But his eyes are slanted and heavy-lidded, and his complexion's more olive than cream. This has got to be Professor Kimura.

"I would like to know," he declares, in a strong, deep voice that I could easily imagine shouting from the Highlands, "precisely where we are and what we are doing here, thank you. Much as I enjoyed the intellectual exercise of formulating an Einstein-Rosen Bridge from this point to a space that had been phased out of the normal reality—twice—I am still smarting from the indignity of several government goons abducting myself and many of my former students and dragging us to some unknown location, then abandoning us here."

Yep, definitely a college professor.

I don't really know what to say to this guy, but fortunately Mary does. "You are here at my behest, Professor Kimura," she answers, stepping forward, and the old guy brightens when he sees her. To me it looks less like "you're so dreamy!" and more like "ah, one of my favorite students!" but the facial hair makes him tough to read for certain. "I apologize if the agents were less than considerate in their handling of you and the others, but time was of the essence."

He frowns. "Perhaps so," he concedes, "but that is no excuse for sloppy math, my dear." Ouch. Mary pales but holds up a hand when I take a step toward him. Aw, c'mon, let me bite him just a little!

"You are correct, of course," she agrees, though her voice wobbles a little as she says it. "I apologize. The pressure was considerable, and I allowed that to unsettle me." She takes a deep breath—which every guy here can't help but notice—and then continues, "Now I would be happy to explain this location and its basic function, and the part you and the others have played in preserving it."

She launches into a brief but all-big-words summary, and I take a step or two away out of the line of fire before my eyes glaze over. I love her dearly, and it is hella sexy when she makes with the science talk, but lectures put me to sleep. Ask my old college professors—school was the six best years' sleep of my life! Instead I start toward the archway. I'm hoping I can find Ned or Tall or Heidi and get them to come back with me before Mary's done. I've got this feeling we may need extra sitters for these kids.

As I walk away, glancing back once or twice, it occurs to me that, in this situation, I am definitely the parent or at least the responsible adult rather than the bratty kid.

Suddenly I've got a whole new level of appreciation for every sitter I ever had. And I realize that Ma probably deserves a medal. Or to be sainted, if they do that with us heathens. Or to be both—would that count as being bronzed?

Tall ducks back into the chamber just as I'm nearing the archway. "Dude!" I shout, hurrying over to him. "Where the hell've you been? Smith took off and ditched the Genius Pack with us!"

"I know," Tall says. He's got the big gun still but it's down at his side now, and he looks both tired and annoyed. "I told him he needed to take them back where they came, but he said 'the Matrix is not my responsibility, you've all made that very clear, so that means it is not my job to police it.'" He shrugs. "Sorry. He's a tool."

"Yeah, and not the handy kind," I agree. I look over at Mary, who is still fielding questions from the crowd. "So, what're we gonna do with these guys?" I turn to him. "Can your ship fit 'em all?" Tall and Heidi are interstellar truckers, after all—how hard can it be to herd a group of nerds into the cargo hold? Give 'em a copy of *Eggheads Weekly* and the DVD set of *Star Trek* and a few six-packs of Mountain Dew and they'll barely even notice when the ship leaves orbit.

Tall frowns, considering. "We can fit them," he acknowledges finally. "But it's a long ride back. They'd be better off if Mary took them."

Which makes sense, since she can be back on Earth in a heartbeat and for Tall it takes a few days. But I don't know how many she can bring at once. Plus there were those odd glitches before. I'm not entirely sure the system's that reliable right now. At the very least we should probably do the whole swim-after-eating thing and give it an hour or two to settle back down.

We're clearly gonna need to figure something out, though. And fast. Because it looks like the Q & A just ended, and as I watch the Nerd Herd disperses, scattering its awkward geniuses to every corner of the room.

What follows is maybe the most exhausting hour of my life

since the time I agreed to run the Boston Marathon. Backward. And naked. While still hungover. And lugging a half-empty beer keg.

Hey, I wasn't about to waste it! Or lose my deposit!

"Put that down!" I warn one egghead—a slick-looking Asian dude in a fancy suit—as he hoists what looks like something between a plant spritzer, a remote, and an arcade claw. It's actually a pinpoint wormhole-actuator, designed specifically for snacks. You type in the right code, extend the arm, and fish with it, and when it pops back it's clutching a bag of Doritos. Or something a whole lot like 'em except these taste a little bit like liquid smoke and too many of 'em make your teeth glow. I only just found the right setting and perfected my wrist flick, and now he's gonna mess it all up!

"That is not a toy!" I scold Cab, who's poking at something like a constantly rotating mural. Actually it *is* a toy, I just don't want them to know that. Most people, when you say "that's a toy," what they hear instead is, "Oh, that's not something we still need or even want but we don't know exactly what to do with it, so if it breaks it wasn't all that important anyway." Yes, it's a toy, but it's my toy, damn it, and I don't want them messing it up. The last time that happened it went into a sulk and wouldn't show anything but the Battle of Hastings over and over again for nearly a week.

"I should just let you fry your brains," I tell Jerome, who's just about to reach out and grasp one of the conduits from the Matrix. "It'd serve you right." He looks properly chastised, and appropriately terrified, and backs up a step, hands safely stowed in his pockets. I sidle on past him, putting myself between him and the Matrix, but what about the others? Especially anyone I don't know by name. I don't even remember who-all Mary invited. How'm I supposed to keep track of them if I don't know what they look like or what to scream at them?

But Mary does. I find her in the mayhem and grab her hand like it's a lifeline and I'm about to go under for the fifth time. "You know all these people, right?" I ask, pulling her in to talk.

She nods. "I am familiar with them, yes."

"Okay, great." I think for a second. "Do you still have that list you sent Smith?"

She produces a phone from somewhere I'd be only too happy to inspect for any other stray electronics, thumbs it to life, taps the screen once, twice, and then hands me the phone.

"Perfect." I study the tiny list it's showing. "Okay, we've got six of 'em in all, including the professor." I do a quick head-count, then try it again. Crap. "And we've got four here with us now."

Mary and I stare at each other, and this time it's a lot less "aw, aren't you sweet!" and a lot more "oh hell, we're doomed!"

Because two of these awkward, arrogant, inattentive boobs are loose in the Matrix building.

I hope we find them before they do something stupid like set off the security systems. Or eat all of my mascarpone.

Or decide to play a quick game of baseball, with the Matrix as both the catcher and all the bases.

Which definitely wouldn't be my fault. I stopped running the bases ages ago. Now I just cut straight across, lobbing balls of my own at the refs to keep them busy. Hey, it works! Especially when I use the ones made of dwarf star alloy. Nothing like getting hit with a fist-sized ball that feels like a cannonball to make you sit up and pay attention to that and not a whole lot else.

This may be why I never managed to stay on any sports team for very long.

That and the fact that I don't play well with others. Some might call that a character flaw. I say it's a finely honed survival instinct. When you look an awful lot like some people's idea of a main course, you learn to be a little wary.

Especially right around dinnertime.

Chapter Thirteen
Perfectly safe as long as you don't move

"Tall!" I spot him and wave him over. "Heidi!" His partner floats over from the other direction. "Great! Listen, we need you guys to sit on the Geek Elite, okay? Maybe herd 'em toward the bleachers?" The Matrix chamber isn't just as big as a football field, it's actually set up like one, right down to the rows of bleachers at either end. At the far end those are still unaltered, but at the near end I've replaced the first row with a bunch of comfy couches and a handful of coffee tables. Sometimes I sit in here and hang out rather than in the living room. Watching the Matrix cycle slowly around is soothing, and out here I can legitimately claim I couldn't answer any emails or calls because I wasn't anywhere near my computer.

Besides, sitting out here makes the living room couch jealous, and I want to keep it from getting too full of itself.

"What're you going to be doing?" Tall asks suspiciously, eyeing us both. Like we're gonna just ditch all of them and go make out in a corner somewhere.

Damn, why didn't I think of that?

"Two of my former classmates are presently unaccounted for," Mary explains. "We must locate them before they tamper with anything that puts themselves or others at risk."

Tall nods. "Go. We've got this." Heidi glows green in agreement.

"If Ned turns back up, tell him to come lend a hand," I holler over my shoulder as Mary and I take to the hall. We're out of sight before Tall can respond, but that's fine. I know he got the message.

"Okay," I say as much to myself as to her as we traipse down the corridor. "If you were an ornery genius who'd just been shanghaied to the Galactic Core and dropped into a psychedelic house made from a giant skull and filled with all kinds of wild alien tech, where you would go first?"

She frowns, then her expression clears as the answer hits her. I get it at the same time, and we blurt out, "the living room!" in perfect synchronicity. Take that, Mormon Tabernacle Choir! In your face, Donny and Marie! Though, admittedly, they actually managed to sing that way, not just shout out room types. Still, it's a start.

Mary takes off like a shot down the hall, and I'm right behind her. We burst into the living room—

—just in time to see my couch engulf some guy in a nice suit.

"No, bad couch!" I shout, rushing to it and swatting the thing. "Bad couch! Spit him out right now!"

The couch curls away from me and turns into a papasan. The fabric of the seat cushion is interspersed question marks and teardrops.

"Okay, fine," I tell it, calming down a bit. "You caught the intruder. Thank you. That part was good. Now please spit him out before he suffocates."

It sulks a little more, reshaping into a beanbag but still with the same fabric pattern. Great. Of all the semi-sentient furniture in the universe, why did I have to get the one that's super-sensitive? It doesn't seem to care much when I spray crumbs or spill drinks all over it but it's upset because I won't let it eat intruders? Is this one of those weird diet things?

"Please?" I ask it. "You don't want to get dead nerd stuck inside your seat cushions, trust me. You'd never get the smell out."

That seems to do the trick, and it turns into a rigid futon, all hard wooden slats and stiff cushion. Upon which sits a rather dazed-looking nerd. It's the slick Asian guy I saw earlier. He looks like a cross between a science geek and a day trader. Maybe a science trader? Day geek?

"Hello, Taki," Mary says, stepping cautiously into his line of sight. If she was worried about this dude bolting, though, she needn't have. He's still looking pretty out of it. But he's breathing, and his eyes follow her motion, so he's probably just a little shellshocked from finding himself on the wrong side of the upholstery.

"Hello, Mirabella," he responds finally, his voice just above a whisper and his eyes wide. He's sitting so still and stiff he might as well be made of stone, but after another second or two he adds, "I would very much like to stand up now."

"Yeah, go ahead," I tell him. "It won't do that again. Right?" The couch quivers a little but doesn't respond otherwise. Fortunately it also doesn't move as I wave Taki to stand and step past me, which he does, slowly at first and then with a little jump like—well, like he was in danger of being eaten by a couch.

I have a feeling it's gonna be a while before this guy goes anywhere near a furniture store again.

"Why don't you take him back to the others?" I suggest to Mary, since I figure he's gonna trust her a lot more than me right now. "I'll keep looking for—"

"Nathan," she responds. "Very well." And, resting a hand on Taki's shoulder, she steers him toward the door. The couch quivers once, like a leashed dog straining after a squirrel, but I pat its back and it settles down.

I wonder if they make Taki-shaped couch treats anywhere? Given the wonders of the Internet, I'm guessing the answer will be yes, but I'm also not sure I should encourage my furniture's new carnivorous tendencies. Y'know, lest it develops a sudden taste for poultry.

Once I'm sure Mary's got the guy under control and the couch isn't going to sneak after them, I turn away and focus on the other doors out of here. One of them leads to the locker room. The other leads to the kitchen. I don't hear any rustling sounds through that second arch, so I'm guessing this Nathan guy isn't rummaging through my spices and my cookbooks or raiding my fridge. Which is a good thing because I've still got at least a few pieces of flarb casserole left and I'm not sharing.

That leaves the locker room or farther down the hall. I scan the locker room quickly, but there's nobody in there. Unless he's hiding in one of the lockers, and if that's the case he's on his own—I still don't know what's in half of them, and I'm a bit afraid to find out. He could emerge as a superhero, or one of those dried-out husks you see in Mummy movies. But there aren't any screams, or any movement at all, so my guess is he didn't stop off here. Which means I keep going.

I really hope this guy isn't in my bedroom. Both because I don't like other people snooping through my stuff and because I might have a few weapons squirreled away up there and at least one of them could level a small continent if not handled just right.

What can I say? I take home defense seriously. You have to when the ones most likely to break into your house are an entire freaking army from another reality! And when you have neighbors who just don't accept "no, sorry, I don't have any gluon-heavy sugar substitute you can borrow."

I'm halfway down the hall to the stairs when I hear something up ahead. Something that sounds like—singing?

Racing toward it, I round a corner and there, coming out of the coat closet, is a tall African-American dude who's swaying like he's stuck on a boat during a storm or like he's just coming off a week-long bender. When he staggers into me a few paces later, his breath smells of lavender and chai, with a hint of kerosene.

"Hey, you must be Nathan," I say, catching him before he goes sprawling. "We've been looking all over for you. Come on, everybody's waiting." And I do my best to turn him around so his feet are pointing toward the Matrix again.

"I...am Nathan," he agrees with that ponderous slowness only the really old or the really drunk can have. "Who . . ."

"My name's DuckBob," I answer. "This is my place. Which means that stuff you smoked? That was mine, too."

Because yes, I know exactly what did this to him. Or rather, how and what he did to himself. It's those jewel-light sticks. I thought I'd gotten rid of all of them—Mary insisted—but I must have missed a pack somewhere. And Naughty Nathan here found it and decided it'd be a good idea to swipe somebody else's stash of unknown origins and light up.

The good news is, you can't really hurt yourself with these things. You just feel all light and floaty for a while. Which doesn't mean he couldn't get hurt while on one, like by walking into a laser-mesh or tripping over a pointy stick—not that I have either of those laying about, but you never know when I might get hit with the urge to redecorate. Or that you couldn't hurt somebody else, especially by pushing buttons you shouldn't have in a place you shouldn't be.

Global Thermonuclear War, anyone?

Nathan's got the decency to look a little ashamed at having broken into my stash. In fact, he gets downright weepy. "I'm so sorry," he wails, and I swear he's leaking giant tears like some Anime character. Any second now his mouth is gonna expand to fill nine-tenths of his face. "Please don't hate me!"

"Dude, I barely even know you," I tell him. "You gotta work a whole lot harder to get me to actively dislike you, much less hate you." His sobbing diminishes a little, but he's still sniffling as I lead him back down the hall toward everybody else. This is one of the reasons I didn't fight Mary very hard about giving up those jewel-light sticks, actually—I'd started to wonder if they were affecting my moods. Like I'd be all happy and giddy as I was smoking one, but then right afterward I'd start to feel really down, like I wanted to cry over even the littlest thing.

I'm not a big fan of something outside me manipulating my emotions. It's fine if I do it to myself—like watching the opening to *Up* if I wanna feel sad, since you're pretty much not human if that doesn't make you bawl like a baby, it's basically a Turing test for the entire human race—but not if something else is doing that without my say-so. Nobody gets to mess with my feelings but me!

We're just passing the door to the living room when I hear a commotion from up ahead. There's screaming and shouting and maybe some cheering thrown in? Did we miss Tall forcing the eggheads into his version of *Fight Club*? I have no idea, but I latch on tighter to Never-Pass-Up-Free-Smokes Nathan and increase our pace to a trot. They'd better have saved me ringside seats, at least!

Someone appears in the archway up ahead, and then comes racing toward us. As he nears I'm surprised to see Jerome, his face scrunched in concentration—

—and in his other hand?

A gleaming tiara.

Okay, that can't be right. I look again, and realize it isn't exactly a tiara, though it does have the same sort of circular shape that flares up near the middle of one side and dwindles down to nothing exactly opposite that. But this one isn't worn with the flared point up front, that's actually the back.

I know because I'm wearing one almost exactly like it.

This idiot with his pencil mustache and his five PhDs somehow got hold of my spare Matrix interface. Which Ned made for me and dropped off after I called him at three am one morning wailing that I'd lost the darn thing and now the whole Matrix was gonna shut down and the universe would implode and it was all my fault. Fortunately, like any good techie he had spare parts on hand and was able to whip up a replacement, which he rushed on over—

—only to glare at me when I answered the door. Wearing the original. Which I hadn't realized I had on the whole time.

Yeah, so maybe trying slogga-gin for the first time by making triple-strength G&Ts—and substituting Tentori vodka for the tonic because I was out of tonic and, hey, it starts with T!—wasn't the best plan.

On the plus side, I now had a spare if I needed it. I usually left it sitting on the coffee table in the Matrix chamber—where Mustachio must have found it and decided, "mine!"

If he tries putting it on he really will fry his brain, PhDs and all.

Which is why, as he comes zooming past, I toss the biggest obstacle I have directly into his path.

And that obstacle is a nogoodnik named Nathan.

I see Jerome's eyes widen as his former classmate stumbles into his path. But there's nothing he can do about it—this corridor is barely wide enough that three, maybe four people can walk abreast but no more, so it's easy to get in someone else's way.

Especially when you're as broad as Not-Yet-Steady Nathan here.

Jerome's right leg slams directly into Nathan's shoulder and it's ass-over-elbows for him. Both gents go tumbling past me, and Jerome finally comes to rest halfway down the hall. The interface gets knocked out of his hand and rolls a bit farther before it, too, slows to a stop. I scoop that one up fast—I'll have Ned run a check on that later, make sure nothing got broken. Nathan I let cartwheel away before finally slamming into the wall and collapsing from either the rapture of interpretative dance or swift contact with the nearest section of ancient, sparkly pink glitter.

It's a pretty good trick when you don't have to be the one policing your house but can let the house do it for you.

"Okay, naptime's over, time to get back to class," I snap, reaching down after a minute and hauling Jerome to his feet. "Let's go." He's still pretty dazed, which is good because it means I don't have listen to him babbling on about how awesome he is. Nathan's equally pliable, so in a second I've got both geniuses on their feet and on the march.

It occurs to me, as I lead these two back toward everyone else, that one of my new charges was felled by my furniture, and the other by the walls themselves.

Which maybe explains why I still can't get any sort of cleaning crew to set foot inside this place. Either that or the dust bunnies have been issuing ultimatums again.

Chapter Fourteen
In brain we trust

My first thought, when we emerge back into the Matrix chamber, is that somebody changed the channel when I wasn't looking, and put on America's Worst Dogpiles or Funniest Scrimmages. Because where I thought I'd find all the nerds sitting in a row against the back wall, possibly in takedown position with their hands on their heads, or at the very least them sitting on the bleachers like well-behaved little children who know the nun's just itching for an excuse to whack them with the ruler, instead I see what looks suspiciously like a human pyramid.

I just hope it's not a food pyramid, because "pasty geek turnover"? Yuck!

Tall's standing off to the side, arms crossed, looking mighty pleased with himself, so at least I know this isn't some crazed attempt at a jailbreak with him in the scrimmage playing the part of the ball. Ned's next to him, looking mildly put out. Mary looks amused. And then positively sunny when she sees me. And my two tagalongs.

"You have successfully retrieved Jerome!" she states. "And located Nathan! I knew you would be able to accomplish those tasks!"

"Yeah, two for two," I agree, herding the pair ahead of me. "Um, what's going on here, though? Somebody drop a solid-gold pocket protector?"

"Something like that," Tall agrees. He's actually in full-on smirk mode, and the fact that Ned is fuming slightly only seems to amuse him more. "After that one"—a bob of his chin indicates Jerome, who is only just recovering enough to start sneering again—"took off with your interface, I decided the rest of this lot needed something to keep them occupied."

"You could've asked!" Ned bursts out. He turns to me, looking all aggrieved, and I feel like I've just wandered into the pro version of "He's on my side of the couch again!" but in the role of "Disapproving Dad." "He just grabbed! That's one of my favorites, too!"

I'm not getting anything useful out of Ned, and Tall's too pleased with himself to enlighten me, so I turn to the floating bowling ball for answers. As long as it's not "Results cloudy, please check again later," I should be good.

"Tall waved one of Ned's tools at them," Heidi explains, "shouted, 'genuine alien tech!', and then threw it onto the field. Hence the pileup."

Ah. Okay, that's actually pretty clever. These guys are all frothing to get their hands on anything extraterrestrial, and at least half of the stuff here could kill them—including some of the snacks! And, evidently, my sofa!—so distracting them with a nice little shiny that probably won't hurt them much and keeps them all focused and contained? Yeah. I give Tall a quick thumbs-up, and he actually grins at me. Grins! Who is this guy, and what happened to the stone-faced, humorless monolith who helped drag me into this whole life all those months ago?

"Sorry, Ned," I add, catching the put-upon look he shoots me. "Tall should've asked permission first, sure, but otherwise? Definitely a smart move." I glance at the mass of over-educated and entitled people writhing on the ground in front of us. "So, uh, the one he did toss them—anything we need to know? Could it up the gravity here a hundredfold and squash us all flat? Open a tiny wormhole to a nearby sun and incinerate everything within a ten-mile radius? Merge everything organic and electronic within two blocks into a single cyborg mega-mind determined to take over the galaxy?" Okay, maybe I watch a lot of B-movie sci-fi flicks. So what? At three a.m. there aren't a lot of choices, even in this day and age—it's that, the Home Shopping Network, self-help shows, or reruns of *Dallas* or *Dark Shadows*. They should merge those last two—I would totally watch a show called "Dallas Shadows" that's about a rich Texas oil family whose forebear is actually a vampire.

Ned scuffs his feet on the ground. "Oh, uh, no, that shouldn't be a problem," he admits slowly. "It's just a tool for de-oxidizing and de-calcifying surfaces while neutralizing certain olfactory tags."

Tall is too busy laughing at one of the struggling geeks—who just elbowed somebody else in the head and got slammed in the gut by a third person, probably by accident but it's hard to tell, it's like the old cartoon images of a fight with nothing but a dust cloud and the occasional limb—and Mary is stepping in to separate them, but I turn and stare at Ned, and I notice that

Heidi has shaded to a muddy brown with splotches of yellow, which I think means confusion and suspicion. Exactly like I'm feeling.

"De-oxidizing," I repeat slowly, "and de-calcifying." Ned nods but he's not meeting my eyes. "And neutralizing olfactory tags." I frown, studying him while I puzzle through those terms in my head before finally bursting out, "It's a toothbrush! Tall tossed them your bloody toothbrush!"

It's like somebody just hit freeze-frame. Everybody stops dead. Then the pileup breaks apart, turning into four geeks all staring resentfully at me. Why me? I'm not the one who threw them Ned's dental gear! And they could've kept fighting over it all day if I hadn't said something. They should be thanking me!

Tall seems remarkably unconcerned. "So what?" he says, waving away both Ned's dismay and the nerds' irritation. "It's still alien tech. He's an alien, he's got alien teeth, he uses an alien toothbrush—alien tech." Very helpful, Tall.

Ned takes advantage of the sudden cessation of hostilities to stomp into the dissolving crowd and snatch the gadget in question from one guy's hand. "Give me that!" he demands, cradling it close. Ned's always had a bit of an unhealthy attachment to his gizmos.

"Okay, so what now?" I ask once he's returned to us, toothbrush safely in his grasp once more. "Do we just pack 'em up and ship 'em home?"

Tall's already nodding, and Heidi's glowing green in assent. Even Mary seems to feel it's best to get her former classmates out of here as quick as possible, before they do actually break something. But Ned, who you'd think would be eager to send 'em all packing, shakes his head.

"Not yet," he says, and his eyes start glowing just a little. "I think we should put 'em to work first."

"Doing what?" I ask, scanning this sorry-looking crowd, hands on my hips. "I've already got a lawnmower, and I doubt they're any good at grazing, anyways."

But Mary's perked up. "An excellent idea," she agrees. "We have a current conundrum that could benefit from additional brainpower."

I actually get her meaning right off. "You wanna use them to help us find the Grays?" I ask. It was either that, getting rid of the invaders, or unclogging the toilet in the guest bathroom, and I doubt any of these guys can even handle a plunger. Which is typical of geniuses—ask 'em to calculate pi to at least ten places (and no cheating by just having it memorized!) and they're all over it, but ask 'em to plunge a toilet or load a dishwasher or fold some laundry and they're either "huh?" or "such menial tasks are beneath me." Yes, I had a genius for a roomie for one semester. Just one. That was the soonest they'd let me kick him out.

This makes sense, though. Because we've got nothing to go on and no good ideas. But maybe one of these guys will.

Of course, that means getting them on the case first. But I'm good at motivating people. I once considered a career as a motivational speaker—until I found out you actually had to motivate them toward an actual life plan, rather than just to get up and jump around and maybe punch the guy to their left. Now I step forward and clear my throat. "Yo, listen up, you lot. How'd you like to help us find an entire alien race?"

Several of them glance at each other. One or two harrumph. Nathan, good ol' Nathan, leaps forward, throws his arms around Ned, and shouts, "Found one!"

"Uh, yeah, thanks heaps, bud," I tell him, helping Ned extract himself, "but obviously we already know where Ned is. And he's just one guy. I'm talking about a whole race. They've gone missing, and we've got no idea where or how."

Professor Kimura clears his throat. "How exactly does one misplace an entire race?" he asks in that deep voice of his. "Or perhaps are you referring to a theoretical displacement, such as being unable to reconcile a particular species' spot on the evolutionary chain? That we could possibly assist with, assuming you can provide us with a full morphology of this displaced race and obviously a detailed map of the other races to be found throughout the galaxy." Some of the other geeks look excited at that, but I got lost when he said "theoretical" and still haven't found my way back to shore. Huh?

Mary must sense my distress, 'cause she pats me on the arm in what is totally a "tag, I'm in!" move. Which we've used before, when . . . never mind.

"This is not theoretical, unfortunately," she explains. "An alien race has been taken or hidden or destroyed, we know not which. Their planet lies empty, all traces of life removed. We must locate them and, if possible rescue and restore them to their rightful place." She bites her lip. "Time is of the essence."

Her old prof nods like he understands, but he's the only one. Which, actually, seems to be because he was one of the only ones paying attention. Oh, sure, Nathan was, and so was Hornet Harriet, but he looks more interested in Mary's hair and she's just busy glaring daggers. Or possibly falchions, which is a lot more impressive but takes practice—and a certain amount of open space. The rest of the Nerd Herd are talking amongst themselves, checking their phones, or just studying their surroundings and not-so-subtly looking for anything they can snatch and sneak back home.

"Hey!" I shout, getting everyone's attention. "Mar— Mirabella's talking! Listen to her!"

Jerome and Taki and Cab all glance over, study Mary for a second—and then decide that there isn't anything important enough going on here and turn away again. Which astounds me, because the mere notion of turning away from my girl seems utterly impossible.

I look up at her, one eyebrow rising of its own accord, and she frowns. She's clearly not happy.

"I can furnish details about the race," she offers, "and a rough timeline for their disappearance. I may be able to transport one or more with me to investigate the incident site more closely, as well."

Not one 'em budges. They don't even so much as glance her way.

Now, somebody tried that with me, I'd be pissed. Of course, that almost never happens—I may be a lot of things, but "easy to ignore" was never one of 'em.

Mary's starting to get pretty steamed, herself. She marches over to Taki and Cab, who are standing near each other, and stops right in front of them, arms folded over her chest. "Are you willing to assist us?" she demands.

Taki glances up at her, smirks, then looks away. Cab smiles, but follows it with a chuckle. "No offense, Mirabella," he says in that watery little voice of his, "but—and don't take this the wrong way—how important can it really be? I mean . . ." He trails off, flushing as even his lack of social skills catches up and whaps him upside the head, but the implication is glaringly obvious, painted in great big neon letters a couple hundred feet high. And then lit on fire:

How important can it be . . . if they put *you* in charge.

This is that same 'but you're a *girl!*" B.S. I saw at the reunion, but there it was hiding behind pleasant smiles and mild platitudes and only emerging in the occasional sneer. Now it's right out in the open, and it's clear all the others feel the same way, even Professor Kimura. I glance over at Theresa, the only other woman from their class, but she's got her head down and appears to be performing a detailed study of her cuticles. Yeah, nice to see you sticking together there, sister.

I've also got an eye on Mary, though. I don't know quite how she's gonna take this. I mean, it's now abundantly clear why she was so hesitant to attend the reunion in the first place, and why she was so glad I agreed to go with her. But it's also obvious she had to put up with this attitude all through school, and she probably did her best to distance herself from it and forget it in the years since. Except that now it's right back in her face again, and trying to make up for lost time. A lot of people would crumple under that much pressure, fall right back into old behaviors, no matter how self-destructive. And I know it's already gotten to her some, like back in the hallway.

Now, however . . . Mary smiles. Big and wide and beautiful. Like Cab just paid her a compliment.

She's still smiling as she reaches out and caresses his cheek with one hand, and Taki's with the other. Neither guy moves, though both are flushed and wide-eyed. I'm sure this is how a lot of their college fantasies started.

I get a little jealous as her hands slide up to nestle in each of them's hair—until her fingers tighten, gripping tight.

Then, without changing her expression, Mary slaps their heads together like she's a cymbalist and they're nearing the end of Tchaikovsky's Fourth. Whoom!

I have never appreciated classical music more.

She releases her hold and both dudes fall away to the sides, clutching their wounded noggins, their eyes slightly glazed. But glued to Mary, as are everyone else's.

"Perhaps I was unclear," she states clearly, wiping her hands on her sides like she's just had to pick up something distasteful. Which she basically did. "You will assist us. This is not a question, nor is your participation optional. You will all put forth your best efforts or I"—and here she crosses her arms again and frowns at them, the perfect combination of a supermodel and a drill instructor—"will be displeased. Is that clear?"

All of them nod quickly, even the yellowjacket in a skirt. Taki and Cab a little more gingerly than the rest, but with no less enthusiasm.

"Excellent," my lady love concludes. Her smile is back in place, though it's less forced now and has a tinge of smirk to it. "And my name is no longer Mirabella. You will address me as Mary."

That's my girl!

Chapter Fifteen
It's not a game plan

Professor Kimura is the first to recover. No doubt he's been browbeat plenty of times before, though maybe not by a female former student. "What, exactly, would you have us do?" he asks. Then adds, "Mary," which earns a smile and a nod from her.

"We must determine exactly what befell the Grays," she explains, "and how it was done. Then we will be able to analyze whether there is any way to reverse that outcome." In other words, if it turns out they were lasered out of existence, there probably isn't much we can do about it except call around and see if anybody's got a time machine handy. If they're just locked up somewhere, though, time to mount Operation: Rescue the Grays!

Kimura nods. "You said you had relevant data," he reminds her. The way his mustache is twitching and his eyes are staring off past Mary at some indeterminate point, I've got the feeling he's already working on the problem.

"I do," she confirms, and produces a small disc from her purse. It looks like a cross between a CD and a prism. Holding it between forefinger and thumb, she concentrates for a second, and I'm surprised to see the thing start glowing. That fades, and

Mary offers the disc to her old professor. "This contains all we know about the Grays themselves, their homeworld, and their disappearance."

He accepts the disc eagerly and holds it up to inspect it. It's clear he has no idea how to use the thing. I can hardly blame him since he doesn't exactly have a "little crystal disc" drive handy. After watching him for a minute Mary takes his hand, flattens it, and sets the disc firmly in his palm. Then she taps it once and light erupts from the top, projecting a bunch of numbers and graphs and text and even pictures at about head height.

I had no idea she could do that, but if she can download anything from her own head into one of those things—well, we could have a very lucrative little side business going here. Especially since I'm already practically an exhibitionist and Mary's becoming surprisingly uninhibited. I wonder if there's a galactic equivalent to the movie ratings system, and if so what it takes to hit NC-17? I do love a challenge!

The rest of the Nerd Herd gathers close around Kimura, all staring at the disc and its display, and Mary quickly pulls out a few more of those discs and repeats the process. "Here," she says, distributing those, and her former classmates are eager to accept them. This is certainly way cooler than an alien toothbrush! Sorry, Ned. Soon each of them has his—or her—own disc, and is engrossed in its contents.

"Okay, that's pretty bad-ass," I tell Mary as she steps back to watch our own little think tank at work. "You did great, babe." I wrap an arm around her waist and give her a peck on the cheek.

"Thank you, my love," she replies, smiling and leaning into

me. "We shall see if their efforts yield any new insight."

Well, I figure we've got bubkus now so it's not like they can do any worse, right?

An hour goes by. Then another one. I rustle up some grub, going for the least exotic stuff I can find, and set out a decent little spread for our unwilling guests. Hey, geniuses gotta eat too, right? But most of 'em could be munching on cardboard for all they notice—they wander over, make up a plate, find a spot to sit or stand and eat, the whole time still studying their discs. At this point I'm pretty sure Steve Jobs could walk by wearing a piñata for a hat and they wouldn't even look up.

"So, how long you think this is gonna take?" I ask Mary. The four of us're sitting on two of the couches at the near end, having just eaten a bit ourselves. The geeks are spread out all through the Matrix chamber, but at least none of 'em are trying to touch it anymore. They've got something else to play with now, and this time it was actually given to them! Problem is, except for the occasional question or request for clarification on something in the files, none of them are saying a thing, so I've got no idea if we're minutes away from a solution or another three months.

If it's the latter, I'm gonna need to go shopping for camp beds, more food, and some extra toilet paper, stat!

"There is no way to be certain," Mary replies. "Not unless they inform us."

"I hate waiting," Tall grumbles. Which is funny, because as a MiB half his job consisted of standing still and looking menacing. But I guess that's not exactly the same. "Why don't we ask for a status report?"

Mary starts to object, but I cut in, "that's a great idea! It could be like a class presentation, right? They show us what they've got so far, and we can give 'em feedback, tell 'em if they're on the right track, which paths to look into more, stuff like that."

"Yeah, I agree," Ned offers. "Nothing wrong with a progress report, I've had to do plenty of those on a long project." Heidi is glowing blue and green, and after a second Mary nods as well.

"Yes, that does make sense," she agrees slowly. "I will inform them that they have another thirty minutes and then should present their current findings and their working hypothesis, if they have one." She rises to her feet and slides past me, heading for the open field and the brainiacs scattered about it. I resist the urge to ask her to bring along a trash bag—once again, geniuses and their complete inability to clean up after themselves. I might wind up having to sandblast the whole room after all this is done.

I hear grumbles as Mary stops by each person to explain about their new deadline, but when she returns she's smiling serenely.

"They understand," she informs the rest of us. "They will be ready with their presentation."

What's weird, though, is that I had to do plenty of group projects back in school and they all went more or less the same way—the teacher tells us the assignment, we divvy up the tasks, we each go off and do our own thing, then we meet a few times and toss everything in together, leaving some poor schlub to collate and clean and coordinate and make sense of it all, then we present it as a group, usually with that same schlub handing out sections for each of us to explain. And yeah, admittedly I tended to phone in my share of the project, but I was always the most comfortable talking in front of the class and often took on more of the presentation—sometimes even the whole thing—so I figured it balanced out a bit.

But that's not at all what happens here.

There's no coalescing, no gathering of all the nerds to pool their results, no frantic "oh, crap, nobody did the bio on Tesla? Quick, somebody Google him!", no "no, no, the timeline on the Industrial Revolution has to come before the essay on the Gilded Age."

And absolutely, positively, undeniably no glue sticks. No glitter. I don't even see a tri-fold board.

Where the hell did these guys learn about class presentations?

Finally, since they're all still just milling about in front of us, Tall stands up. "Are you ready to present?" he roars in his "I am waking a slumbering dragon from deep beneath the ocean waves" voice. Everyone nods. "Then begin!" He sits back down, and I'm disappointed that he didn't add, "I declare mortal combat!"

I am still hopeful that, if he doesn't like the way the presentation goes, he'll give it a thumbs-down and sneer, "Your soul. Is. MINE!"

There's some muttering among the nerds, and finally Professor Kimura steps forward. Which makes sense—he's the oldest, and probably the most practiced at public speaking.

"I have analyzed the data you provided," he starts. "And given the lack of remaining structures on their world, and the correlating lack of damage to the strata, I can only conclude that they were transported from that place, along with all their buildings and possessions, by some form of matter-transmitter. Most likely in a widespread beam form." He starts to explain exactly how such a thing would work—which is funny, since he's talking to some people who teleport on a regular basis—when a loud, braying laugh interrupts, cutting him off mid-babble.

"A matter-transmitter!" It's Jerome who pushes his way past the others and confronts Kimura. With his pencil mustache and the professor's big bushy one, I feel like I'm watching a showdown between Fu Manchu and Scotland Yard. Or maybe between a Pekingese and a sheepdog. "That's preposterous!" he continues, getting in the professor's face. "Did you find any residue from displaced ions? Any shattered chemical chains from the sudden transition? Any massive pressure sinks from the displacement of so much matter all at once? Of course not!" he answers his own question, which I've always considered incredibly rude. Not to mention a waste of everybody's time, because if you already know the answer, why ask in the first place? "Because that isn't even remotely what happened!" He holds up a hand for quiet, though nobody else is speaking anyway. "What happened here," he declares, "is glaringly obvious. It was"—he pauses dramatically, and I want to leap over the coffee table and rip that mustache from his face, one pretentious little hair at a time—"transmogrification! That's right, you cannot find any trace of these Grays' departure because they have not left. They are still there, all around, in the shape of rocks and stones! You were walking on the very beings you sought to save!"

Huh. Could that be true? It would make sense, actually. The invaders are reality-manipulators—who's to say they couldn't have turned all the Grays and their cities into rock? Though I would've expected to just find them as statues, then, instead of rough, unmarked stone.

I'm still trying to wrap my head around this possibility, though, when someone else says, "That's the stupidest thing I've ever heard." It's Cab, who steps up to sneer at Jerome just like Jerome did to Kimura. "Transmogrification? Really? That's the best you've got?" He starts to say more but at that point I stop listening.

Because my eyes drift to the rest of the Nerd Herd, and I see each of them shaking their head, laughing, rolling their eyes, and so on. And suddenly it hits me:

The reason I didn't see them coming together to organize their presentation is because they don't have one. Not a single one, at any rate. They didn't treat this as a group project, not at all. They each took this as an individual assignment, determined to solve it on their own.

We're not looking at one presentation, we've got six. And from the sound of things, each of 'em is going to offer a different answer.

I glance over at Mary and Tall and Ned and Heidi, and I can see by the looks on their faces—and the colors of Heidi's sphere—that they've just grokked the exact same thing I did. And we all realize something else, too:

It is possible that one of these guys could have spotted something we missed, or put the pieces together in a way we couldn't. One of them might have figured out the answer to our little riddle.

But the odds aren't good. Because Mary's smarter than any of 'em, maybe than all of 'em put together. And Tall's a damn good investigator. And Ned and Heidi are both crazily tech-savvy. And me? I make intuitive leaps like I'm the Hulk and logic trains are the buildings I'm jumping between.

If the five of us together couldn't figure this out, what're the chances that any one of them could, when they don't even know the Grays and none of 'em have ever been out into space before? We thought we were getting six geniuses combining their brainpower to form an organic supercomputer. Instead we got six geniuses competing to show the others up.

Chances are, that's not going to help any, which means we've just wasted a whole bunch of time for nothing.

"We can just cut this short and send them back," Tall suggests quietly, though Cab and Jerome and even Kimura are now outright arguing so it's not like anybody's gonna hear us anyway.

This time I'm the one to shake my head. "No, we can still use 'em," I insist. "We've just gotta get 'em all working on it together instead of against each other."

The look Tall shoots me is Number Eleven, which isn't exactly one of my favorites. It translates roughly as, "Okay, clever guy, what's your plan, then?"

Oy.

Chapter Sixteen
An elephant would be easy!

"Right," I say, rubbing my hands together. "Here's what we do."

Only problem is, I don't have a freaking clue.

How the heck do you get six geniuses to work together on a single problem when each of 'em has their own idea on how to go about things, their own pet theories, and the unshakeable conviction that they and only they are absolutely in the right?

This is totally the blind men and the elephant, only instead of an elephant it's a chimera, so there's actually multiple heads and different body parts from different creatures, all shoved into one.

And the blind men are each speaking a different language.

I'm tempted to turn to the crowd—or maybe the heavens—and shout, "Anybody a master translator?" Because that's what we need here—somebody who can translate what each member of the Nerd Herd is thinking, distill that down, and then plug it into the whole so that we get a single answer instead of six. Like piecing together a puzzle—it's fine if they're each working on their own area initially, as long as we can connect them all back up into a single picture of Big Ben by the end.

And that, I realize, is exactly the solution.

"We treat this like it's Big Ben," I tell my pals, then when they all give me shades of Four ("How can anyone talk so much and make so little sense?") I add, "a puzzle of Big Ben. Or any puzzle, really. It doesn't have to be Big Ben. It's the puzzle part that's important. It could be the Eiffel Tower, or the Statue of Liberty, or Mount Rushmore, or—"

"Get to the point," Tall growls.

But Mary nods. "I believe I understand, my love." She rakes her gaze across Tall, Ned, and Heidi. "What DuckBob means is that we must divide the problem into discrete sections, and assign each of my former classmates one section and one alone. Then I will collate their results and assemble that into a full picture. This will end the current disputes because they will each be working on different aspects of the problem, rather than each attempting it in its entirety."

"Dude, that totally makes sense!" Heidi bursts out, shading green. "And I ain't no scientist but think I grok enough of what's going on that I can help—I can check in on each of 'em from time to time, see if there's overlap, point 'em toward each other if it turns out two or more need to compare notes, stuff like that."

"Yeah, I can handle that, too," Ned offers. "Mary can field the tough questions, Tall can prevent any fights, and Heidi and I'll keep 'em on track and pointed in the right direction."

"Great!" I squint at the loosely assembled geeks. "I'll offer moral support—and refreshments."

Everybody from ol' Fartcap is still arguing with each other, which is at least keeping 'em busy. "So we need six pieces," I point out. "What've we got?" There's a yellow legal pad sitting on the coffee table—I like to doodle sometimes, or to play Hangman with the others when they're over—and I scoop that up, turn to a clean page, and detach the pen that was clipped to the top. Then I write, "What Happened to the Grays?" on the first line, and number the next six lines in order.

"We need to know how they disappeared," Tall suggests. He didn't specifically say that he was onboard with this plan but since he's contributing I'm going to assume that's a "right, let's do this!"

"We need to know where they went," Ned says.

I start to write those down. But the first one, "How they disappeared," is really the big question, same as "What happened to them?" and that's what we're trying to break down into smaller pieces. And where they went feels more like the answer than the question. What're we missing?

"It would be useful to analyze the energy readings the invaders left behind," Mary contributes. "That might lead to clues as to how and what they have done." Okay, that's good. I put that one as the first piece.

Heidi is a swirl of yellow and brown and orange. Thinking colors. "They'd been there a while, right?" he asks now. "The Grays?"

Most of us shrug—it's not like any of us took "History of the Grays" in college—but Ned nods. "From what I heard, that was where they evolved," he answers. "So we're talking thousands of years, maybe more."

"But there wasn't any trace of them left?" Heidi follows up.

"Nothing left but bare rock?" Ned, Mary, and I all nod. "That doesn't make any sense. Never mind removing the Grays themselves. If you take the buildings, like shear 'em off at their base, okay, that's nuts but whatever. But what about everything that's below the surface? Cities thousands of years old, they've gotta be dug deep."

"Sewer lines," I say, seeing where he's going with this. "Power lines, too. Subway tunnels. Foundations. Sub-basements." I look at Ned and Mary. "We didn't see any of that. If you yank a city out by the roots, there'd be big gaping holes everywhere. But there weren't. Nothing."

"Indeed," Mary agrees. "Whatever method the invaders employed, they removed all traces, aboveground and below. As if the Grays had never been there."

I add that to the list: "How did the Grays disappear without leaving any trace, even underground?"

That's two. Ned offers another one: "When did it happen, exactly? If we could figure that out, it might help us figure out what they did."

"Did it affect anyone else?" Tall pipes in. "If you fry a server, there'll be system outages all through its system. What did taking the Grays—and especially their Singularity—do to everyone around them? And everyone who depends on them?"

"Ooh, good one," I tell him, adding that and Ned's to the list. Four. "Hey, what about warning signs? The Grays are scarysmart and kinda paranoid—they must've had some kinda security system in place. And any decent alarm system has a backup off-site. Did that get tripped? We could analyze that data, too."

Ah, Stare Six ("So your brain does sometimes work after all!") is way better than Four!

Now we've got five on our list. One to go.

"What of the neighboring systems?" Mary suggests. "Perhaps they detected signs of the invaders as they approached, or as they set their trap into effect. We could study the data from those other planets and cultures for the time right around when we received the distress call." That's a good point, but it's really part of "were there any warning signs or tripped alarms?" so I just add it to that one instead.

"Hey, the distress call!" I practically shout that, and a few geeks glance up but quickly return to belittling their peers. "That'll tell us when it happened, at least ballpark, but there might be more info there, too! Like embedded code or something. Maybe a snippet of their sensor readings. All I know is, the Grays're way too sharp to just send the word 'help.' We've been a little too busy to look at that signal again, but that's what these guys are for." Everyone nods, so I add that to Number Three.

Which just leaves one more task and then we can put our little herd of nerds to work.

Mary clears her throat and we all turn to her. "There is another incident that is almost certainly directly related," she reminds us. "The teleportation array has been erratic since we received that distress call. That cannot be a coincidence."

"You're right," Ned says. "Let's get one of these guys to go over the readings and code for that system. I can help get 'em set up with that. If we can figure out what's wrong with it, we might be able to tell what messed it up, which could lead us right back to what the invaders did."

"Perfect!" I jot that one down and hold up the legal pad. "And we're set! Now we just need to break up the fight, divvy up this list, and start cracking the whip."

Tall smiles and straightens, cracking his knuckles. "Leave that first part to me." Then he turns and strides out into the crowd like a bull elephant that's just spotted a small, untouched grove and is eager to turn it to kindling.

"I will determine which individual is best suited to each task," Mary offers, taking the pad and pen from my hands. Can't argue that one—she knows these guys, so she'll know who can handle what.

"I'll collect those holo-discs Mary doled out and restructure their contents," Ned says. "I'll highlight the relevant info for each task, and add whatever new data they need for some of those that aren't directly about the Grays, like the neighbors and the teleport." He follows Tall, who has already started physically separating people and barking orders that have them all stiffening in place like good little soldiers.

Or corpses. Tall sometimes gets carried away.

Of those two options, I really hope it's the former. The latter won't be much use except as compost or maybe insulation, and I don't need prize petunias or a lower heating bill *that* badly!

"I can start calling up some of that secondary data," Heidi tells me. "That way Ned'll have it available once he's ready." He twirls in place, his colors going black and white and mottled rather than swirled or striped.

That just leaves me. It's too early to provide moral support, and I think the others all have their own tasks well in hand with no help from me.

Which leaves refreshments. But that's fine—I know only too well how important it is to stay fed and hydrated. So I start gathering up plates and cups to bring back to the kitchen. I'll toss those into the dishwasher—at least I think it's a dishwasher, admittedly when I open it back up I usually find my dishes've changed size and shape and texture, and sometimes increased or decreased in number, but they're always nice and clean so that's really all that matters, though I have to remind myself not to get too attached to a particular mug or steak knife—and then put together something for these guys to eat, something clean and simple.

I'm thinking sandwiches. I don't have actual Cheddar or roast beef out here, but what I do manage to order tastes close enough, and looks close enough, that nobody should notice the difference.

As long as they don't start humming while they eat. Because whatever these deli meats and cheeses are out here, turns out they're highly sensitive to music.

To the degree where, if you wind up singing under your breath while you're putting together a nice tray of luncheon meats, you might get treated to an impromptu deli chorus line.

Which, let me tell you, is as entertaining as it is delicious. Provided you don't have a problem eating something that was just doing a high-kick and a soft-shoe two seconds before.

At least they've never started singing, which is good, because that's probably right about where I would draw the line. Though there is something to be said for food that provides its own musical accompaniment. Problem is, I'm betting all deli meats would know is eighties hair bands, and while I like Metallica and Poison and Whitesnake as much as anybody, they're not what I'd call conducive to digestion.

Chapter Seventeen
Anybody got any Super Glue?

It takes another hour or so, but soon the whole place is humming along like a good little think tank. Tall had to pull out some of his best scowls and glares but he managed to get all the geeks to back off each other, and then he and Mary got them all to agree to each focus on their own little piece of the puzzle. We warned that they weren't supposed to talk to each other unless they felt one of the others had information that would directly aid in finding their own solution, or if they realized that something they'd figured out would directly benefit somebody else.

Then I had a brainstorm on how to motivate them all. "You're each getting just one piece of the whole," I told them all, which earned me a few sour looks. Nobody likes being told they're not good enough to do it all themselves, especially geniuses who are used to beating any intellectual challenge thrown their way. "Just remember, time is of the essence."

I frown and squint up at the skylight like I'm just now thinking of something. "Of course," I say slowly, "I guess the smartest of you will come up with a solution to your piece first, right? That makes sense. Just like the smartest one always finishes the test first." Now there's some teeth-gnashing going on as well, but the glares are being spread around, aimed at each other instead of just me. The hard part is not grinning or laughing as I head back down the hall afterward. Because if there's one thing overachievers hate, it's coming in second. Just ask me about the Limbo Challenge at the office work party at my old job. I still say Beverly from Accounting cheated—it's not fair that she modeled part-time and had already had a few ribs removed!

Anyway, I know that they're all gonna be super-motivated to finish first now, just to hold that over the others. Which is fine by me. The sooner they can solve this riddle, the sooner we can get the Grays back and have everyone and everything back where they belong.

I conk out on the couch a few hours later. It's exhausting watching geniuses at work! Actually, no, it's just dead boring. All most of them're doing is standing around staring off into space, or staring at their holo-discs so hard it's a wonder their eyes don't burn holes straight through. Occasionally one of 'em'll emerge from brain-fog and look around, like a diner hoping desperately to catch a waiter and ask for more coffee. Ned's taken a break too, but Heidi and Mary're both still going, and they're both keeping their eyes peeled for anybody needing help. One or both of 'em will head over to that geek and answer any questions they might have—Heidi handling a lot of the "where do I find this data?" stuff but leaving the actual math queries for Mary—then leave 'em to work on it again. They're like a roving IT team, circling users and pouncing on problems. Which of course makes me think that the next thing should be an IT ninja squad, where you've got a problem and then suddenly you don't because they snuck up on you and fixed it without you even knowing. Maybe that's what happens every time your computer freezes but then starts working again—it's actually thanks to an IT ninja. Who may still be standing right behind you making sure everything's running properly again.

Suddenly I wish I didn't spend so much time surfing the web in my underwear. Man, I hope those IT ninjas aren't laughing at my beachball boxers!

Tall's still awake as well—I've always wondered if he just saves up sleep when things're quiet, so he'll be like, "Nothing much doing today, think I'll rack up fifteen hours of nap time," and then he somehow siphons that off into a sleep-battery or something, so whenever he needs to just push on through he's like, "Hm, better use up some of that sleep from the other day to make sure I'm wide awake throughout this."

I'm the same way except I think something's wrong with my battery—no matter how much I nap, I don't seem able to siphon that off to use later.

When I wake up, still a little hazy, my first thought is, "Hey, they've made themselves into a solar system!" Because all the geeks are circling Mary like she's the Sun and they're each planets. And moons. And maybe a comet for Cab, who's sort of corkscrewing his way in a big looping path around the whole crowd.

"Hey, what's up?" I ask, sitting up and rubbing the sleep from my eyes.

"A lot of 'em have figured out their pieces," Heidi answers. I hadn't noticed him floating by the arm of the couch. "They're telling Mary what they've learned so far."

"Yeah? Nice!" I glance around. "Where'd Ned and Tall go?"

"Tall's taking a power nap in one of the other rooms"—aha, that battery ran out!—"and Ned muttered about needing to check on something on your computer."

"Huh." That sounds a bit ominous, so after I manage to haul myself back to my feet I toddle off toward the living room to see what's going on.

I find Ned hunched forward, staring at my computer screen so close I'm worried his eyes'll frostbite. My computer's made of some kind of liquid ice display, after all. That's why I keep a parka on the back of my desk chair! "Hey, whatcha doing?" I ask, crossing the room to see. But, after jumping slightly, Ned clicks a few buttons and whatever was on the screen disappears, to be replaced by a shot of the Milky Way Galaxy. Subtle.

"Oh, nothing," he answers, turning to face me. "Just wanted to take a look at something. Thanks." He hops out of the chair and makes to slide past me, but I'm crowding him just enough that he can't.

"Come on, man," I tell him. "We both know you're holding out on me. What's really going on? It's true, Ned's a terrible liar. It doesn't help when your eyes light up whenever you're excited, nervous—or lying. In order to fib he's basically got to close those peepers completely, and that's not a giveaway!

He sighs. "I want to wait and confer with Mary about it," he tells me finally. "I promise if what the rest of her friends've found lines up with what I'm thinking, I'll tell you. Okay?"

I study him for a second. I trust Ned completely, just like I do Tall and Mary and even Heidi. So after a second I nod. "Yeah, all right." And I step back, giving him room to slip by. Then I turn and follow him back out to the others.

Mary's still talking to a few of the eggheads, so I head over to the buffet table I set up, grab a drink and a cookie, and then wander back to the couch. Maybe twenty minutes later, the last of the geeks finishes talking and Mary steps over to join me. She looks a little tired—still amazing, just tired—which makes sense. I'm pretty sure she hasn't slept since before we headed to her old alma mater. She also looks—not pleased, exactly, but satisfied. Like it's a job well done, even if she doesn't like the ultimate results.

"You got the goods?" I ask as she seats herself beside me. I offer her a water bottle and half the cookie, both of which she accepts.

"I do," she admits after munching and sipping. "I still need to collate all the data they have provided, in order to be absolutely certain, but we now have a working hypothesis as to what has happened, and I believe it to be correct."

"Nice!" I peer over at the nerds currently milling about on my lawn. They're like the geekiest set of deer ever. "What do we do with them in the meantime?" I turn to Ned, who quickly slaps a hand over his tool belt, lifting his chin defiantly in return. "Hey, I was just gonna ask if you could come up with some kinda brainteaser to keep 'em occupied," I assure him. "No theft of personal items necessary." Which isn't strictly true, but I'm too far away and he reacted too fast for me to make a grab for anything.

"Oh." He unwinds a little—though he keeps his hand there, which just shows that he knows me really well—and gives that some thought. "Got one!" he states after a minute. "Back when I was in school, there were always a few problems the teachers would dangle over our heads, usually with statements like 'well, nobody's ever solved this one, but if you think you're smart enough . . .' I still remember a few of those." He gets up, scooping up my pad and pen along the way—now who's making off with whose stuff!—and ambles over to the geeks.

"I'll go get Tall," Heidi offers, flashing blue. "No sense you having to repeat yourself." He floats away at a decent clip, and a few minutes later he's zooming back over, with Tall right behind him. The big guy looks fresh as a daisy, which totally isn't fair—I got in a much longer nap and I'm sure I still look dazed and confused. Even moreso than usual.

Ned's finished sketching and explaining this Gordian knot of his, and looks awfully smug as he returns. "Good luck with that one!" he declares, sinking back down onto the same spot he left. It's the same place he usually sits when he visits and we're out here, and I suspect it's got a permanent Ned-shaped dip in it by now. Me, I tend to switch things up more. I like to distribute my lumpiness evenly.

Once Ned's ensconced again and Tall's perched himself on one arm of the couch, Mary states. "Now that I have all the analyses and hypotheses generated by my colleagues, I have what appears to be the answer to our question: What occurred to the

Grays?" She takes a deep breath, lets it out, then continues. "The first portion of that question was 'where did they go?' And the answer is 'nowhere, for they still exist in the same location as before." She frowned. "Not in the same space, however."

"Um, okay, once more for the slow kids?" I ask. "They're in the same spot but not the same space?"

She smiles. "Precisely! They have not in fact gone anywhere. They have, instead, been phased out of our reality. But only by a tiny increment, half a step at most. They are, mathematically speaking, hovering just beyond our perception."

"Huh." That does explain how they could all be gone, and so fast, and the buildings and everything. And the invaders can manipulate reality so doing something like this is absolutely within their capabilities. "Is that why the teleport array's been on the fritz?" I ask. "'Cause the Grays built it so I'm guessing the heart of the system is on their homeworld, and now that's been phased out?"

Mary nods. "That is exactly why, yes. The teleport array, like the majority of the Grays' creations, is powered at least partially by the Quantum Singularity. But with that out of phase, the array can no longer draw power from it, and thus has difficulty gathering enough energy to operate."

A horrible thought hits me. "Does the Matrix draw power from the Singularity?"

Mary looks away, but finally nods. "It does," she admits. "And if the Grays and their Singularity are cut off from us for too long, the Matrix will suffer. It may even shut down completely." Which would do the invaders' work for them—that was how all this started, with the Matrix shutting down and the invaders being able to shove their way through from their reality once that border fence collapsed. If it drops again they'll hit us with everything they've got.

"Damn." I snap my fingers. "I bet that was the point of this whole thing. Wipe out the Matrix without even having to touch it. Wait, but if that's the case, why attack us here at all?"

"Maybe it wasn't working fast enough for them," Tall points out. "They got tired of waiting, or weren't sure it was going to take down the Matrix after all, so they went to Plan B."

Ned's wriggling in his seat like he needs to go and is afraid to ask to be excused. "All right, dude, spill it," I tell him. "What's going on?"

He sighs and deflates into his seat. "Like I said before, I wanted to be sure first," he explains slowly. "Now, though—yeah." He scrubs at his head with one hand. "Like Mary said, the teleport array and the Matrix both draw power from the Singularity, and now they're starting to have trouble 'cause they're basically running on reserves instead of tapping into it fresh." He squirms a little more. "But I've been wondering for a while if things didn't run a bit . . . deeper than that."

I look at Mary and Tall, but they don't seem to know what Ned's getting at, either. "Deeper how?" I ask.

"The Grays . . . used the Singularity to power just about everything they built," Ned answers, twisting his fingers together. "Everything . . . and everyone." He looks up at me, and at Mary. "Their alterations are dynamic, not fixed—they're always in flux, which actually makes them stronger 'cause they're more adaptable that way. It's like in metals, you want a little bit of give, otherwise it'll be strong but brittle. And that's great as long as the Singularity's there to pour more power into it, just enough to keep it fluid. But when that's cut off . . ."

"So, wait," I say, standing and starting to pace between the coffee table and the couch. "You're saying that, with them out of phase, me and Mary might . . . what? Freeze? Crack?" Another possibility whispers itself in my head, and I spit it out before I even realize I've said it: "Revert?"

Ned looks like a kindly neighbor having to admit he just ran over your dog. "Maybe. I don't know. Obviously this hasn't ever happened before. But yeah, could be. Depends exactly how they made the modifications, and if they built in any fail-safes. It might just lock into its current state, which could give you some negative side effects. It could split or crumble away somehow. Or it could start to fade out the way they did, the way the Matrix might. Returning to the original structure."

"Whoa." I have an instant flash of me walking around and my bill suddenly cracking and crumbling away, or just fading, and leaving behind—me. The old me. Bob Spinowitz. Not Duck. Not anything.

I don't like it. I don't like it a lot.

And Mary—I can see in her wide eyes that she's just as worried as I am. But is she worried about her, and what she'll do without the Grays' enhancements—or about me, and how I'll manage if I'm just plain ol' Bob again?

Or whether she'll want anything to do with me if that happens?

"Okay, let's not worry about that now," I say, forcibly shaking the image from my head. "First things first. We need to get the Grays back, simple as that. We need the Matrix to stay intact, we need the teleport array back up and running, the whole shmear." I look at them. "So, how do we do that?"

The blank looks I get in return aren't exactly reassuring.

Chapter Eighteen
It's like UHF all over again

Time to rally the troops," I decide. I stand up and holler, "Yo, brainiacs! Over here!" Amusingly enough, this actually works, and they all come trotting over, looking various shades of amused, annoyed, and just plain arrogant. Gee, I can't imagine why none of them were able to find a date for the reunion!

"Okay, first off, good job on cracking the riddle of what happened to the Grays," I tell them once they're all glaring at me. "Top marks all around. But now we move on to Stage Two, where things really get tough." I rest my hands on my hips. "You know where the Grays are? Swell. How do we get them back?"

That causes a bit of excited murmuring. Typical eggheads—can't resist a brainteaser.

"We're not gonna divide things up this time," I continue, "mainly because we have no idea how to do that. So try to work together, huh? See if you can build off each other." That's met with a lot more sneers and some scoffs, maybe even a few scowls. "Oh, and first one or group or whatever to solve it?" I add. "Gets a proper sit-down with the Grays. You get to play 'Ask the Alien' for a good thirty minutes, no interruptions." The murmurs rise to an excited gabbling. Who says I don't know how to motivate people?

"You really think the Grays'll go for that?" Ned whispers as I plop back down.

"Who knows?" I admit. "Maybe. Especially if they're gonna wipe their memories anyways." No, I didn't mention that part to the Nerd Herd. It's like the verbal equivalent of reading the fine print, only this time it's more like hearing the unspoken disclaimers. But we'll cross that bridge when we come to it. Assuming there's even a bridge there, and that we've got enough to pay the toll.

Yeah, I know. I never met a metaphor I didn't like enough to take home and introduce to the family and start converting to a small shed out back.

Mary starts to get to her feet, mumbling something about needing to keep the others on track and field any questions, but I pull her back down. Gently. "What you need to do is get some sleep," I correct. "You're gonna be dead on your feet otherwise, and while I'm sure zombie Mary would still be hella cute, I prefer the live version."

She starts to argue, saying she's fine, but I cut her off. "How many digits can you calculate pi to?" I ask. "A trillion? Two?" She told me once that some guy claimed he'd worked it out to 2.7 trillion digits. Then she scoffed and called him a piker.

Now, however, she frowns. "I . . . do not know," she admits after a moment. "Several billion, perhaps." I don't have to say anything more, just wait for it, and finally she glances up and nods. "You are correct, my fatigue is beginning to impair my thought processes," she confesses. "If allowed to continue, I will be unable to adequately synthesize any solutions and theories they might propose." This is one of the reasons we don't fight much—Mary's big enough to admit when she's wrong about something, and I'll admit to pretty much anything, so we never have that awful "well, I know you're right but I'm never gonna give you the satisfaction!" standoff.

She starts to stand again, and this time I let her because I know she's gonna head upstairs to my bedroom and collapse for some much-needed rest. I consider joining her, but somebody needs to keep an eye on these yahoos. Besides, I already took a short nap, so I'm fine to play watchdog for a little bit.

Ned stretches out on the other couch, feet on the coffee table, and promptly lists to the side and starts snoring. There isn't a warm-up—one minute he's sitting there, awake, and the next he's asleep and drooling. I wish I could do that, but my switch only does "bleary to blinky" and then through a couple more notches before it finally hits "unconscious." I think Tall's is set permanently to "alert and dangerous," and it's just a question of whether his eyes are open or not.

I do kick back a bit, leaning my head against the back of the couch, feet up on the table as well, arms crossed. This is pretty comfortable, and I let myself zone out a bit, aware of the Nerd Herd but as background motion and white noise more than anything. My thoughts start to drift a bit.

What would it be like, being normal again? I wonder. It's been so long since I was, I barely remember it—when I think back to times growing up or in college, the glimpses I have of myself are hazy but do still look vaguely duck-shaped, like I started to hatch that particular silhouette at a young age and it just solidified and clarified as I got older. Which isn't true, of course—I was completely normal (at least on the outside) and then, blammo! I was abducted and returned like this. It's just that I'm so used to being DuckBob now, and images of Bob are starting to fade a bit.

No feathers. No bill. No webbing. Hair. Bare skin. A chin.

It all seems so weird.

No more Matrix gig, either. Both because I wouldn't be modified anymore, so I wouldn't be attuned to it, and because the Matrix would probably have disappeared before I fully changed back. So if I wind up normal again, we're pretty much done already. Good to know.

I try to imagine myself and Mary, me completely normal-looking and her just your average super-genius without the mods, going out to dinner. In Manhattan, most likely—if I'm gonna be not only earthbound but restricted to a single city, I'd absolutely choose New York, no question. Although then there's the question of what to do for a living. I've got the apartment, of course, and it's practically rent-free—the MiBs made an arrangement with the landlady—but even so, Manhattan real estate is crazy expensive, and "practically rent-free" isn't far off from "would bankrupt a non-New Yorker or cause suffocation as they gasp in shock." No going back to my old cubefarm job, not that I'd want to but at this point, having saved the universe a bunch of times, I can't exactly bring myself to care about TR-40s and 1099s and whatever. I wonder if the MiBs would hire me? I've got a lot of experience working with aliens, after all, and I bet Tall would give me a recommendation. And they've had agents who aren't exactly svelte before—Tall's old partner was shaped like Mr. Potato Head. Smith would probably love to hire me, if only so he could boss me around with impunity, but I guess I'd put up with that for the paycheck if I had no other choice.

Of course, if the Matrix fails and my duckness goes away, the invaders are practically home-free, at which point they're gonna rewrite the universe and we might all die horribly, so I guess there isn't a lot of reason to worry about this, really.

I must've fallen asleep worrying, 'cause when I suddenly jerk upright I've got a pain in my neck, my legs are asleep, visions of me trying to tie one of those skinny black ties are still circling, and none of the nerds I was watching before are still in view. Crap. If those little buggers waited until I passed out and dove for the Matrix again, I'm gonna pulverize whatever the Matrix itself didn't already turn to ash.

Grimacing, I manage to yank my feet off the table. I try not to wince too much as they hit the floor, sending jolts of pain woven through the pins and needles in my legs. Man, you'd think the Grays could've at least improved my circulation when they made all these changes! It's like they wanted me to suffer. Which, actually, having met them a bunch of times and worked for them the past year or more, I can believe.

Now that I'm a bit more upright I can see that the geeks've all migrated to the bleachers at the other end of the field. From here it looks like a few of 'em are stretched out—but who'm I to judge, when I do half of my best thinking while I'm asleep? (The other half is in the bathroom, whether in the shower or on the john. What?)—and the rest are either doing their impression of The Thinker or scribbling on a legal pad or, in one case, actually talking to each other.

At a guess, I'd say they're still on the case but haven't come up with any brilliant solutions yet.

Ned's still passed out. Tall is still perched on the arm, his own arms crossed, his eyes closed but his body still upright, his back still straight. The man probably has better posture when pretzeled into an old VW Bug with twin basketball stars than I do when I'm trying to stand up straight. And I know from experience that anything gets too close to his face, or moves too loudly, he'll be instantly awake.

Like I said before, creepy.

Heidi's hovering over the other arm, so it's like I've got my very own pair of sentries. I hope he's still awake in there—it occurs to me that, short of talking to him, there's no way to know. He could have a version of autopilot in that thing and have programmed it to just float in place while he curls up on the world's tiniest waterbed and catches a quick nap. Or maybe he's watching a movie, catching up on the latest TV, something like that. Whatever he's doing is fine, of course, and I know if I shout for help he'll be awake and on it in a heartbeat. But that doesn't mean I can't make fun of him sometimes. And right now, hanging in mid-air, when all he's missing is the "Check back later" sign out front, is definitely one of those times.

With a groan that could probably wake the dead—and does have Tall on his feet and in a combat stance, eyes scanning for the attack moose he just heard—I lever myself up off the couch and stretch. Man! Why didn't I go up with Mary and use the perfectly comfortable bed instead of passing out down here?

I catch sight of the Nerd Herd again. Oh, right. That.

"Everything okay?" Tall asks. He straightens back up, having confirmed that the only threat right now is me, and only to his hearing and maybe his delicate sensibilities.

"Yeah, fine," I tell him. "Except that I'm suddenly a hundred and three and my whole body's complaining that it hasn't felt right since I was a hippie."

He smirks at me. "Should start doing those exercises again."

"What, the ones you forced on me? Those weren't exercises," I retort. "Those were torture programs cleverly disguised to get past the Geneva Conventions. I'd have told you everything I know to get you stop, if only I knew anything."

"You tell me everything you know anyway," he points out. "Repeatedly. Without any coercion. Despite my best efforts to make you stop." I never know if I should be proud for having awakened Tall's snarky side or annoyed that he now talks back instead of just being the straight man for all my jokes. This must be how every teen's parent feels. Especially when he comes over, eats all my junk food, and drinks all my beer.

At least he never asks to borrow the car, or for any money. And I've never had to explain sex to him.

Which is a shame, because I rock at Pictionary.

A motion catches my eye, and I turn toward the distant bleachers. One of the geeks—I think it's Cab but I'm not sure from here—is standing up and waving his arms at me. Maybe he's trying to start a wave. Or maybe he's trying to signal for a menu.

Either way, I guess I'd better see what he wants.

Only, that proves to be a problem. Because I navigate my way between couch and coffee table just fine—grimacing a little, since the pins-and-needles still haven't faded and it feels like I'm walking through a cactus grove without any pants—and then start across the lawn.

And keep walking.

And keep walking.

But, after a few minutes, I haven't gotten any farther.

Now I realize that Cab's not waving, he's moving. Walking toward me, to be precise.

Or at least he's trying to.

Because it doesn't look like he's getting anywhere, either.

"Oh, hell," I groan. I glance back over my shoulder at Tall, whose frown shows he knows something's wrong, even if he hasn't figured out exactly what yet. I wave at him, and mime hoisting his big gun and preparing to shoot at things. "Here we go again."

Chapter Nineteen
Out walking Zeno's Paradox

Tall hasn't picked up on my cues—he's a terrible Charades partner, unless your word has something to do with the military, Boy Scouts, aliens, or fifties show tunes, in which case he's practically telepathic—so I shout, "We got trouble! Right here in Matrix City!"

That gets his full attention and he leaps off the couch—or tries to. Because he isn't moving, either. Or not properly—it's more like if somebody filmed him leaping down, then ran a loop of just the first part so he's continuously spring upright and levering himself into the air but somehow he's never quite managing to touch the ground. It could be an art installation, "The Futility of Struggle" or "Shades of Blue in Monochrome Severity" or something. After a minute he gives up and flops back down, chest heaving. "Looks like I'm stuck," he states.

"Yeah? No kidding. I thought you were just inventing some new calisthenics." I glance over at Ned, who's just starting to stir. I swear, the entire building could collapse on top of him and he'd just roll over, brushing debris off his shoulder, and mumble something about not liking the draft. Then I look up at Heidi. "Yo, you stuck too?" He was last time, but this seems like a different trick than before. Never let it be said these guys don't know how to adapt.

Heidi zooms toward me, stopping mere inches from my eye, then curves up over me and around, describing a quick circuit of the nook we're in. "Doesn't look like it. Maybe because I'm not ground-bound I'm not affected as much?"

"Sure, could be," I agree. Or it could be that whatever the invaders are doing doesn't work as well on the color puce. Or that Heidi's level of radioactivity is keeping their mojo at bay. That's a puzzle we can worry about later, though. "Hey, Ned, can you move?"

He sits up, groaning, and rubs a hand over his hair, which just makes it stand up more. "I dunno," he says softly. "Does this count as moving?"

"Technically, sure, but just to win over the Romanian judge let's see you get up and walk to the Matrix," I reply. "You do that, we've got ourselves a winner."

People're funny. I haven't said there was so much as a contest. I haven't said what the rules are. I haven't said anything about any potential competition, any time limit, nothing. But somehow when you use words like "winner" and "judge," that ol' competitive spirit rears its ugly head once more. Which is why Ned growls, grits his teeth, and forces himself to his feet. "Ha-ha!" he shouts, throwing both arms up over his head.

"Yeah, you're a real Muhammed Ali," I tell him, "overcoming obstacles left and right. Now take a step, champ."

He does—and almost kicks himself in the butt, as his right leg has somehow relocated to a spot behind him. I can still see it where it's supposed to be, but at the same time I can see where it is instead. Mind-blowing enough for me, and I'm just watching. I shudder to think what that crap feels like. "Look, Ma, I'm in two places at once, and neither of 'em have that ice cream you like!"?

Just then the air next to me shivers like it's cold—and try knitting a sweater for that!—then shimmers, warps, and steadies again, unfolding like a giant flower with the most beautiful woman I've ever seen standing in its midst.

"Hey, babe," I tell her, exchanging a quick kiss. "Love ya, but don't touch the floor or you'll be stuck here same as us.

Mary frowns and looks down at her feet—she's barefoot, and her feet are resting comfortably on the ground. She doesn't ask what the hell I'm talking about, though. Instead, she cocks one eyebrow. "I take it the invaders have launched a second assault."

"We're stuck," Tall replies, neatly summarizing several minutes of struggling and, equally importantly, cursing, in those two simple words. "I'm guessing you are too, now." I watch his eyes narrow and his jaw harden—it's like watching flan dry. "How did you manage to reach us, anyway?"

Mary smirks at him, lifting her chin in stately triumph. "I teleported to DuckBob," she answers, making sure her voice is loud enough for the others to hear without having to really crowd in. "Since he is still carrying the fob, I was able to home in on that signal instead of the mess of signals bouncing around everywhere else." She wraps an arm around me, then the other, hugging me tight. "You are my fixed point in space."

You know you're in love when even a flat-out geometry pronouncement comes across as dead sexy.

I do get what she's saying, though. It's like when she used her access to the array and my fob to get us to Obscura Major. Only in this case it's like she was trying to toss a magnet at a metal pole—but cheated by sticking another magnet on the pole already, and the two magnets had opposite charges, so when she threw hers it zoomed straight at the other one and, voila! Perfect shot!

Huh. I guess it *is* possible for smarts to rub off on people!

Excited as I am to have her here, though, I still ask, "I don't suppose you can reverse that trick and get back out of this funhouse ride? Like, to go get help?" I gestured toward the Nerd Herd, who are all either still clueless or doing their own personal impressions of Mime-in-a-Box. "I don't think they're gonna be much use this time. Besides, we still need to them focus on getting the Grays back."

She shakes her head, though. "Now that I am here, I seem to be as trapped as you," she confirms. Damn.

"I can call in the agents again," Tall offers, holding up his cell phone. "Whatever it is the invaders do, it doesn't seem to be affecting cell reception."

"Yay, we can stream movies while the universe ends," I retort. But, I follow that with a sigh. "Yeah, fine, go ahead. I know Smith'll be thrilled, but not sure we've got a lot of choice."

Tall makes the call. Then Mary makes one of her own, to Kimura. She explains the situation to her old professor, and assures him that the bubbles aren't dangerous—which honestly

I think is just guesswork on her part, or a straight-up "oh, yeah, it's fine"—and to let the others know. And to keep working. Might as well, it's not like they've got anything else to do!

While we're waiting for the MiBs, I ponder our situation. "So this is different from last time, right? Before, we were all trapped in the hall together. Now it's like we're each in our own little bubbles." Except that, because she teleported straight to me, Mary and I are in a bubble together. Good thing it doesn't come with soundproofing and blackout curtains or I'd worry about getting distracted!

She nods. "Before, we were able to formulate a mathematical bridge from the rest of reality to our location," she reminds me. "That would not work now, however—we would need to craft bridges to each of us individually. I might be able to calculate my current position, and Ned may have devices that could do the same for him, but Tall would be unable to provide those coordinates for his own, nor would my former peers. All of them would remain trapped indefinitely."

"Or until the invaders managed to shut down the Matrix and everything else with it," I mutter. "Okay, so you're saying they got smarter, learned from their mistakes. Swell. How do we beat this one?"

"I do not yet know," she admits. "I am considering strategies, however." Which means her mind's racing a million miles a minute, cycling through all the different possibilities we could try. And I have trouble sometimes deciding what to order for dinner!

I don't want to interrupt her calculations, so I keep quiet, which takes some effort. I spend the time scanning the area, searching for any sign of the invaders, but I don't see that telltale flickering anywhere. Nor are there bug-zapper flashes of light all up and down the Matrix like there were last time. "I get the feeling they phoned this one in," I tell the others. "Or at least they're attacking from cover somewhere. I'm not seeing any of 'em."

Ned nods. "The new security measures should be keeping them out," he agrees. "Apparently they can affect us from outside the building, but probably right outside it." He grimaces. "'Course, if they can get the Matrix to go down, or fade out enough, they'll be able to just waltz in like they own the place."

"Damn." I turn to Tall. "Any idea on an ETA from our suit-and-shades friends?"

He starts to answer, but stops as we suddenly hear loud pops that are unmistakably gunfire, coming from right outside. A slow smile spreads across his face like sunrise—or glaciers. "I'd say right about now, actually."

"Great!" I rub my hands together, which not incidentally means giving Mary a squeeze at the same time. She giggles, but quickly puts her "serious business" face back on. "Hey, you might wanna let Smith know not to even try coming in this time. We don't want them getting caught in bubbles of their own." I'm picturing the entire chamber like a giant bubble pit, and anyone trying to enter just gets sucked into the first one they touch. At least this'll keep the Nerd Herd out of trouble—they can look but they definitely can't touch!

Tall nods, his phone already to his ear. Good. Much as I dislike Smith, and can't stand his "I've gotta control everything, all the time" attitude, we are ultimately on the same side. And right now the MiBs are the only defense we've got.

Mary makes a quiet humming sound, and when I look her way I see she's got her brow furrowed. "What's up, babe?" I know that look, and it means she's got all that lovely brainpower focused on a single problem—and the problem's beginning to crack under the pressure.

"You said bubbles," she replies slowly, clearly still a million miles away. "I believe you are correct. Which means"—she looks up, and her eyes latch onto Tall. "Come here."

He's still sitting on the arm of the couch, and shakes his head. "I can't."

"You cannot charge forward," she counters. "But think of it as being trapped inside a giant bubble. You cannot run. But you can creep forward, inch by inch."

He frowns but gets to his feet, moving slowly and carefully. Then he takes one step forward, just a little one, barely six inches.

And when he plants his foot, it stays put. He isn't suddenly back where he started. So he takes a second step, equally slow, equally small. That one sticks, too.

With all the speed of a geriatric snail caught in drying jam, he inches his way along the front of the couch. Closer and closer.

Ever been in a car or an office or something like that and the heat was cranked and everything was hot and humid and muggy around you? And then someone opened a door or a window and you could feel the fresh, sharp, cold air blow in from outside, like someone puncturing a bubble? After a minute everything started to equalize, but for that first second it really did feel like two separate environments colliding.

That's what happens here. Only they're not so much two separate environments as two pieces of a larger whole, and they're not clashing, they're reuniting.

There's a faint pop, and the space around me and Mary suddenly feels more expansive, more open.

And Tall's in that same space.

"Sweet!" I hold up my fist, and we bump. "Dude! You just bridged reality through sheer force of will! And the power of your feet!"

He tries to stay all stoic but can't manage it, and a big, shit-eating grin covers his face. "Ha, that's right!" he declares, raising one booted foot. "Altered reality's got nothing on these!"

I'd never say it to his face, but having smelled his feet when he's ditched those boots and stretched out from the couch, Tall's right. Certainly the odor is otherworldly!

Instead I turn to our other buddy. "Ned, your turn."

He does his own turtle impression and, after a few minutes, expands our bubble even more. It now encompasses the whole couch, and most of the coffee table. Heidi, of course, just drifts in and out—he says he doesn't really notice any barrier, though the air consistency is different.

Now we're all together again. "Maybe we could do that bridge thing now?" I ask Mary, but after consulting with Ned and Heidi she shakes her head.

"It appears they have learned from that error as well," she admits. "This area is shifting its relative location to normal space-time, much like a radio cycling through frequencies, but seemingly at random. Without knowing the correct sequence, we cannot lock its position, and thus cannot establish a bridge." Why can't we have stupid enemies for a change? That would be really great.

I'm wondering if we can make it all the way out across the field to the Nerd Herd, or down the hall and out the door to help put down the invaders themselves, when Tall's phone rings. He answers, and after listening a second his face twists in disgust.

"They're getting their asses kicked," he explains once he hangs up. "Smith sounded as close to panic as I've ever heard him. He said it's bad enough fending off invisible enemies but these can change reality around them. It's like swatting at dragonflies or something."

Damn. I should've realized this wouldn't work. The MiBs are formidable, no doubt about it—some more than others—but they're a government agency. Which means they've got all kinds of rules and regulations. They're all about following protocols and filing reports and such. That's not going to do it right now. We need the opposite—people who can act totally off the cuff, so the invaders can't predict what they're gonna do.

Fortunately, I think I know just the candidates.

Chapter Twenty
No extra charge

"This is a really bad idea," Tall warns.

I shush him and listen to the phone ring. Then there's a click. "Yo." I have no idea if Grant knows it's me or just answers everyone that way, like they're old pals who just talked recently but it's cool that they're calling again now. Possibly the latter. He probably even answers that way when it's insurance salesmen or people calling to ask him to vote for a particular candidate, and by the time they get off the phone they've invited him over for dinner and promised to swing by with that brownie recipe. He's just like that.

"Hey, Grant," I tell him. "It's me. I need a little help."

That gets his attention. "You okay?" he asks, and now he's only about half as laidback as he was, which is still more relaxed than most people can be and still be conscious. And sober.

"I'm fine, yeah. Just got some trouble here at work. We're . . . we're under attack." I deliberately turn so I don't have to see the agonized grimace on Tall's face. Last time this happened, over on Ned's world, I turned to my family for help but I didn't tell them exactly what was going on. Some of them—mainly Lizzy—figured it out, of course, but at least I could say I hadn't revealed any secrets myself. And then the Grays wiped their memories, at least enough so they couldn't remember any specifics. Or anything about space and aliens and other planets.

But the Grays aren't here, we've already told the Nerd Herd, and right now I need my family to believe me.

Fortunately, Grant does. "Who?" is all he asks. "And where?" I hear metal clanking, and I know I caught him in his garage, and that he's just picked up a big wrench. That's partially because I really do have good hearing, partially because I've heard that particular sound before whenever somebody threatened anyone in the family and Grant was around to put a stop to it, and partially because I know that's what he'd do.

"Right, this is where it gets tricky," I answer. I take a deep breath, then plunge in. Remember before, when you guys came and helped in that big fracas?"

"The one down in Brooklyn?" That comes out as a lot more of a question than you'd expect, but I'm not surprised. Because it wasn't really in Brooklyn, it was on Ned's world, which looks a lot like old Brooklyn, but they got there through a wormhole that was in Brooklyn. So, yeah, kinda.

Which is exactly what I tell him. Followed by, "So, this is kinda near there. Only, the easiest way to get there is Manhattan." I give him an address in Midtown. "When you walk in, ask for—" I stop and look at Tall.

He grinds his teeth for a second before muttering, "Metro Investment Brokerage." Oh, right—that was the company he called the time he had to break into MiB headquarters. "Ask for the Actuarials Archive."

I relay that, then add, "Tell 'em I sent you. They'll be waiting. And, Grant? This is a big one."

"No worries, little bro," he assures me. "We got this. See you in a few." The line goes dead, and I nod to Tall, who takes up his own phone and calls Smith to let him know that they're gonna have to play ferry service again, but this time not for a bunch of eggheads.

No, this is gonna be a whole lot worse.

The good news is, it's only an hour's drive from Little Neck to Manhattan if the traffic's not too bad. And my family's good at mobilizing, especially if there's the possibility of violence, crime, or mayhem—or all three.

Okay, that last one might be a good thing. Certainly other local clans haven't found it to be so. Nor have local authorities. Or, one time, a visiting culinary institute. They shouldn't have challenged us to a chili cook-off and then dissed Ma's recipe. We did seriously impress several athletics coaches, though. And one Army recruiter, who got really depressed when his superiors vetoed the idea of enlisting our whole family at once and deploying us as a single unit. "They don't need any additional training!" I can still remember him wailing into the phone. "Trust me, these guys could destabilize a third-world country in an afternoon! Less, if they thought there were snacks involved!"

Of course, in the meantime there's nothing we can do but sit and wait. Mary checks in with Kimura again, but nothing new there. They are still chewing on the problem, though, which is good. It's more critical than ever that we get the Grays back as fast as possible.

"Hey, what if they're gone for good," I ask Mary and Ned. "What if the invaders melted them to sludge or burned them to ash or transformed them into spaghetti and ate them in one big bowl of pasta with pesto sauce?" You wouldn't want to use Alfredo or even marinara for that, though fra diavolo would do in a pinch. "Is there anything we can do to keep the Matrix running?" And keep me and Mary the way we are, I'm thinking but don't say. I don't need to. They both know that question is hanging over us, too. "Like maybe we can hook it up to something else instead of the Singularity?"

Ned shakes his head. "It's not like swapping out a car battery," he points out, "or even switching a monitor or replacing a hard drive. They draw on the Singularity throughout the process, so its energies are all mixed in right from the start." He frowns, thinking, then adds, "it'd be like wiring an entire house with fiber-optic, then deciding you wanna run it all off ambient electricity instead—you can't just flip a switch or plug the wires into something else, you've gotta basically start all over from scratch."

"Oh. Right." Damn, I was really hoping it was more like a car battery. Should've known the Grays'd go with something a lot more proprietary.

Ned clears his throat. "Even if we can't keep the Matrix up and running," he offers slowly, "there might be something we could do . . . for you." He glances between me and Mary, and I try not to get my hopes up. "Since the Matrix is drawing off the same energy source you guys are—the Singularity—we might be able to rig it up as an interface, converting some other energy into enough Singularity juice to keep your transformations going."

"Oh?" For a second, I let myself get excited about staying DuckBob. Then I think it through. "That'd mean we're basically taking the Matrix offline for good though, right? Just so we can use it to keep us this way? Like shutting down a lighthouse so we can use the reflector in the light in order to shave?"

"Something like that," Ned admits. That's one thing I've always liked about him, and about Tall and Mary, too. They all shoot straight. No beating around the bush with these guys, and no sugarcoating. Which may seem harsh to some, but I much prefer straight answers to half-truths and vague replies. I'm the same way, of course—I may blurt out all kinds of stupid stuff, but I don't lie. Ask me a direct question, I'll give you a flat-out answer. Unless I think the question's so painfully obvious it's stupid, in which case you're gonna get an equally ridiculous response. But still direct.

"No way," I tell him now. "If there's even a chance to keep the Matrix active, we've gotta take that. The whole universe's a lot more important than just saving this pretty face."

Mary kisses me on the cheek. "It is pretty," she agrees, "but I concur." She squeezes my hand, and her eyes are bright. I know what she's saying without a word: "Even if you don't look this way, I'm still with you. And I wouldn't have respected you if you'd given any other answer." I feel the same, of course, but for me that's a no-brainer—even if we revert to our pre-altered selves, Mary's still gonna be off-the-charts smart and mindbogglingly hot.

I'll just be some shmoe who used to look like a duck.

That does give me an idea, though. "Hey, if we could use the Matrix to power us up," I ask, "could we use other Gray stuff to power the Matrix?" I tap a finger to my bill. "Like maybe something they've got strung up from one end of the universe to the other like my cousins' old Christmas lights, every strand all tangled up with every other one into one huge snarl?"

"Oh, of course!" Mary laughs. "The teleportation array!"

Ned's eyes light up, making Mary and Tall squint and look away. Me, my nictitating membranes drop into place. Heidi just polarizes. Showoff. "Hey, that could work!" Ned agrees excitedly. "It's an ambient array that draws on Underspace for both power and connecting points, exactly like a wireless network. If we can get into the heart of the system and reroute the lines, we could funnel all that energy into a single spot."

"The Matrix." I glance over at it, out on the field. Is it my imagination, or is it rotating a little slower? And starting to look a little see-through?

"The Matrix," he parrots. "And since the array was built using the Singularity, I think we could figure out how to output its energy in that format. But it doesn't get all its power from there, it's pulling from cosmos too, like a dual power source."

"That is why it has been more difficult to access and control of late," Mary confirms. "With the Singularity currently inactive, the array has only the universe to draw from." She smiles. "But that would still be enough to maintain the Matrix at full strength, and perhaps retain a handful of specific teleport locations as well." So it'd be like my fob or like the wormholes, with fixed routes instead of all-purpose.

I could live with that. I'm betting we all could. We could use Tall and Heidi to get anywhere else we need to go—might not be as fast, but that's all right. Especially since, if we can beat the invaders back for good, we wouldn't have to worry about speed so much.

I don't ask whether the array could keep me and Mary in our current state as well. Though if we're gonna maintain the Matrix, we'll still need at least one person with full alterations intact.

That puts another thought in my head. "The other abductees!"

Three heads and a bowling ball, all staring at me in confusion. "Who's been abducted?" Tall demands, leaping to his feet. Which nearly knocks Ned off his, since we are dealing with a limited amount of space here at the moment.

"No, you know who I mean," I correct. "The others the Grays've abducted over the years. The others they modded out like me." Well, not exactly like me, but in a similar style if a different part of the animal kingdom. I've met a bunch of 'em over the years, there's even an annual convention, though I stopped going after the first few times. It just felt too much like being part of an odd indie film where the metaphor was a petting zoo. Or in one of those kids' flip books where you mix-and-match tops and bottoms.

And, if I'm being totally honest, part of it may've been that I didn't like just being one of the crowd again. Normally, I stand out—kinda hard not to, since it's not like anyone's gonna say, "Which guy?" and after being told "The one with the head of a duck!" follow up with, "Yeah, there's like twenty of those, can you narrow it down some?" But at those gatherings, we were all hybridized. There were lion-men and deer-women and snake-boys and rabbit-girls, and not for nothing I wondered if the Grays were just indiscriminately grabbing whatever two beings they found nearby and shoving them together or if they were building some kind of organic chess set like, "right, we've got four lion rooks, now we need two more bear bishops."

In which case, as the only duck-man I ever saw or heard of, I'm clearly the king.

Oh yeah.

It takes an effort, but I drag my thoughts back on track. "Each of us has some Singularity energy, right?" Ned nods. "And that's fading now." Another nod. "So if we gathered all the others together, could we consolidate what's left into a single charge?" I do feel a twinge of guilt for suggesting it, except that most of the others I've met aren't nearly as comfortable with their alterations as I am. The vast majority of 'em would kill to go back to being the way they were before.

Ned's considering the problem. "Maybe," he says finally. "I'd have to run some tests, see just how much energy each one's got—and then figure out how to draw that out before it fades completely. But it might work."

I'll take "might" right now. It sure beats, "no, sorry, you're doomed to go back to having a weak chin and a pudgy nose and floppy ears. Suck it up and deal."

Of course, all of this is assuming we can fight our way out of here and send the invaders packing, at least long enough to test my theory and come up with a way to implement Ned's plan.

But the odds of managing at least the first two parts increase dramatically when I hear a whole bunch of new noises spring up outside.

Including what I'm pretty sure is someone bellowing about pie.

Sounds like my kin have just arrived.

Chapter Twenty-one
Think on your feet—or someone else's

The hard part is that the fight is taking place outside and we're stuck within. There aren't even windows—not on ground level—for us to be able to see what's going on. All I can really do right now is listen and try to picture what's happening:

"Pie! Give me pie!" That's Andy. He shouted something similar the first time we met some wiseguys from Ned's world who'd been altered by the invaders. I guess he's adopted it as his own personal war cry now. I imagine he's using a wrench whose top is as big as my head, like he was last time—it'd take most people a partner and a winch just to lift, but Andy swings it onehanded like it was an oversized Swizzle stick. Those invaders had better hope they're not even remotely solid when he connects!

"Get 'em! Don't let up!" That sounds like Grant. He's probably wielding a wrench too, though it's nowhere near as big as Andy's. Still not something you wanna get clocked with, though.

"Out of my way, you! Or I'll dice you up and spread your puree on a slice of toast!" Bonnie's not really a hands-on brawler—she tends to do most of her damage psychologically.

I'm sure whatever invader's right in front of her is cowering in terror right now.

"For Bobby!" That's Cousin Jimmy, or maybe Frank, or possibly both. Not exactly the best fighters in the bunch, or the sharpest, but they're loyal, you gotta give 'em that.

"Are we sure this is a good idea?" That sounds like Matt. "Hey, whoa! Hold up! Oh, fine!" Followed by a clang. Yep, definitely Matt.

"Put me down, you big bully!" Uh oh. What is Lizzy doing here? She's gonna get—"Ha, take that! Gee, were these important?" Never mind.

And then there's the other noise. The one that almost brings tears to my eyes, though for most it'd cause an instinctive tightening of the privates, and the uncontrollable urge to cower and protect your head:

There's a certain sound that can only come from a small, hard, round object—like, say, a hot pink baseball—striking something at professional-fastball speeds.

Which means Lila's here.

There's a few other shouts and smacks mixed in. Grant heard me when I said this was a big one. He brought the whole clan.

Which means the Galactic Core is about to see a level of mayhem that probably hasn't been loosed since the first time an alien race decided, "Hey, what'd happen if we just unbounded all the atoms for a three-square-light-years radius, all at once? And then added saltwater taffy, a couple dozen hot fudge sundaes, and some blackberry jam?"

The answer, btw, is a great big sticky, gooey, highly radioactive—but tasty—mess!

"So," I say to no one in particular, "how do you think they're doing?"

Mary starts to answer when suddenly my ears—or where they should be—tingle painfully. Beside me, Tall and Mary both clutch at theirs, grimacing, and Ned's actually curl in on themselves.

It feels a lot like when you're in an elevator and it drops all of a sudden. Or when it just starts pouring out of nowhere, then stops just as fast and the clouds scatter before an angry Sun.

In other words, it's like a rapid pressure change.

"D'ya think?" I start to ask, but Tall has already grabbed up his gun and is marching for the hall and the front door beyond that. He doesn't get yanked back to us or tossed aside or trapped halfway between couch and archway, and a second later Mary and Ned and I are scrambling after him. Looks like the invaders' little bubbles have just burst.

I'm inclined to take that as a good sign.

I manage to catch Kimura's eye across the field. "Stay put and don't touch anything!" I bellow. He nods. Let's hope he and the rest of the Nerd Herd actually listen!

Then we all sprint down the hall, catching up to Tall just as he throws the last of the deadbolts—I don't enjoy door-to-door salesmen, and around here some of 'em can get a bit pushy and a bit cavalier about little things like invading someone's home to prove a point and try to sell some cable package—and yanks the door open.

Okay, so I knew it was going to be chaos. I didn't expect it to look like a cross between a Dali painting and the food fight scene in *Animal House*. But it does, and for a second I just stand in the doorway, staring.

At first glance, my sibling and cousins appear to be swatting at empty air. There's an awful lot of shouting and cursing and flailing about, though—a lot more than you'd expect even from my relatives if they're all by themselves. Plus if it was just us there'd be a lot more physical contact.

If I squint, though, I can make out shimmery patches interspersed throughout the whole mess. And those are what're getting pounded. Repeatedly.

Yep, I'd say we're winning.

Of course, that's just when the invaders decide it's time to change things up a bit.

The first one I notice is Lizzy. She lets out a confused cry as her feet leave the ground—not because she's leaping on someone, for once, but because she's suddenly floating like an extra in a Mary Poppins scene. Only without all the laughing.

"Lizzy!" I charge through, but there's no way I'm gonna reach her before she's well above second-story levels. I see someone who will, though. "Frank!" I shout. "Grab Lizzy!"

One of the good things about Frank is that he responds quickly to authority. Of course, that's scotched at least half a dozen schemes, too, when a cop demands to know what's going on and Frank tells him. At length. But this time it means he turns and lunges for his cousin, catching her hand just before she drifts too high. Whew!

Of course, his feet lift off next. I haven't heard a yelp like that since someone thought it'd be a good idea to shave the dog's fur into a map of the U.S.

And, for the record? Don't start from either end, because you'll never get the Mississippi to line up right.

"Jimmy! Get Frank!" Jimmy's used to being linked to his brother, so it's a no-brainer for him to latch on tight. Which he does, just before he finds himself floating, too.

Bonnie and Grant both see what's going on, of course. "Andy!" Grant shouts at his son. "Anchor! Everybody else, tug-of-war mode! Now!"

I can't help laughing, mainly because I can only imagine the invaders' confusion—and it probably mirrors the looks on the faces of Tall, Ned, even Mary, and all the MiBs scattered about. But yes, my family has a strategy for tug-of-war. This is what happens when there's a whole lot of you, and you're always getting challenged by other families or small gangs or visiting Boy Scout troops whenever you're in the park. This is also exactly why I wanted my family here. The MiBs are floating too, but they're just flailing about individually, which isn't helping anyone any. My relatives took one look at the situation and instantly adapted. We're used to thinking on the fly.

It's just a shame there isn't a high-speed chase involved, because that's where we really shine.

Andy's taken two Hulk-sized steps forward and grabbed onto the front door with his right hand. Grant loops his arm through Andy's left, Bonnie's next in line, and so on. They look like a swing-dance troupe that got caught in zero-G. Lizzy's at the end, as both the smallest and the highest up, and she lets out a triumphant yell when she sees everyone's connected now. "Time to play Crack the Whip!" she shouts. The others all holler in agreement, and Andy grits his teeth, heaves those continent-wide shoulders of his, and spins his body like he's hurling a fast-ball of his own.

Only this fastball consists of my whole family, all linked up. And ending with Lizzy, who's holding what looks like a pair of garden shears in her free hand.

Ever see an expert whip-cracker perform? It's something. We had a guy at a nearby county fair, once, and watching him work was amazing. The whip is huge, over six feet and as thick at its base as a kid's forearm (we know, we checked). He uncoils it, lets it drape on the ground by his side, and then almost lazily lifts his arm, swings, and then suddenly jerks his wrist like he's tossing a Frisbee. The whole length of the whip is already in the air at this point, and when he flicks his wrist it comes hurtling forward, the tip gaining speed and momentum as it moves. Do it right and you can crack the sound barrier.

I'm pretty sure Lizzy does exactly that as she hurtles into the crowd of invaders, those shears gleaming.

They scatter. And I don't just mean "they all run away"—I'm pretty sure she cut through about half of 'em just now. I'm not dumb enough to think that's the end of these guys—if you can alter reality, you can probably put yourself back together after a high schooler's sliced you up with a straight-edge—but it's still gotta hurt. And be more than a little demoralizing. Especially since she's giggling like a toddler and shouting, "Again! Do it again!"

Have I mentioned how much I love my niece?

You can also tell the invaders are hurt because their concentration dips again. Which means gravity reasserts itself—and my family all comes tumbling down like the world's weirdest rainfall. Those closest to the ground are fine—Andy's only six feet up, maybe, and acts like he's just jumped down off the porch, and Bonnie and Grant manage fine as well—but Jimmy and Frank are at least twenty feet in the air.

And Lizzy's more like thirty.

I look around, fast. And spot exactly who I need. "Lila!" I shout. My little sis turns her head, acknowledges me with a quick, "Yeah, you really think now is the time for hellos?" nod. "Clothesline!" I holler at her, and see her squint and then give me a quick little smile. "Andy, get ready! Lizzy, be prepared to hook on!"

Beside me, I know Mary and Tall and Ned are wondering. But there's no time to explain. Instead, I turn to the one person I know can get the job done. "Heidi, I need your help."

"You got it," he says at once. That's one of the things I like about this guy. We roped him into our craziness back when Tall needed a ride to another planet, and he's been with us ever since, but he never questions if we're nuts or not. Probably because he made his mind up about that a long time ago.

I point at Lila, who's just hauled a rope from her messenger bag and tied to a baseball. "She's gonna need some extra pull."

"On it!" Heidi shoots forward like a rocket and Tall takes off after him on foot, clearly aiming to lend a hand. I don't know if he'll get there in time to make a difference, but I sure appreciate the intent.

Lila hurls the baseball at Andy, who grunts as he catches it. Even without trying to wound, those things hit hard! He quickly drops the ball and winds the rope end around his forearm, tugging it taut. Lila's got the other end, and Marty's next to her, but I'm worried that they won't be strong enough to keep it tight. This only works if there isn't much give.

But then Heidi's there. He seems to pass right through the rope, or maybe it passes through him, and now he's got it clamped down somehow, adding his weight but more importantly his thrust to keeping it straight.

Jimmy hits first—and throws both arms around the rope, swinging for a second before dropping to the ground. One down.

Frank is next, and fumbles it a little, like usual, but still manages to get one arm over it, which is enough to slow him down. He lands in a graceless heap, also nothing new, but it doesn't look like he's broken anything.

I see that Tall's made it to the others and added himself to the chain, but most of my focus is on Lizzy, who's falling fast. She passes the rope—

—and loops both arms over it, tucking her knees in and swinging up and over it once, twice, three times before letting herself get flung free again. She lands with feet apart, arms up, straight and tall, shouting, "And she sticks the landing!"

This kid, I tellya.

I kept back by Andy in case he needed a hand—not that he'd require extra ballast unless we were catching a blue whale or something—but the minute Lizzy's got the rope I'm in motion.

Which means she only gets to hold her dismount pose for a few seconds before I've got my arms around her. Then the others all pile on, and for a few seconds we're just a big family dogpile filled with laughter and cheering and backslapping and hugs.

Through all that, I catch Lila's eye and do my best to convey "Thank you, sis." She shrugs, but I'm pretty sure there's a smile tugging at her lips when she looks away.

The MiBs are regrouping as well, ringing us like a protective detail, and I disengage as gently as I can from the crowd as Smith approaches. "Well played, Mr. Spinowitz," he tells me, shaking his head a little like he got caught napping and knows it. "Much as it galls me to admit it, that was not something my agents were prepared to handle. Your family, however, seems to have adapted nicely."

"Yeah, we're good at rolling with the punches," I reply. I hold out my hand, and after a second Smith takes it. His grip is as dry as he is, firm but not bonecrushing, and only lasts a second, but I feel like we've reached a new understanding. Which hopefully doesn't involve him trying to take possession of my couch anymore.

"Looks like they're gone," Ned reports, joining us. Mary is right beside him, and slides under my arm in a way that makes Smith green with envy. Poor guy, I could've told him she's more into the Hawaiian-shirt type than a stuffed suit. Which is definitely good for me because I can't even see my neck, let alone get a tie around it.

"They'll be back," Tall warns as he enters our little confab. "Unless we can put a stop to this once and for all."

Someone clears their throat behind us, by the door, and we all turn. It isn't the Wasp, though. It's Professor Kimura. And beneath all that facial hair, he's smiling.

"I think we may be able to help with that," he says.

Chapter Twenty-two
Pick me, pick me!

"It was Taki who had the initial idea," the professor's explaining. We're traipsing back down the hall toward the Matrix chamber, leaving the MiBs to establish a perimeter outside—Smith still seems hesitant to enter after last time, which is fine by me. My family is trailing along behind the rest of us, and I know I'm gonna have a lot of questions to answer soon, but right now I really need to hear what Kimura's saying. Of course, half of it is over my head, but my takeaway is this:

We know the Grays are out of phase with our reality. Not too far off, though—just half a step, like me during fourth grade dance class. Sorry, Catherine Lucinda, but hey, at least you never had to worry about high arches again!

So, the trick is how to resynch them. And it turns out it's actually not all that complicated. At least in theory.

"When a computer system is out of synch with its database," Kimura tells us, "all that is needed to resynch them is to re-import the data, overwriting any inconsistencies. That is exactly what we must do here."

"You're gonna overwrite the Grays?" I ask. "How's that gonna help any? Ooh, wait, but can we turn 'em yellow and make their heads into smiley faces? That'd be cool!" Okay, sometimes my glass-half-full perspective gets a little carried away.

"We will not overwrite them," Mary answers for the professor, who's got that knitted-brow, pursed-lip look I used to get a lot from my own instructors, back in the day. And from Tall a whole lot more recently. "This will affect their world instead."

"The invaders couldn't go through and shift each individual Gray," Ned chimes in. "So they had to do 'em all at once. Easiest way to do that is to just put a big bubble around the whole world and move all of it. Or at least all the important bits."

"So all that rock we saw, that was just what was left?" I ask. "Like stripping a car and leaving the frame behind?"

"Right!" Ned grins. "Which makes it easier for us, too. We can latch onto the bubble, inject reality back into it, and bring them back all at once."

"Oh. Okay. Sure." I rub my bill. We've reached the Matrix chamber now, and I stop just inside the doorway, staring at the Matrix where it occupies most of the space, and the eggheads who've all gathered by the couches now that they can move again. "And how do we do that, exactly?"

"That is the difficult part," Kimura agrees. "We must, in essence, boil reality down to its base elements, encode that into a set of parameters, find a way to bridge the gap between our reality and this bubble, and inject that code in such a way that it corrupts the bubble and forces it to reset itself back to those guidelines." He grimaces. "And all without harming the structures contained within, or injuring their inhabitants."

"Yeah, wouldn't do us much good to bring back a whole

lotta squashed Grays," I agree. Though, if it comes right down to that, we'd be better off with Gray mush but a working Singularity than without either. "I'm guessing, though, that you guys've figured it out?"

"Of course." That comes from Jerome who saunters over to join us. I swear, this guy looks more like a comic-book villain every time I see him. "It was child's play."

Nathan follows him, looking a lot more focused than earlier but still just as laid back. "Yeah, right," he says with a laugh, slapping Jerome on the back in a way I can immediately tell he hates. "You were practically tearing your hair out, Jerry. We all were." He offers me his hand. "Sorry, we didn't really meet properly before. Nathan Sutter." Then he turns and gives Mary a quick hug. "Heya, Mirabella. Sorry—Mary."

The fact that she hugs him back tells me all I need to know about this guy, even before she graces him with a smile. "Hello, Nathan. I did not get a chance to say so before, but thank you for agreeing to come."

"Are you kidding?" He grins like a little kid. "A chance to go to another planet—well, sort of—and help figure out things like Einstein-Rosen bridges? Hell, yes!" Okay, now that he's sober again this guy is definitely my favorite Fartcap.

"So, what'd you work out?" I ask. "How're we gonna do this?"

"We?" That's Taki, who's clearly recovered from his own excursion through my abode and is once again all Nerd Goes Corporate. "I'm sorry, but how exactly are you contributing to all this, again?"

I bristle at his tone, but the thing is, this guy's barely half my height and yeah, he might have twice my IQ but he's still not in Mary's league, so I'm not exactly intimidated by him. Plus, once you've had Tall get on my case as many times as I have it's tough to feel threatened by anybody. I'm pretty sure if King Kong suddenly appeared and roared right in my face I'd just be like, "Dude, two words: Breath. Mint."

"I'm contributing by not kicking your silk-suited ass out of my house," I respond, waving a hand around us. "You're just a consultant, Slick, and don't you forget it. I'm the Guardian, dig?"

He starts to reply, clearly not happy with the fact that I'm not bowing down to his evident intellectual superiority, but Tall cuts in. "DuckBob is the one who suggested calling all of you in the first place," he points out, stepping forward and looming over Taki, who suddenly realizes that, fancy suit or not, he's still a geek and he's facing a guy who's practically the entire football team rolled into one. "Show some respect," Tall finishes, and Mr. Suit gulps, nods, and backs away a few paces, just to be safe.

I turn back to Kimura. "You were saying?"

He seems to have been amused by that whole little scene, which I get—he's probably used to having to school kids a quarter his age but brighter than he is who think they're God's gift to everyone, so seeing one put in his place must be refreshing. "We will need to go to where they are, obviously," he continues now, "because the code will need to contain those coordinates, the atmospheric elements, and other local details. Once we have that"—his eyes twinkle under those bushy brows—"we can condense that into mathematics and beam it across."

The light dawns. "You're gonna use a bridge," I say. "Same as we did before. Only maybe even easier, because if they're exactly half a step off they're fixed, too."

"Indeed." He beams like I'm a difficult student who just got a tricky question right, and out of the corner of my eye I see Slick glowering. Yeah, I may not be in your league but I'm not an idiot, thanks. "It will still be tricky to link the bridge to their end, since we do not know the exact distance there, but we will do our best."

I shake my head. "Nah, this one's a no-brainer," I tell him. "The Grays built the Matrix and powered it through the Singularity. Same with me." I don't mention that they also did that to Mary because I'm not sure she wants her former classmates to know she was altered, and that's entirely up to her. "Which means I'm linked to it. Ned can help you lock down the frequency I'm picking up, then you'll home in on that and bingo, you've got it in one."

"Of course!" Kimura looks thrilled. "That will indeed solve that! Thank you!" Ha ha, Suit-man looks pissed! "Now we only need to determine how to make sure the signal propagates correctly throughout their bubble."

"That, too, may be a simple matter," Mary offers. "As DuckBob pointed out, the Grays power all of their work through the Singularity. If you transmit the code directly into it, the Singularity itself will act as the propagator, sharing the data throughout its network to all of its creations." She smiles. "All of their world will be affected at once."

"Brilliant!" The prof rubs his hands together, and Mary flushes a little. Yeah, always nice to get praise from your favorite teacher. Especially after that earlier crack about her screw-up on the bridge calculation. "We are nearly ready with the code, as much as we can be from here. Is there some way to bring us to the location in question?" Ha, dude does a commendable job trying to hide his excitement at that one. "Hey, um, can we go to another planet now? Please?" But I don't blame him. Before all this happened, I'd have been super-excited at the prospect too, and I'm not even a science-nerd like these guys.

"DuckBob and I will ferry you there as soon as you are ready," Mary promises. She frowns. "I would prefer to bring only as many as necessary, however—the array is not as stable as it should be, and larger numbers may interfere with its func-tion. Ned will be necessary to help calibrate the actual trans-mission—how many others will you require?"

Kimura stops to think, and behind him all the eggheads freeze like somebody threatened their pocket protectors. I actu-ally sympathize with 'em—well, most of 'em, anyway. To have the idea of teleporting to another planet dangled in front of you and then be told, "eh, sorry, you're nonessential, you stay here on the bench"? Harsh.

Slick isn't having any of it, of course. "You will need me, obviously," he insists, stepping forward, though I notice he skirts Tall to do it. "I am the only one who can perform the necessary calculations."

"I wouldn't say the only one," Jerome drawls, sneering down at his old classmate. "I can handle them without a problem, thank you." Wow, it's like "Anything You Can Do, I Can Do Better," only with calculators and code instead of rifles and horses. I wonder if any of these guys can carry a tune?

"Pretty sure several of us could handle it," Nathan adds. He doesn't look entirely happy about it as he adds, "Though, yeah, Taki's probably the best at coding on the fly." The Suit preens.

"Agreed," Kimura declares. "I will need Taki. And Jerome." Mr. Arch-Villain smiles, nods, and then shoots an acid look at Slick, who returns it with interest. Ah, ain't class rivalries grand? "Between them, myself, and Mary, I believe we will have everything we need." Nathan, Cab, and Theresa deflate a bit. Sorry, kids. You can go on the field trip next time, I promise.

I tap the prof on the shoulder and gesture him to step back with me, and wave Mary and Ned along, too. "So, when we do this," I say once the four of us have retreated a few paces, "assuming it works, everything Gray gets tugged back into our reality all at once, right?" Everybody nods. "On Obscura Major?" More nods—it's like my own little collection of Bobbleheads. "Which is where we'll be standing?" The nods stop mid-motion. "Yeah, what's gonna stop us getting squashed by an entire city that wasn't there a second ago?"

"That . . . is an excellent question," Kimura agrees. He's looking at me with what looks suspiciously like Tall's Stare Number Eight. Boo-ya, it's spreading! "I see what Mary means," he adds. "You have an agile mind." Thanks, prof. Always nice to be appreciated.

Ned's considering the problem I just posed. "We could activate the data dump and then teleport out," he suggests. "Timing'd be tricky, but if it takes a second or two for them to re-integrate, that might work."

Mary's frowning, though. "We cannot be sure how long the process will take," she argues, "and we must be present throughout in case there are last-minute corrections required." Makes sense. We're gonna be the engineers at the control panels, typing in commands and monitoring screens while the powerplant fires up. Only we'll be in the same space as the control rods when it happens.

Or will we? "Is there any way we can get a look at their world?" I ask. "The way it should be, I mean."

"Sure," Ned answers. "Now that we know exactly what's going on with it, I can set a scanner to that frequency. Why?"

I've got a second question in response. "We just need to be on-site anywhere within that bubble to inject the data, right?"

Ah, we're back to synchronized nods again. And Mary breaks into a big, beaming smile. "I understand," she says. "We will locate a suitable spot within their city, one that has nothing atop it currently. That will be safe for us to stand upon, because when their world returns will not need to worry about displacement—or about being crushed beneath any existing structures."

"Exactly. Find us a park, or a plaza, or a parking lot," I tell Ned. "Something flat and empty and ground-level."

He grins. "You got it."

I turn to Kimura. "Okay, get your guys together, and the rest of your code buttoned down. Let's do this."

"Indeed." He claps me on the shoulder, smiles at Mary, and turns to gather the Geek Brigade, Strikeforce version.

Which just leaves me and Mary. She raises a hand to stroke my cheek. "Do not let Taki bother you," she urges quietly. "He has always felt the need to establish his superiority in every situation. He does not like knowing that he is not in control here."

"Yeah, no worries," I assure her. "I'm good." I place my hand over hers. "Are you?"

She nods. "Yes. Seeing all of them again . . . is difficult. And some of them still believe they can belittle me." The smile she gives me is a little grim and a whole lot proud. "But I am not Mirabella Rosalind Jost any longer. I am Mary, and I will not let any of them, or anyone else, convince me that I am not their equal. Or their better."

"That's my girl." I give her a quick peck. "You're the best, and I mean that." I thread my fingers through hers and lower our hands to our sides. "Now, let's go get our bosses back."

"Indeed." And together we turn and walk back to the others.

It's time to saddle up.

Chapter Twenty-three
Nobody likes to auto-tune

"Do not stray from the circle," Mary warns. It's maybe twenty minutes later, and the six of us are standing together in a rough chalk circle Ned drew on the ground.

Jerome scoffs at that. "Why not?" he asks. "Is this some Dark Ages superstition? Are we casting spells now? Summoning demons?"

"Try 'holding in oxygen,'" I tell him, which shuts him down real fast. "We're going to another planet, genius, and even if it normally has a breathable atmosphere it might not now. Ned's rigged up a force screen to keep the oxygen in this space, and a filter to process it and keep exchanging oxygen for carbon dioxide, so as long as you're standing in the circle, you're fine. But you wanna step outside and suffocate or depressurize or whatever, be my guest."

That shuts him up real fast, and wipes the smirk off Taki's face. Man, out of all the eggheads in the room, why did Kimura have to pick these two? I'd have preferred Nathan, or Cab, or even Stinger Girl.

Well, whatever. This isn't a social engagement, it's business. We get there, we zap the Grays back, we come home. Done deal.

Because, of course, things always go that smoothly.

"What are you doing, exactly?" Taki demands. Mary's closed her eyes and started the process. I can tell because the world outside the circle is getting all wavery and fuzzy. Or maybe that's me.

"She's taking us apart, transmitting us across half the galaxy, and putting us back together, Nimrod!" I snap at him. "You wanna wind up with my head on your body, or a few extra feet? Then keep distracting her!" Sorry, but these two are really getting on my nerves!

Fortunately he takes the hint—look, in my family it's still just a hint if it doesn't involve bludgeoning—and doesn't ask any more questions. And yes, I get that this's gotta be killing him. He's a scientist, and a serious brainiac, and he's being teleported across the galaxy without being told how or given an instruction manual. But it's gonna kill him for real—and the rest of us with him—if he makes Mary screw up, so I'd prefer to err on the side of caution.

The world's going all wobbly, and I squeeze my eyes tight. Then my conscience twinges. "Shut your eyes," I warn. "Trying to watch will only mess you up." I've no idea if they're complying, but whatever, that's their problem. I did what I could.

I feel that blurring effect again, like my body is unraveling at the edges, followed by the weird stretching like I'm a rubber band being pulled back and then shot across huge distances. My extremities are tingling like they've gone to sleep but feeling creeps back in, the edges solidify, and after a few more seconds I'm feeling back to normal.

I open my eyes.

Yep, Obscura Major looks just as amazing as it did before. Meaning it's just as much of a blasted-rubble landscape of boring brown and red rock, with no hint that life or civilization has ever existed here at any point in the planet's history. There isn't even a Starbucks, and that'd be stretching the definition to begin with.

The three geeks are peering around, all wide-eyed, and it occurs to me that, except for the starry sky, you wouldn't know the Matrix wasn't just housed in some really funky art-installation-style building in the West Village or Rodeo Drive or something. It'd be very easy not to think about how far from Earth you really were there, especially when the only people you see around you—aside from me, Ned, and Heidi—look completely normal.

But this place is clearly a whole other world. And it's blowing their oversized minds.

"Right, welcome to Planet 4593 of the Virulga system," I tell them, sweeping an arm about. "Also known as Obscura Major by the neighbors, and Prime by the locals. Who we are here to rescue." I cup my hands to my bill. "You hear that, Grays? We're here to save you!" I don't have any idea if they can see and hear us, but I figure just in case, it pays to give 'em the heads-up. Last thing we want is to manage to bring 'em all back, only to get shot because they think we're the invaders returned to finish the job. Or the neighbors, come to steal all the silver.

Kimura nods, visibly forcing himself to concentrate on the task at hand. I can see why he's a good teacher—it can't be easy to keep yourself on track, much less your students, when presented with an opportunity like this. But now he breaks out a small tablet, and two smaller devices that look a lot like old-fashioned light meters. He hands those to his former students, who both start scanning their surroundings. Okay, good, they're on the job.

Ned's got his own doohickeys out as well, and he's waving them around like he's conducting an invisible orchestra using a small extendable rod made from toothpicks and wilted celery. As I watch, the tip of one wand turns blue, then the other. "I've got a lock!" he shouts, lowering his voice after the rest of us wince. "Sorry. I've got the frequency locked down. They're definitely all still here. I'm working on getting a topographical map now."

"Cool." I look at Mary, who shrugs. Yeah, neither of us are needed just yet, not until either Ned or the Geek Trio finish their work. Shame we're all stuck in this circle, or she and I could nip off behind a rock somewhere and make out. But even I'm not shameless enough to do that in front of an audience, especially one that's practically sitting in my lap. So we wait.

Fortunately, it doesn't take long. Kimura finishes first. "We have the rest of the data," he announces, and Mary steps over to join him as they, Taki, and Jerome all start analyzing the details scrolling across the tablet. Once they plug in the local specifics, they'll be able to compute the exact formula needed to bring the Grays' back to our reality.

A minute or two later, Ned looks up. "Got it." He waves me over, and I move in close as he taps the two wands together, rubs them back and forth a bit, presses them together length-wise, and then pulls them slowly apart like they're the ends of a small scroll. As he does, an image forms between them. A glowing, three-dimensional representation of a city.

And what a city! Even at this scale and semi-transparent, it's gorgeous. I can see exactly what Mary was talking about—this looks like the "City of the Future" you used to see in old artists' conceptions, all sweeps and curves and arches, every building tall and graceful, every street and walkway gently curved, every surface shimmering. But there's also a precision to it, like you can tell every inch was mapped out precisely, and every ratio carefully calculated. It's like someone managed to combine soap bubbles, glass sculpture, modern skyscrapers, a space station, and a Mandelbrot all into one place.

"Okay, yeah, that's pretty cool," I mutter, and Ned nods beside me. That's right, he's never seen it before, either. Right now, though, we're not here for artistic appreciation, so I squint and start studying the layout. A red dot glows about a third of the way toward the right corner, which I'm guessing is us, and I start from there, working my way slowly outward, one grid section at a time.

"What about there?" I suggest, pointing to a flat spot not too far away. But when Ned taps that section and it expands, we can see that there's actually what looks like an elaborate fountain there. Pretty, and if we could guarantee we'd wind up standing in a fancy wading pool I'd say sure, but for all we know that water's rushing up from a thousand-foot hole, and isn't even water but instead molten metal. Or lava. Or acid.

Better to stick with solid, dry ground, just to be safe.

"How about that?" Ned offers, pointing to another spot just a little past that first one. Several of the bridges and lanes converge there on a blank, flat circle, and estimating it against the towers I'd say it's actually at least a hundred feet across at the middle. In other words, a nice open plaza.

I clap Ned on the shoulder. "Perfect." Then I tap Mary. "We've got a location," I tell her once she looks up. "You guys good to move out?"

She nods. "We can complete the final calculations once we are in place," she agrees. "Changing our physical location will not alter the data significantly."

"Great." A thought occurs to me. "Ned, you can move the bubble with us, right?" Because that would suck—"Sorry, guys, you either stay here in this spot so you don't suffocate but you might get crushed, or you come with us and won't get crushed but might suffocate. Which death sounds better?"

Fortunately, he grins. "Yeah, easy-peasy." Then, crouching down, he taps the circle—and it lifts up off the ground, floating about an inch above. "It's keyed off this," he explains, standing up and waving another of his gadgets, this one short and stubby and shaped a lot like a little toy airplane I had when I was a kid and lost in the bath. Hmmm. "As long as the circle's active, it'll maintain the bubble roughly four feet around me in every direction." Four feet? Whoa, good thing Ned isn't that much shorter than me or we'd all be doing a lot of walking stooped over! As it is, we'll need to make sure he's in the middle of the group, otherwise there won't be room to fit everyone.

"Okay, hand me the map," I tell him, and he offers up the two wands. I take them, a little nervous that they're gonna feel sticky and gross or try to nuzzle my hands or whatever, but they just feel like sticks or maybe metal rods or somewhere in between. Then I turn toward the spot we've picked, which he's helpfully marked in green. "Okay, roll 'em out!" I announce. "Yeeha, Rawhide!"

Yep, this is officially the smallest wagon train EVER.

It takes us a few minutes to get the hang of moving like this—the geeks keep stumbling and slowing or straying to the side, forcing us to all stop and wait until they're back in line again, and I've gotta keep to a snail's pace so I don't cause the circle to slam into the backs of their knees as Ned hurries to keep pace with me and the circle stays centered on him and they don't keep up. But gradually we get into a rhythm, everybody moving more or less together, and start to cover some real ground. Another five minutes after that and we've reached the area Ned had marked. I take us to roughly the center of that circle before I finally stop. Unless they built a new high-rise here in the last few minutes, we should be safe.

"Okay, your turn," I tell Mary, Kimura, and the boys, giving Ned back his wands and trying not to watch how he turns them off or where he puts them after. "Let me know when you need me, and what you want me to do."

They don't reply, but a minute later they all look over at me. "We are ready," Mary declares. "The code packet is complete and we have begun the process of constructing the bridge." We brought a small portable generator Ned promised had enough juice to do the job for that, and it sits at her side right now, humming with energy, a light on the top blinking in time with one on the tablet.

"Great." I step closer to join them. "What now?"

In reply, Taki grabs my right arm and Jerome jabs it with some kind of needle. Typical super-villain!

"Whoa!" I shout, flailing at him, but Mary takes my free hand and I stop. "A little warning next time?"

Jerome half nods half shrugs, like, "yeah, sure, okay, I guess." The needle's actually a lead, I see, and the wire from it stretches back to Kimura's tablet. I guess they decided to link me in literally!

"My apologies," Mary tells me. "We felt the only way to utilize your link to the Matrix was to tap into that directly, through you." She tightens her grip. "It was not my intent to harm you."

"I know," I promise her. And I do. I'm also willing to put up with a little pain if it'll bring the Grays back and banish the invaders for good. "Okay, prof, hit it," I tell Kimura.

He nods. "We have calibrated to the extraterrestrial energies coursing through your veins," he replies, "and are now downloading our code packet directly into that energy, where it will be drawn inexorably toward the energy's source." He gives me a mild grimace. "This may hurt a bit." Then he taps a spot on the tablet and my head erupts in flame.

At least, that's what it feels like. Turns out, having someone use you as a living antenna so they can beam a transmission through your body? Feels a lot like if they'd just slit a vein and poured in some battery acid, then covered the wound, lifted you off your feet, and shook you like a ragdoll. I suspect I'm screaming, but I can't hear over the roaring in my head, like when you're on a plane that suddenly drops out of the sky and the pressure threatens to pop you like a grape. Every inch of me is sizzling from the inside out, and my heart is pounding fit to burst, going at least quadruple time.

Then it cuts out, as rapidly as it started. I gasp and topple forward, my knees buckling, but Mary grabs me on one side to keep me up and Ned quickly ducks under my other arm and props me up there, too. I feel like I just ran a marathon covered in honey and fire ants and then got struck by lightning right as I crossed the finish line. I'm still gasping for breath, sweat pouring out of me, as I manage to ask, "That it? Hope so, 'cause I don't think I'm up for a Round Two."

"That was indeed it," Kimura replies, checking his tablet. When he looks up again, he's smiling. "The packet has been transmitted successfully through the bridge!" He sighs and lowers the tablet. "Now we must wait and hope we were correct."

"Yeah?" I'm still utterly wrung out, but manage to ask, "What if—" before an entire world starts phasing in all around us.

It's incredible to watch. If you had really bad eyesight, and somebody stole your glasses and then tossed you into a car and drove somewhere super-fast and then stopped all of a sudden and handed you back your glasses, it'd be something like that— there's a feeling of motion even though we're standing still, then a whole lot of color and light all around us, then all that starts to take on blurry edges, which slowly get sharper and sharper until all of a sudden everything around us is crystal clear. It's like adjusting the lens on your camera until the image pops into focus all at once, only we're in the middle of the picture.

What a picture, too! If the map Ned pulled up was breathtaking, the real deal is enough to make you forget you ever knew how to breathe in the first place. Buildings tower above us, delicate and airy-looking but so perfect and solid they don't sway at all in the gentle, slightly spicy-scented breeze. There are bridge and arches up there linking them together, and I don't know if people walk across those or travel through them or even if they're just decorative, but they give the whole place a feeling like it's all just one big building with a whole bunch of spires growing out of it, rather than separate spaces that were then linked together. That's also because of the color scheme, which has subtle shifts but is overall so harmonious it's clear either the entire city was built at once or every time a new building was added a whole committee got together to work out exactly what color it would need to be to fit in perfectly with its nearest neighbors. The air is filled with the tinkling of water from the many fountains, and the light ruffling of the breeze, and the low murmur of conversation.

And that last sound is rapidly getting louder.

We all turn as one as a group of three figures appear over one rise, emerging from behind a building there and striding quickly down the long walk toward our circle. I'm always a little creeped out by the Grays, to be honest—too many episodes of *The X-Files* and too many late-night B-grade alien invasion movies—but right now I'm thrilled to see them in all their smooth gray skin and oversized eyes and teardrop-shaped heads on stick-figure bodies. And, judging from the smiles splitting their faces—literally, because when a Gray smiles it looks like somebody just unzipped their head from side to side—they're just as excited to see us.

I am not even a little bit surprised that the Gray in front is wearing a pair of footie pajamas. After all, it has every other time I've seen it. This time they've got a flying saucer motif, which is just a bit on the nose but still pretty darn cute.

"DuckBob Spinowitz," the one in the lead declares as they approach. "MR3971XJKA. Ned. We had hoped you would find a way to restore us to reality. We thank you." It stops and bows, and so do its buddies. Which is nice, but I'd really prefer a raise, thanks. Or at least a party.

Still, I know I'm grinning too when I respond, "Hey, no worries, guys. Like we were gonna let you waste away in a pocket reality? We're still waiting on our paychecks!"

The Grays glance back and forth between themselves like they don't quite know what to make of that. Which is typical, really.

"What DuckBob means," Mary cuts in, "is that rescuing you was our top priority." That has them all grinning and beaming again.

Behind us, someone clears his throat. Oh, right. "We couldn't have done it without help," I tell the Grays. "This is Professor Kimura, Taki, and Jerome, from Earth. Mary's old professor and classmates. There's a few more back at the Matrix, too—Tall's keeping an eye on 'em, don't worry." I don't mention the fact that they've been there for a while, or that my whole family's there, too. First things first.

One of the other Grays is speaking. "The invaders did this," it states, and I swear it gnashes its teeth a bit. I'm gonna have nightmares about that for years to come. "They must be dealt with, once and for all."

"Yeah, that's what we thought, too," I tell them. "Maybe we should all head back to the Matrix and talk it over, figure out a game plan."

The next thing I know, the world's going wobbly around me again. I slam my eyes shut fast as I can, but not before I see those three Grays twist and deform like they were drawn in foam on top of a coffee and somebody just stirred it with one of those little motorized whisks.

I swear, I'm never gonna be able to use a straw again without worrying that there's a Gray spinning around in my shake or smoothie and about to get sucked into my mouth.

Ick.

Chapter Twenty-four
Obliterate is just a fancy way to say smush

When I feel like the world's stopped spinning—or at least like I'm now spinning with it instead of being frozen in the middle like the eye of a Technicolor storm—I cautiously open one eye. I immediately see grass, a sparkly pink wall, and something long and twisted and golden floating at about chest height and rotating in a slow, stately loop.

I'm back at the Matrix.

I crack open the other and see that Mary, Kimura, Ned, and the two obnoxious eggheads are here as well. Whew! We made it!

Then I see the Grays. But they're not looking at me. They're turned away, eyeing the couches—and the others from Mary's old class, who're sprawled or sitting or standing by or leaning on that furniture, with Tall posted between them and the hall, arms crossed, legs apart, clearly prepared to keep them from going anywhere but this room.

And, spread out on the field itself, are Lizzy, Grant, Bonnie, Andy, and all the rest of my kin.

It's like a company picnic for some cheeseball entertainment site, with the on-air talent on one side and the IT crowd on the other, and that lone HR employee trying to keep it from turning into a gang war.

I should tell Tall to just switch on the karaoke machine. In under an hour we'd have Jerome and Jimmy doing "Despacito" and Cab and Frank trying to pull off "Smooth" and we'd all be one big happy family.

Until somebody got all uppity and decided to select anything at all by Rod Stewart. Wars've been started over less.

But we're back now, and the minute we appear everyone perks up. "Yo, wassup?" I call out, holding my hands up and showing off two V is for Victory signs. "Check it out, it totally worked! We are back in business!"

Both camps cheer, and I catch a few of them shooting each other "Wait, why did we think you were so bad, again?" glances. This might work with no singing necessary, which, believe me, would be a good thing for everyone.

But then the lead Gray speaks up. "Who are all of these interlopers?" it asks in that high-pitched "I may look like a small child but I am several thousand years old, vicious, brutal, and easily bored" voice it has. "And what are they all doing in such close proximity to the Matrix?" It bares its teeth like an angry cat, and beside it I see the other two reach for their sides, where suddenly there are nasty-looking ray guns. Hm, maybe we should've told 'em we had a playdate scheduled?

"Hold on!" I shout, putting myself between them and the crowd. "Remember I said we had a few others who helped us get you out? This is them. Those are all Mary's old classmates"—I indicate the Nerd Herd—"and those are my family, the same ones who helped us against the invaders that time on Artelusia IX." There's movement behind Tall, and my heart sinks as I see a familiar squad of black-suited goons appear in the doorway from the hall. "And that's Agent Smith and his men," I add with a sigh. "Though they were supposed to be manning the perimeter."

The Grays seem to consider this. At least they haven't actually drawn their guns. Mary approaches them, and for a minute the four of them are all still as statues, heads tilted slightly to one side. I know they're talking mind-to-mind—that was one of the ways they altered Mary, so they could communicate with her directly. It really creeps me out to not be able to hear what they're saying. If it was me, everyone would hear it anyway because I basically just say whatever I'm thinking, but I get that not everyone is built that way. Which is a shame, because it would sure cut down on lousy second dates: "I actually don't like you at all." "Oh? Well, I don't like you either, and I don't find you attractive." "Really? Perfect. Bye!" "Bye."

Eventually they all stir, and Mary retreats a pace or two and rejoins me while the lead Gray opens its trap again. "MR3971XJKA has pointed out that we are, in essence, at war with the invaders," it declares. "During times of war, normal rules involving security, access, and compartmentalizing information may be suspended in order for facilitate broader alliances. We accept the necessity of this. All of those present here have agreed to participate in this war and to fight on our side. Therefore, for now, we bid them welcome."

In other words: I need you right now, so I won't kick you out. We'll revisit this topic later, though, provided we win.

It's only delaying the conversation, but right now I'll take it.

"Okay, time for a full-on pow-wow," I call out. "Everybody, gather 'round." I stomp over to the couches and eye Cab, who is sprawled across on one of them. "Do you mind?" He gets to his feet, looking a little sheepish, and shuffles out of the way so Mary, Ned, and I can all sit down. My family drape themselves over the back of our couch, while the eggheads crowd onto their remaining couch and the MiBs line up behind them. Tall perches on the arm on my side, Heidi hovers on his other side, and the Grays themselves choose to stand between the couches and beside the big coffee table, which still has Ned's panorama map stretched across it.

Yay, the gang's all here.

I turn to the Grays, but like usual they've gone back to their whole "don't mind us, we're just gonna stand over here and look creepy" stance. We're not gonna be getting much direction from them, and probably not a whole lot of answers.

Which means it's up to the rest of us.

"Okay," I call out, making sure I've got everyone's attention. "So, Phase One complete—the Grays are back, safe and sound, and that means the Singularity is back, which means the Matrix should be back on full power now. So the invaders shouldn't be able to get in again."

"That's what we thought last time," Tall mutters, and I glance his way.

"True, and yet somehow they did," I agree. "Which means we need a more permanent solution." I look around the room. "Any ideas?"

Of all people, Joe raises his hand. "Just reverse the polarity, man," he says. Half the eggheads snicker. So does Marty—and one of the MiBs, standing in back. Great, we've succeeded in uniting all the SF geeks in the room. I'm not entirely sure how that's useful, but I'm willing to give them the benefit of the doubt.

"Care to explain for the class?" I ask.

Joe's chuckling a little at his own joke but manages to get past that. "Yeah, sure, dude," he replies. "We just, y'know, turn the tables on them, right? Do to them what they did to us. Or them." He waves a hand toward the Grays.

Nathan stands up. "I think what he means," he explains, "is these invaders can warp our reality, right? Including making little bubbles outside our reality, where certain natural laws don't work quite the same? So, in theory, we can turn their own power against them—force them into a feedback loop where they create a bubble around themselves, altered in such a way that their powers no longer work." He smiles. "It's the classic 'create something he can't lift' dilemma, only this time the answer is 'yes, and it'll leave him stuck in hole for the rest of eternity.'" He sits back down, and from across the aisle Joe gives him a thumbs-up, evidently grateful for the translation from stoner-speak.

I rub my bill. "Okay, so you're telling me we could beat 'em at their own game? Trap 'em in a bubble they can't ever get out of, just barely out of phase with us so they can never cross over but they can't ever go home, either?" Joe and Nathan both nod. Huh.

"An excellent suggestion," I hear a certain, familiarly slick voice declare. And there's Smith, looking just as smooth and dangerous as ever, a shark in a silk suit. "How long would it take to implement, and what do you require in the way of tools or data?"

"No." The objection doesn't come from me, or Tall, or any of the eggheads, or even the Grays. It comes from the lovely lady by my side, as she stands up and turns to face Smith. "We will not do such a thing, not even to them," she insists. "It is an act of utmost cruelty to trap someone in such a half-life, outside reality and unable to reach it. Ask them." She points to the Grays, who still haven't said a word during all this, just stood around watching like this discussion was the world's most boring tennis match. Which is saying something, because you're not even allowed to tackle the other guy! Or at least so my high school PE teacher kept insisting. I think he was just annoyed because I always got the hit in first. I never understood the problem—after all, I cleared the net!

"They did the same to the Grays," Smith argues. "This is just turnabout. If anything, it's what they deserve."

"No one deserves that," Mary counters. "And whether they behaved in such a fashion should not and does not dictate our actions. We must rise above our basest natures, not give in to them—and if our foes do give in, all the more reason for us to rise above." Ah, the old "they go low, we go high" argument. She's got a point, though. It's easy to stoop because your opponent is. It's a lot harder to stick to your guns and your moral compass, but that doesn't make doing so any less right. If anything, the challenge makes it that much more important for you to hold fast.

"You're an idealist," Smith tells her. "And that's all well and good—except that this is war. And in war, the idealists are the ones who wind up dead in the dirt while the realists fight on. If we're going to win this war, we have to use every means necessary, no matter how dirty that makes us." Not that he looks at all concerned about that kind of dirt. I guess his suit's the only thing he's worried will stain.

"I'm with Mary," I declare, rising to my feet beside her. "Nobody deserves to get ghosted like that. Not even the invaders." I cross my arms. "I mean, sure, they broke into our reality and tried to reshape it, but that's just because they can't live here otherwise. Have we ever wondered why they don't just stay in their own space instead? Why bother coming here at all when it's so unpleasant for them, and takes so much work to fix up, and has people already here who keep shoving them back out the door?"

"Huh, you're right," Ned agrees. "They do come across as pretty desperate, don't they? Like they're running from something, and they don't have a choice but to come through here."

"That's not an excuse for invading, though," Tall says. "It doesn't excuse what they've done."

"No, it doesn't," I admit. "But maybe they had reasons, could even be good ones. You can see where a guy's coming from, and sympathize, even if you wouldn't have done what he did yourself, right? We've never really sat down and talked to them, found out what's going on back where they come from, why they're so eager to come here, stuff like that. Maybe we should."

Little Lady Wasp is shaking her head. "You don't try to find common ground with a grizzly," she argues. "Last guy who did that, after years of hanging out with them and palling around and snuggling, one of them bit his head off. Why? Because they're *grizzly bears!*" Yeah, okay, point taken, though I'm guessing she just doesn't like bears. The whole honey thing and all that.

Lizzy pipes in next, and despite being the youngest person here, she doesn't waver at all. "Maybe there's a way to bring them in peacefully," she suggests. "Does it have to be 'our way' or 'their way'? Couldn't it be both ways?"

Jerome takes it on himself to answer. "Their reality is antithetical to our own," he explains, but he's clearly too intrigued to be up to his usual level of snootiness. "But they've appeared here, which means there's some way they can cross that barrier safely, at least for short periods. If we could find a way to extend that..."

"No!" Smith looks furious as he shoves past Tall to confront the rest of us at the couches. "This is war, and in war you don't compromise with the enemy! You eliminate them! Because it's us versus them, it's that simple! The more you sit around trying to find ways to compromise, the weaker your position, and that's how they win! Do you think they'll sit around wondering if there's some way to co-exists with us, if that happens?"

He's clearly not gonna budge—I've met enough people like that to know when they've not only planted the flag but dug it in so deep a tornado couldn't budge it. This is his position, and he's gonna stick to it, no matter what. We could argue till we're blue in the face and never convince him.

At the same time, Mary and I are pretty determined to find

a way for everyone to exist together. Lizzy's clearly onboard, and I think Ned and Tall could be swayed.

And just like that, we've gone from karaoke to *Family Feud*. Only this time it's a lot more vicious than calling out answers and turning over signs. This is a whole lot more Hatfield-McCoy than Richard Dawson.

Chapter Twenty-five
Our survey said . . .

"**Okay, hold up,**" I shout, raising my voice to be heard over the sudden shouting. "Let's all just dial it down a few notches, 'kay? This is just a friendly little discussion, nothing more. Blowing your stack doesn't get your point across any better, and most of the time it's a whole lot worse."

Smith is still red in the face, though, and I think he may be past the point of no return. On the other side, Mary might as well be carved of marble, she's so stern and unyielding. Some of the eggheads've jumped to their feet now too, and they're starting to separate into two groups, the one migrating toward our couch while the other edges to the side, toward Smith and the MiBs. For the first time since moving in here, I wish I had a proper gun safe. Instead I've basically treated the whole base like it was one giant safe—after all, it's supposedly one of the toughest places to break into in the entire cosmos in order to the protect the Matrix—and that's all well and good. Unless you happen to be trapped inside said safe. With a whole bunch of slightly crazed, slightly unstable, slightly confrontational people with a hatred for traditional authority, a history of breaking rules, a propensity toward casual violence, and a complete lack of concern about consequences.

And opposing the MiBs are my family and friends and some of the Fartcaps.

I'd be tempted to back away too if there was any way to clear the couch with my feet.

Glancing around and looking for possible exits, though, my eyes slow to a stop directly across from me, where a trio stands completely silently, watching the mayhem unfold.

"Yo," I shout in my best school-principal voice, and a hush falls over the crowd as three dozen or so heads, maybe four, all swivel in my direction. Old Mr. Levine would've been proud. "Look, we can argue til we're blue in the face, and probably will," I continue. "Or—we can listen to what they have to say." And I point at my three bosses. Which sounds like a sitcom. In which case, one of 'em must be too serious, one not serious enough, and the other is a teen heartthrob for half the galaxy and will ultimately marry an evil mutant librarian. Or something.

Everyone's staring at the Grays now. And they're staring back. Not at anyone in particular, just at all of us in general. Sort of a diffuse, wide-angle stare. Which, come to think of it, looks an awful lot like zoning out. Maybe they didn't hear what I said? Maybe they haven't been paying attention at all? Maybe Lee's been letting them sharing his stash?

But then the one in the footie PJs shifts, stirs, blinks—and that's creepy, since its eyelid is big enough to cover half of Miami—and then opens its mouth to speak. What it says is:

"We have no opinion in this matter."

Everybody just stares at it. Somebody lets out a startled, slightly outraged yelp.

Oh, wait, that's me.

"Whaddya mean, you don't have an opinion?" I demand. "You've been standing in their way this whole time! You built the Matrix that keeps them out! You're the ones they banished to a pocket dimension exactly because you were the biggest threat to their plans! How can you not have an opinion after that?"

The Gray studies me a second. I feel like I'm back on the table, and my whole body starts to itch with the need to curl up and hide. I wish my stare could do that. I'd totally use it on door-to-door salesmen and on delivery people who forget my graxlenut shake.

"Perhaps," it says after a long pause, "it would be inaccurate to claim we have no opinion. Instead let us say that we understand both sides of the argument you have all engaged in here." Ah, okay, now we're getting somewhere! Hopefully somewhere with food. And a view.

"We agree, obviously, that these invaders are currently a significant and repeated threat to our very existence," it continues, clasping its hands together. "That cannot be allowed to continue. And, in the past, we have certainly removed species from existence for less." Really? Crap. Suddenly I'm dreading my next performance review. I didn't realize "obliteration" was one of the possible determinations! Hopefully they'll grade on a curve!

"However," it declares, "we have matured as a species, and now prefer to find less aggressive, more elegant solutions to our problems. And MR3971XJKA is correct, subjecting anyone to the fate of being permanently imprisoned in isolation seems unnecessarily cruel. Although," it continues, showing its teeth in what could be a smile or a snarl or a "hey, there's my dinner—yes, I mean you!" opening sneer, "if such a sentence is the only outcome which will ensure the safety of our reality, then that is what must occur. And if it is a choice between that or annihilation, is exile the more merciful option?"

Damn, I feel like I'm back in college again, stuck in freshman-level Intro to Philosophy and forced to listen to a couple of my frat brothers, all either hungover or still drunk, present their logical arguments. This makes my head hurt in exactly the same way.

"So you're saying," I reply slowly, trying to piece it together, "that we might need to destroy them, or exile them, but we might be able to find some other way, and perhaps we should?" It nods once. Oy, now I've made my own head hurt!

Smith cuts in. "I say it is a clear choice," he declares sharply. "Us versus them, with us being the entirety of our universe and them being only a single race. I think we can all agree that we need to give the preference to us, and that we should do whatever is necessary to protect and defend and preserve us. *Whatever* is necessary."

"Absolutely," one of the eggheads agrees. It's Taki. Because the fact that he's utterly ruthless comes as a total shocker. "The math totally vindicates us. We're talking, what, a few hundred versus trillions upon trillions upon trillions? It would be criminal to even consider anything but doing whatever it takes to defend that vast majority."

"Math has little to do with morality," Jerome retorts. "Not that you'd know anything about that. Cold and calculating as usual, but these are still lives we're talking about, and every single one is precious." It's a good reply, though I do have to wonder if he really means it or if he just can't help putting himself on the opposite side of whatever Taki picks. I can tell that, back in school, these two were the ones everyone else rolled their eyes at whenever they got into it, which would have been all the freaking time.

"So go ahead and save theirs," Taki shoots back. "And doom the entire rest of our universe as a result. Let's see how morally superior you feel when none of us even exist anymore!" Okay, that's at least half a point for him, even though we're talking about trying to find a way to save the universe and everyone in it too. Just without necessarily killing or marooning the invaders in the process.

It occurs to me, though in a surprising show of restraint I don't mention it out loud, that even the name we have for them prejudices us against these guys. "The invaders." What if we called them "the refugees" instead? That automatically makes you more sympathetic. Or "the visitors." Okay, that's a little creepy. Or maybe "the wanderers." Or "the unexpected guests." Or "those guys who keep showing up at your door when you thought you had the place all to yourself and were just kicking back to watch Hyper-Venusian slip-wrestling while eating a large sundae made of not one or even two but three full pints of Ben & Jerry's and an entire bottle of Hersey's Syrup and now have to set that aside and hope it doesn't melt and figure out what you did with your robe no not that one the other one that doesn't have the horrible burn patches where you dripped flame-jell-o on it that one time and wonder if you should just give up and drape a sheet over yourself toga-style and add a wreath to your head and pretend it's ancient Rome or that you're going ultra-retro for a personal style choice."

Right, I'll stop now.

"I'm glad to see at least one of you has some sense," Smith is saying with a sneer, gesturing toward Taki. "Are the rest of you really that naïve, that dewy-eyed and idealistic that you'd sac-rifice reality for something as petty as a so-called moral code?" Gee, Smith, spoken like a true villain. Why don't you twirl your mustache a little bit, while you're at it?

Cab gets up and moves to join Taki. Then Kimura stomps over to stand beside them. Aw, really? I like the prof! But I guess he'd rather be safe than sorry.

Meanwhile, Nathan moves to our side, where Jerome has already stationed himself. And, much to my shock, Theresa does, too. Go, Team Friendly! First task, come up with a better team name!

Mary glances around us and smiles at those of her class-mates who stepped over to our side. And of course my fam-ily, who are all solidly behind us—though that could just be because they're too comfortable to move. "I believe," she states slowly, "that the numbers stand in our favor. We will seek a way to protect our reality without exiling the invaders to one of their own phased bubble-dimensions."

But Smith shakes his head, and for all that I know he's still crushing on Mary his smile is sharp and nasty. "You are assuming that this is a democracy, my dear," he states, and behind him I see a bunch of the MiBs reach for their guns. Tall stiffens and starts to raise his, which had been resting in his lap in a way I only now realize was a little too "I love you, my Precious," but fortunately the Grays intervene.

"There will be no violence within these walls," Mr. Footies announces, glancing between our two sides. "Especially not between allies. We will not allow it." I'm not sure if that means they'll make all weapons spontaneously turn into bananas and mangos or just that they'll frown and speak sternly to anyone who shoots anyone else or something in between but I know I'm not keen to find out, and I suspect no one else is either. Even Smith frowns but finally nods and his people reholster their weapons. Tall takes a bit longer to stand down again, but finally settles back into "wary guard" mode.

"Very well," Smith says. "But I cannot be party to such idiocy. I will continue to protect our reality as I see fit—with or without the rest of you." He turns on his heel and marches toward the door. And Taki, Cab, and finally Kimura all move to follow him.

Looks like the band just broke up.

Unfortunately, I think they're planning to form their own band, and they're gonna call it Destroy the Invaders without Mercy. Which is an awful title but at least abbreviates to DIM, and now I'm gonna call Smith "Dim Smith," at least in my head, every time I see him. So, hey, silver lining!

"Shouldn't we stop them?" Tall demands, watching Smith

and his goons file out with four geeks in tow. "You know they're gonna try putting his plan into effect."

"I know," I answer. "But no—if we tried we'd only get into a fight, which the Grays already nixed. And what're we gonna do, tie 'em up and shove them all in a closet somewhere? Don't answer that!" I add quickly, cutting him off before he can speak. Tall may be my best friend, but sometimes he's a little too happy to resort to violence. Especially when it's Taco Tuesday.

"Tall is correct," Mary agrees. "They will attempt to enact their plan. And the Grays have already stated that they will not intervene, which I suspect means they will not actively participate in any course of action unless the invaders return and once again threaten them directly." The Grays confirm this with a short nod. "Which means"—she turns and smiles at our group, which consists of her, me, Tall, Ned, my whole family, and then Jerome, Theresa, and Nathan—"that we must develop and proceed with our plans first."

Now we're talking! It's a race! I love those. Especially if there's a way to cheat and take a car to just before the finish line. Or if I'm simply watching it on TV, and can make fun of all the guys beating themselves up to run for a week through the desert or whatever while I lounge on the couch eating sundaes and drinking silly drinks with umbrellas in them.

Don't judge. Marathon eating like that takes just as much training and dedication, and nobody ever gives it the recognition it deserves. I should get a medal or something.

Chapter Twenty-six
It's like tug-of-war but with science!

"Right," Ned says, rubbing his hands together. Which, sorry, just makes me think of tossed salad. "Whaddya need us to do?"

"We must devise a plan that will eliminate the threat once and for all," Mary replies, "without destroying the invaders themselves, or sentencing them to a shadowy half-existence unable to interact with either our reality or their own." She glances at the doorway the others—let's call them Team Smith Sucks—just disappeared through. "And we must do so before the others can finalize a plan that will cause the reverse to be true."

I look around at our team, Team Awesome. Because I'm the one handing out team names, and that's what I'm calling us. It's all about the motivation. "Okay, so anybody got a whiteboard?" I ask.

Ned grins, reaches into one of the pouches on his tool belt, and pulls out—a length of knotted rope. Thin, dirty-looking rope. Actually, it looks exactly like somebody just tied a whole bunch of old shoestrings together in order to create a homemade clothesline they intended to string between two trees across a sidewalk and take out a few older kids who'd been picking on them at school when their older siblings weren't there to look out for them. Just as a hypothetical.

"Uh, Ned?" I tell him. "No offense, but you do know that a whiteboard requires, um, an actual board, right? It's less about the color than the size and shape. And the ability to write on it."

"Nah, this is better," he insists. He dangles the rope in one hand and I realize it's tied in a loop. Then he gives it a quick shake like he's wringing the last bits of water out of a garden hose, shakes it again, and tosses it up in the air. It spins as it rises, opening up like a sideways lasso—and, when it reaches about head height, it suddenly stops. Just stops dead, like somebody grabbed it and is now holding it in place, a frame that's somewhere between a rectangle and an oval.

"Okay, yeah, that's cool," I agree. "Still missing the whole 'write on it' part, though."

Ned just widens his grin—I can see that darn ladybug in his tooth now, and it winks at me again, the cheeky little bugger—and lifts his hand, index finger extended. He pokes the air within the frame, drags his finger down it—and a glowing line appears there. He continues the motion, and now he's drawn a big, glowing circle. He adds two dots and a curve within that. Cute.

I have to admit, though, it does beat pretty much any whiteboard I ever saw.

"Nice," I tell him, and step over to it. I don't even have to ask the next question—he rubs his hand over the "surface" of the board, and the smiley face vanishes, leaving that space blank again. "So," I direct the next question to Mary and the others, "what've we got?"

"Aliens!" Lizzy shouts. She is clearly super-excited about this. "We've got aliens!"

"Aliens beyond aliens," Nathan agrees. "Aliens from outside our very reality. Doesn't get much more alien than that."

"Aliens inimical to our reality," Jerome adds. "And for whom our reality is inimical to them."

I write "aliens," "from another reality," and "inimical" on the board. I'm not actually sure what that last word means, and I have to guess at the spelling, but whatever.

"They've been trying to convert our reality into a place more like theirs," Tall joins in. "So they can live here." I add "can't live here" and "want to convert our reality to theirs."

"Oh, yeah, and they have reality-warping powers," Ned points out. "Kinda important." I put that on the list.

Lizzy's hand shoots up like she's in class and dying to get to the right answer first, but I'm momentarily distracted as a small, hard sphere goes shooting past me at dizzying speeds. A hot-pink sphere.

"Hey!" I shout, before realizing it didn't just miss me, it wasn't even close. Nor did it hit the whiteboard. I don't even know what that would've done—passed through without effect, messed up my writing, or shattered the whole darn thing? But the baseball—because of course that's what it was—went sailing safely past the incredibly inviting floating ring.

It rocketed toward the field instead.

And the Matrix slowly spinning there.

I hear the *whack!* of a baseball hitting flesh at about the same time as the whine of "Ow!" I'm already barreling in that direction. Tall's way ahead of me, both because he was closer and because he's built like a Roman god and has the reflexes of a ninja, which is good because he's able to grab Jimmy and toss him toward the sidelines mere seconds before my cousin grabs hold of a piece of the Matrix.

And becomes a pile of "he never lived up to his potential" ash in the process.

Frank's still clutching his shoulder where the baseball connected, so Tall's able to shove him away too without any problem. Then I'm there, and the rest of my family's right behind me.

"What the hell?" I demand, rounding on these two idiots. "You guys can't keep your hands to yourself for ten minutes?" Actually, they really can't. We timed 'em once, at a family picnic—left an old baseball card where they could see it, sticking out of one of those little closets that's up above a door. Took all of two minutes before they were dragging a chair over to get to it. Grant and I split that one—he had three minutes, ever the optimist, and I had one. Bonnie'd pegged them at thirty seconds and was pissed because she insists to this day that they'd have gone for it sooner if somebody hadn't made a noise and spooked them into behaving for an extra ninety seconds. Eddie, of course, claims it was an accident.

"We were just curious," Frank whines. "Never seen anything like it before."

"And you were hoping it might be worth something," Grant supplies, stepping up beside me. "Never mind that it isn't yours, that it's clearly important, and messing with it could screw something up royally." Frank doesn't answer that. He and

Jimmy both look suitably cowed, but I know from bitter experience that's only because they got caught. These two don't know the meaning of remorse any more than I know "inimical."

I should have realized something was up. I didn't notice that they weren't still over by the couches with the rest of us, which should've been the first warning sign. These two aren't exactly masters of stealth, and they've never known when to keep their mouths shut, so if you aren't shaking your head and rolling your eyes at them, chances are it's because they're off somewhere else getting into trouble. By doing things like trying to pocket anything that isn't nailed down.

So of course a glowing, glittering circlet of metal, light, circuitry, glass tubes, and other elements floating in the air and rotating under its own power out the middle of what's basically a large football field would be like a giant "Hey boys, check me out!" sign. Made out of meat and money and dipped in booze. I doubt I could make a better Frank-and-Jimmy-trap if I tried.

"Just so you know," I tell them, "this is the Matrix. It keeps the universe safe from invasion and running smoothly. So if you'd broken it, those invaders y'all were fighting outside less than an hour ago? They'd've come flooding back in, but this time about ten times as many." Now they do look a little guilty. "Also? Touch it and it'll burn you to a crisp in less time than it takes to say, 'whoops.'"

Bonnie's frowning at the cousins, but also at the Matrix itself. "Really?" she asks. "It's that dangerous? Don't you live here and take care of it?" I wasn't sure any of 'em had picked up on that, but of course Bonnie did. She notices more dead asleep than most people do while wide awake and staring right at you. Which, trust me, is really alarming when you're trying to prank her in the middle of the night and she tells you off without even waking up.

"Yeah, but I can touch it," I assure her now, and maybe I puff up just a little. "The whole 'altered by aliens' thing. That's why they picked me."

"That and your bravery and cleverness," Mary adds. She must've sauntered over while I was lecturing Tweedledee and Tweedledum, and now she links hands with me. "But DuckBob is correct; contact with the Matrix is lethal to those not already attuned."

I look around and spot Lila off to one side. "Thanks." It was her baseball, of course, that just saved me from having to Hoover up "cremated cousin."

She shrugs. "Didn't look like something you wanted them messing with."

"The list of things I don't want them messing with includes just about everything," I remind her, "including old shirts I'm ready to toss and milk I think might be past its Drink By date. But yeah."

She gives me a little smirk at that. "Fair enough." Then she turns and heads back toward the couches, her job here done. Is it stupid that just exchanging those few words has me so happy I could dance a rhumba? Looks like the ice and awkwardness might be melting a lot faster than I thought, which is pretty amazing. I'm gonna try not to get my hopes up, though. Just be cautiously optimistic.

And find some handcuffs for the Dumbass Twins. And a bedpost I can attach them to.

"Okay, everybody back to brainstorming," I declare, and even without my asking Andy and Tall round up Jimmy and Frank and herd them back over with everybody else. Between my nephew and my best friend I feel like a small kid staring up at the Colossus of Rhodes, but I'm comfortable enough in my masculinity to be able to handle that.

Besides, my profile's got theirs beat all to hell.

"Where were we?" I ask once we're all back together again. The eggheads hadn't bothered to follow us over onto the field, but they haven't added anything to the light board, either.

Lizzy raises her hand again. "They can alter reality?" she asks.

"Yep. You saw some of it," I remind her. "The whole gravity thing and all that. It's how they sent the Grays packing, too—no offense." My bosses don't even acknowledge the comment.

"And somebody—I think it was Smiley Guy there—thought we could trick them into changing reality around them and sealing themselves off from the rest of us, right?" Yes, she takes after me, right down to giving people ridiculous nicknames. I couldn't be prouder.

I see where she's going with this, but Mary gets there first. No surprise. "You are suggesting we trick them into altering themselves so that they can exist in our reality," she guesses. "That would indeed be the optimal solution. Then there would be no need for them to alter their surroundings, and they would no longer be a threat to our continued existence."

"Okay, nice!" I write "alter themselves, not our reality" on the board. I add a few exclamation points after it. And some stars. And then a bunny rabbit. And a sportscar. This is why I was rarely allowed to go to the board back in school. Except in art class. "So how do we do that?"

"We need to know exactly how they differ from us," Jerome replies. "Then we can calculate what it would take to convert them into a life-form that can survive here."

"Then we'll need to figure out how to force-feed them that formula," Theresa states sharply. "Which shouldn't be problematic in the least." Ah, clearly the team optimist.

Still, I feel like we've got the start of a game plan going here. There's some rough patches, a few holes, but I've played with a whole lot less.

And the nice thing is, this time we've got a pretty deep bench. With skills ranging from "do complex equations in your head while designing a new supercomputer" to "verbally eviscerate someone" to "beat them upside the head with a wrench the size of a compact car."

Whatever else you can say about Team Even More Awesome, we're definitely covering all the bases.

Too bad this is probably going to turn out to be hockey or water polo instead.

Chapter Twenty-seven
Pretty sure that orange cheese dust is psycho-active

Ned is studying the light board and stroking his chin. "I think I've got something we can use," he says. He pulls out something like a swizzle stick with a bad case of mold on one end, tugs the end out another foot, then twists the bottom to make the top split into three pieces like some kind of tiny fungal missile array. Once he's done, he offers the whole thing to Jerome.

Not surprisingly, the nerd shrinks back from even touching the gizmo. "What exactly is this?" he asks in much the same tone you'd use to say, "and tell me again why I am still in the same city block as this?" Can't say I blame him, really. Most of Ned's gadgets look like they could as easily be found in a terrarium as a tool belt, but this one looks downright gnarly.

"It's a full-spectrum chronometric enzyme sequencer," Ned answers. "With a few little extra bits thrown in." When Jerome still doesn't move, Ned sighs and turns toward Nathan instead. "Hold it over something and stroke the blue light on the side," he instructs.

Nathan doesn't look entirely thrilled about being handed something that could have come from a dorm fridge at the end of a full school year, complete with a half-dissolved note that only has a few random letters left, followed by "Don't overheat." He accepts it, though, holding it at arm's length and with only a few fingers, and turns it this way and that. "Hold it over anything?" he asks.

Ned nods, and Nathan glances around. There's still some leftover snacks on the coffee table, so he holds the device over what I'm pretty sure is a Cheez Doodle—unless those Technicolor caterpillars from Arlus-vega are getting in again, which is annoying except that they hum as they move, so an infestation of them is like having the world's tiniest, brightest choral group in your house. Except they can only hum Bach for some reason. Then, grimacing a little, he strokes the blue light.

And gasps as energy sparks across the three spires at the top, forming a wavering beam that falls upon the Cheez Doodle— and then producing a glowing image over the blue light. I can't make out all the details, but I see what looks like rows of numbers or maybe code streaming past, and alongside that is what I'm pretty sure is a DNA spiral.

"This is incredible!" Nathan gasps, and the other eggheads surround him in a heartbeat. Including Jerome, who looks pretty peeved at himself for passing up ownership of the toy. "Look, that's the chemical composition right there!" Nathan is saying, pointing to a line on the display.

"And that's the same thing but expressed in code," Theresa adds, gesturing to the section below that. She sounds excited, which is the first time I've heard her be positive about anything. I don't expect it'll last.

"If we can find a sample of the invaders' DNA anywhere around here . . ." Nathan continues, but he doesn't get to finish the thought because the others all jump in and do it for him:

"We'll have what we need to calculate the difference!"

That part I followed just fine, which is why I turn to my family, who are all crowded around and hopping from foot to foot or twirling a knife between their fingers or twiddling their thumbs or any of a half dozen other ways to show they're getting bored and antsy. "Okay," I tell them, "the Nerd Herd needs bits o' invader, stat. Go back outside where we fought them and start scouring the place for anything that might be DNA evidence—an ear, a flap of skin, an eyelash, whatever. Go." That command gets greeted with some nods and some stares and some shrugs, until Grant and Bonnie marshal the rest and start them all marching toward the door. Whew!

So that's two of our ingredients we're already working on getting—the invaders' DNA and, from that, how they differ from us, or at least from something that can live in our reality. Two pieces in the works, a few more to go.

"Tall," I call, and my best bud is looming over me a second later. "We're gonna need some kinda delivery system," I point out. "How would you go about injecting code into someone?"

"Dart pistol," he answers immediately. "Like a tranq gun, but fill the darts with code. Somehow." His expression at the last word shows he's not sure how that'd work, either.

Fortunately, one of the brainiacs overhears us. "You need a retrovirus," Theresa announces, straightening from where she, along with the other nerds, was busy waving Ned's gadget over anything and everything. "Program it with the code to change them from their current state to the new one and, when it hits them, the virus'll start overwriting their cells with the new code." She doesn't look anywhere near as bitter and sharp-edged when she's enthused about something. It's kinda eerie.

"Theresa is correct," Mary states with a nod to her former classmate, who surprises me again by acknowledging the gesture with a tiny little smile that's gone almost before I spot it. "We will craft a retrovirus, suspend it in a liquid, and then fill the darts with that solution."

"I'll find us a dart gun that'll work," Tall promises, and stomps off toward the hall. I'm guessing he's going to the locker room, and I have to wonder if he actually stashed a tranq gun there with the rest of the weapons he'd hidden away.

And, if so, who the tranq was for, since it seemed unlikely something like that would work on the invaders. Even if you could see to shoot them.

Which has me wondering how Tall's dart gun is gonna help at all. We can't actually make out where the invaders are most of the time. Nor do we know how many there are. Heck, we don't even know if darts will work on them! Maybe their skin's like metal, or glass, or that plastic coating they seal packages in. He'll have to fire blind and hope he gets them all.

Unless we do something else. "What about a spray?" I suggest. "Retroviruses can be inhaled or even absorbed through the skin too, right? They don't have to be injected? So we could load it into an aerosol instead of a gun, spray it all over them, and—"

"—and then we wouldn't have to worry about hitting the

target," Theresa agrees. "And if we make sure the retrovirus—which we'll tailor specifically to them, so it won't effect anyone else—is contagious, and fast-acting, once one gets it he'll pass it on to another one, and so on." This time that razor-sharp smile isn't aimed at us as she adds, "I like this plan!"

Much as I hate to agree with her, so do I. "Heidi, get Tall back here," I call out, and Heidi winks blue and green before floating away. "Tell him not to worry about the dart gun!" I shout after him. Then, "Ned, you can whip up aerosol containers, right?"

"No problem," he agrees. "And I'll rig something to funnel the retrovirus liquid into them. They'll mix with the aerosol when triggered and spray out in a fine mist that'll coat everything in its path."

"Perfect." I watch him go as well. Now we've got a way to infect the invaders with this, assuming we're right. We just need to isolate their DNA or whatever they have, figure out how to match that up to some other alien race for the other half of the equation, write the code that'll bridge that gap, download that into a retrovirus, load the virus into water, fill the aerosol containers with that water, find the invaders, and hose 'em down.

Piece of cake—if you've just discovered that you're deathly allergic to certain cake ingredients, and aren't entirely sure which ones or what is in this particular cake. But you know you have to take a piece anyway, and at the very least take one bite. And then just hope like hell it doesn't kill you.

It's a really good thing I'm practically fearless, at least when it comes to cake.

A wave of approaching noise precedes my family's return

like a panicked herald, rushing in to fill the gap with sound rather than worrying about precision. They march across the field looking excited, with Lizzy and Bonnie right in front as the bandleaders. Only instead of waving a baton or a staff or whatever that is those people usually carry, Lizzy's got a pair of garden shears.

Ah.

"We were out there looking and looking," Bonnie explains once they've reached me again, "and couldn't find anything." She shrugs. "Doesn't help that they were invisible, or close to it. Then we remembered Crack the Whip."

I nod. "And Lizzy had the garden shears at the end of the whip."

"Exactly. She dropped them when everybody fell"—Bonnie wraps an arm around Lizzy's shoulders, making it clear nobody blames the kid for being more worried about surviving a forty-foot fall than about holding onto a garden implement—"but we managed to find them."

Lizzy holds out the shears like they're some huge prize. Which they just might be. "Here," she proclaims. "I slashed a whole bunch of 'em, so hopefully it's still got a little invader blood on it or something."

"Great. Thanks." I take the shears from her, though not without giving her a quick hug, then turn to the eggheads. "Yo, Nathan!" I offer him the tools. "Try scanning this thing. Especially along the edge. If we're lucky, there's invader DNA on it."

He accepts the shears with his free hand. "Thanks!" And

immediately starts checking for exactly that. Mary, meanwhile, has gathered Jerome and Theresa and moved off to the side to converse quietly with them. I have no idea what they're talking about in particular but Mary catches my eye and gives me a little wave, so it must be something related. Which makes sense. There's no need for all of them to be staring over Nathan's shoulder.

"What else've you got?" Grant asks me. I'm about to shrug and suggest they all take five when Ned reappears with an arm-load of jars, cans, lids, and other assorted parts, all of which he proceeds to dump onto the nearer of the two buffet tables. Fortunately, we'd already cleared most of the food off that one, and if anyone really wants more bean salad I guess they can pick the circuit boards and wires from it.

"I could use a hand," Ned calls out, and my family quickly converges on him. "We're gonna make spray cans," he explains, and then launches into a full breakdown of the process, step-by-step. I stop paying attention after "first, grab a can," but that's fine because the rest of my family seems fascinated, and it'll keep them out of trouble. Nice one, Ned.

"Got it!" Nathan shouts, and I see that Ned's doodad is displaying numbers and code and a DNA spiral again. This time, though, it looks a lot more complicated, with a lot more lines of code and a lot more strands to the DNA. "It's definitely alien," Nathan tells me as I step over to get a better look. "Really alien. As in, most of the chemical composition is wildly different, and the DNA has three strands instead of two. I think this is it. Invader DNA."

"Awesome!" I clap him on the shoulder. "So we've got one end of the equation, right? Now we just need the other end. Yo, Heidi!" Heidi floats over. "You've done a lot of traveling, met a lot of folks. And I'm guessing you've scanned most of 'em." He flushes for a second but doesn't argue the point, "Take a look at what Nathan's got. What race do you think would come closest to that?"

Heidi lowers until he's just above the readout, then a light plays from his underside across that display. Is he scanning the scan? Weird. But after a second he drifts back up to normal head height. "Huh, interesting," he says, his colors flashing some blue but also some gray and a little pale yellow. "Never seen anything like it. But most like it? If I had to come up with something, I'd say the D'n't'ronians."

"Oh, yeah, good call, that makes total sense," I agree. Yes, I've met D'n't'ronians. Not socially, mind you—it's not like we crash the same parties. But I've seen 'em at markets before, and had to fend off one that was going door-to-door selling crappy chocolate bars for its offspring.

Is that like a universal thing for parents everywhere?

But the D'n't'ronians, from what I remember, are small, slight, semi-translucent, and float in the air the same way Heidi does. They do have heads and arms and legs and bodies, and they are visible, and they're missing the whole "weird rustling sound for speech" thing, but still it's a good match.

"I don't suppose you've ever scanned a D'n't'ronian?" I ask Heidi. He just turns a deep, rich blue. Yes, I'm sure you are very pleased with yourself right now. "Can you display the scan somehow? Or send it to Ned so he can show it? Or both?"

"No problem," Heidi agrees. "Just sent the data to Ned, and here it is." And a beam emerges from his front, projecting an image just a little above the table and right beside the one Nathan's already showing.

And, just like that, we've got another piece of the puzzle.

Now we just need to be sure it isn't one of those 5,000-piece puzzles where the whole middle is just endless dessert or the unbroken sea. Because I doubt we'd have time for that. Unless Smith and the invaders both agree to take a short break, maybe catch a nap, and come back later. After all, who wants to subjugate an entire race—or any entire world—on an empty stomach?

Chapter Twenty-eight
No good seal goes undone

"**Houston, we have** a problem."

I look up—I was staring at the two DNA scans, invader and D'n't'ronian, like I could mentally just superimpose them and save us all a lot of hassle. Ha, wouldn't that be cool!? Imagine if I had that power, to just superimpose things and turn them into a combo of the two? It'd be like the Reese's superpower—"Hey, put your peanut butter over that chocolate." "What? Why?" "Blammo! Peanut butter cups!"

Knowing me, if I had that power I'd probably open a sweets shop or an ice cream parlor or something. "You say you want mango *and* mint chocolate chip, but mixed together somehow? No problem!"

But it was Tall who said that, and he doesn't usually make such pronouncements unless there's something going on, so I leave my dreams of food-superherodom aside and step over to where he's conferring with Ned and Heidi. "Yo, what's up?"

It's Ned who answers. "Just got a call from Nessa," he says. That's his wife, nice gal, I only met her the one time but she seems cool. "Some weird stuff happening back at home."

"Weird stuff like 'the kids built a rocket out of spare parts and fired the neighbor's dog off to the moon' or like 'it's raining lava and all the cars just turned into giant snakes'?"

Tall gives me a Look—Number Four, I think, "How could anyone talk so much and make so little sense?" though it could also be Fourteen, "What kind of drugs did you take in college because I want to make sure those are banned for the good of humanity"—but Ned is too worried to even notice. "Our power grid just overloaded," he answers. He's got three different gadgets out now, including his phone—which looks like a swarm of bees around his head except they're little glittery nanites or some such—and it looks like he's trying to conduct a one-man symphony and play a drum solo while juggling tiny pins, all at speed. "I'm tapping into the system remotely to find out why."

I tap my fingers against my bill. "Okay, sorry, the problem is your power went out? That used to happen to me every time it rained, back in one apartment. Couldn't it just be something like that?"

Tall shakes his head, but for once he doesn't give me Stare One, "Are you a complete flippin' moron?" "I asked the same thing," he admits, keeping his voice low so as not to distract our tech buddy from his little dance. "Problem is, Ned doesn't have his house wired into the local grid. He's got it set up with its own power converters, like solar panels and wind turbines but better." Yeah, of course he does—that actually makes total sense for a tech-geek like Ned. "So the fact that it overloaded—"

"—means there's an issue in the area, not in the local power company," I finish for him. "Got it."

Ned's now got his phone screen up, but he's expanded it so

there's a floating, shimmering display in front of the four of us, and instead of a person or a living room it's showing several screens that look like charts and graphs and lines of code. Wasn't I just looking at something like this with the eggheads? No DNA here, though—this is more like what I used to get in my electric bill, only live and in person.

"There," Ned says, pointing. It's a graph showing power usage—no, power absorption, according to the header—and there's a steady rise over the last few days, then a massive spike in the past hour. "That's . . . an insane amount of ambient power," he explains. "Even before the spike, it's easily ten times what we should be able to draw." He frowns as he fiddles with the control sticks some more. "I don't know where all that power's coming from, but it's not normal and it can't be good."

"You've got a neighbor who just installed a power plant?" I offer, but it's weak even for me. A different thought pops into my head, and I hate it but there's no shaking it loose so I spit it out instead. "Uh, Ned, how far are you from the wormhole? The new one."

He takes my meaning at once. It's always weird when he pales, because it looks like somebody just whitewashed a piece of broccoli and is trying to pass it off as cauliflower. "A mile, maybe," he answers, fiddling with one of the sticks. "If I isolate just the influx from one of the collectors, the one aimed in that direction, I should be able to—ah." The numbers at the top of the graph change, but the general shape doesn't. He does something else and the graph changes to a different one that has a much more level input. Same with the next two, then back to the one that looks like a mountain range. "Yeah, it's definitely coming from that direction," he agrees.

"Swell." I'm thinking out loud—I've never been much good at keeping the thoughts in my head. Which didn't work out well on testing days. They started locking me in a sound booth for the state tests, which actually turned out to be good for everyone—until I realized they'd left the power on and I became the official Test Day DJ. For about five minutes, until they could get the door open. "This's gotta be the invaders, right? It's too much of a coincidence otherwise. Right about the time they start messing with the Grays and us again, they do something to or around the wormhole that generates a ton of power." I tap my bill. "Could they've broken the lock?" I tricked them into altering the wormhole to their reality last time, tweaking the transference rate so far that it'd take centuries or more to get through from there to here. Then Ned added some sort of energy lock on top of that, to keep anyone from accidentally wandering into the thing—from either side.

"Maybe," Ned admits. "I'll need to see it and run some tests to be sure. It'd explain the energy readings, though. And the new attacks."

"They might've thought, with the Matrix going down, it'd weaken the lock, too," Heidi points out. "We don't know if the lock's still there or not—that power could be from them trying to bust it open and failing, and that's just the spillage."

He could be right, of course, but my gut tells me it's a whole lot worse than that, and I tend to trust my gut. Except when it claims that two am is a fine time to have a triple-decker tuna melt *and* a giant fudge sundae. Unfortunately, it can be pretty convincing.

"Okay, so you're saying we need to pop over there and have a quick look-see, make sure the hatches are still battened down," I say. "I'm down with that. Mary!" She glances up from where she's been heads-down with Theresa and Jerome this whole time. "We need to hit Ned's world ASAP."

She nods, but a second later that changes to a frown. "His world is currently inaccessible through the array," she reports. "I am uncertain as to why."

"It's the energy levels," Ned answers. "I bet they're so high the array's locked the whole region down to prevent any possible contamination. Standard procedure for a radiation leak and this is too close to not take the same precautions."

Okay, that makes sense. It also makes things a lot more dire for Ned's world, his family, and the wormhole. But I'm trying to look on the bright side. "Okay, to the Party Bus!" I declare, clapping my hands together. "That's you guys," I inform Tall and Heidi. "We'll do this the old-fashioned way—with a roadtrip!"

"We don't have time for that," Tall argues. "Not if it is the invaders trying to bust that wormhole back open. Just have Mary take you as close as she can, and requisition a ride from there." By "requisition" I'm pretty sure he means "beg, borrow, or steal," and I'd laugh if I wasn't so stressed. Back when we first met, Tall was Mr. Law-and-Order—he'd never have even considered taking a vehicle illegally! Hell, he wouldn't have picked up a dollar bill off the street without first launching a citywide search for the original owner. And filing a full report about the incident. In triplicate.

Mary has finished her earlier conversation and is making her way toward us, but she clearly heard what Tall said and she's already shaking her head. "The nearest systems are either under Galactic Interdict or not advanced enough for us to acquire any vehicle capable of covering the distance in a reasonable amount of time," she reports. "Given your ship's speed, we are in fact better off simply taking it from here to there without pause or delay."

We? "Hang on, babe," I tell her. "Ned and I'll go with Tall and Heidi, but you guys should finish what you're working on. That's gonna be crucial."

She beams at me. "We have already completed our task," she replies proudly. "We have computed the necessary changes and devised a code that will force the invaders' cells to reprogram themselves accordingly. All that is left now is to finish Ned's spray cans, fill them, and download the virus into their contents. We will do that while en route." Her smile widens. "Besides, this is the perfect opportunity."

I don't get that last part, but Tall must because he snaps his fingers. "She's right!" He actually looks pleased about the recent turn of events, which may not be a good sign for me because it usually involves me either being used as bait or being forced to do a whole lot of exercise. "If the invaders are messing with the wormhole, we know where they'll be, and they'll all be grouped together! We can infect them all at once!"

Hm, okay, that does sound promising. "Right, everybody to the Party Bus!" I holler, raising my voice enough to be heard by the whole crowd. "Bring the can-making supplies and whatever else we need. And snacks, lots of snacks!" Hey, it's gonna be a long flight, and my family requires frequent distractions. Better junk food than taking the ship apart from the inside out.

Andy wanders over to me, his massive brow furrowed. "We're going to where these things are?" he asks, his voice as soft as usual. I nod, and he looks even more worried. For a second I think he's scared of them, but I should've known better. "Those other guys, they're looking for them too, though, right?" Crap, yeah, Smith and his little dream-team are also on the search for the invaders, assuming they've had time to figure out how to shove them into a bubble and seal it for good. "So if they know about whatever's drawing the invaders to wherever we're going . . ." Andy trails off, but I get his meaning.

Tall was close enough to overhear, and the way he's grinding his teeth I know he agrees. "He's right," he confirms. "Smith'll be headed there, too. They set up sensors around both wormholes after the last time, just in case, so he'll have gotten the same readings as Ned, and the brains he took with him will be able to figure out what that means."

I shrug. "Okay, so we've gotta get there first, that's all. And you know what that means, right?" I clap my hands together. "It's a race!"

"It definitely is," Ned agrees, joining us, "and not just a two-way one, either." He holds up one of his gadgets. "I did a quick sweep of the space between here and home, looking specifically for the invaders' particular energy readings. And I found 'em. They're heading for my planet right now, fast as can be."

"Which means," I point out, "that they aren't all there yet, at least. They must've left one or two to work on the wormhole while the rest came here, and now they're on the way back. Okay, three-way race it is." I raise my voice again. "Listen up!" I announce. "The invaders are headed to Ned's world! If they get there first, they'll crack the wormhole wide open and flood our reality with the rest of their kind. The MiBs are headed there— if they get there before us, they'll set up their invader-trap and pin those guys in a bubble like butterflies in a picture album, only alive the whole time. Which means we've gotta come in first, or else best case the invaders suffer eternal torture, worst case our reality ends and us with it. So let's move!"

It's a bit chaotic after that, as the whole crew grabs everything they think they might need and makes a run for the door, but at least everyone looks properly motivated now. We'll see how long I can keep 'em all fired up once we're all stuck on a ship together with nothing to do but brood and eat and argue.

I just hope Tall's willing to change the music, because if we have to listen to country the whole way I'm starting a mutiny.

Chapter Twenty-nine
"Yellow Submarine"
as sung by Johnny Cash

It's been a while since I've been in Heidi's ship.

Actually, I've never been in it before, not in person. The first time Tall met Heidi I was along for the ride but only in a creepy, stalkerish way—I was using a spycam I'd stuck on Tall's forehead, in fact, so I could see and hear everything and he could see me but I was still back at the Matrix the whole time.

Which is why I hadn't realized just how overpowering the décor really was.

The ship is just as massive as I remember. It looks less like a vehicle and more like an old black iron fortress you'd find up in some mountain pass somewhere, the edge of its walls dusted with snow and its interior lined with old holy symbols to keep some ancient evil imprisoned deep within. It doesn't help that Heidi basically generates his own light so there isn't a whole lot of illumination. Then you get inside and wow.

I still don't know if the walls and floors and ceiling and chairs are really covered in black velvet or if it's just some other material that looks exactly like it. And feels like it, too, I discover as I run my hands over the back of a chair. I mean, it could be, right? There's got to be only so many texture and color combinations out there—we can't be the only race to have come up with stuff like silk and velvet and denim.

Taffeta I'm willing to believe is ours alone. And twill I'm still not convinced isn't some kind of infernal joke that got played on us.

Anyway, that other time I felt like I'd been transported to an Eighties disco lounge. Now, though, it's clear that Tall's added a few touches of his own.

For starters, there's the throw rug over one of the chairs toward the back—they're those funky zero-g recliners, really, and this one has a serape blanket tossed over it. The bright stripes show up nicely against all the black, and there are black lines separating the colors, so it really adds a nice accent piece. There's also a big metal locker up against the wall in that corner, like the kind you'd get in the changing room at a gym, and it's just plain, brushed steel but it also sets off the black well. I'm guessing that's were Tall keeps a few changes of clothing, and that this couch is basically his bed while they're on the road, especially since there's also a little table next to its head. Very cozy.

There's a similar blanket tossed over one of the chairs up in front, too, right by the monitors, so that must be Tall's co-pilot chair. And the clever cuss has added a drink holder to the console right in front of that, which is something every trucker needs. That and a good CB handle.

"Nice, love what you'd done with the place," I remark as we all file in. I'd wondered how this was going to work, actually—I mean, Heidi and Tall are interstellar truckers, so this thing's the starfaring equivalent to an eighteen-wheeler, but if you take on a few extra passengers you don't exactly stick them in the back, you find ways to squeeze 'em into the cab with you. Thing is, this cabin isn't exactly huge—it's got a nice high ceiling but it's only the size of my living room in terms of actual floor space, and there's the two chairs up front and another four back here but that's about it.

There's ten of us, I think. It's hard to tell right now, with all of us shoved in like it's a New York subway train at rush hour. I just hope this thing doesn't suddenly decide to go local, or to hop onto the F line instead!

"Yo, Heidi, I don't suppose you've got an extra cabin or anything tucked away?" I ask, trying not to elbow anyone or, worse, poke them in the eye with my bill. "Otherwise this's gonna be an uncomfortable ride!"

"No extra cabins," he replies, glowing purple, which means he's laughing, "but try this on for size!"

And the back half of the room suddenly rises into the air.

We all go tumbling about as it does; those of us standing in that section, while the few who were in front stare and the ones in between stumble back and try not to topple over. The floor moves smoothly, not rocketing upward but at a nice steady pace, and it comes to a gentle stop when we're maybe ten feet up. Then the front edge sort of bends upward and lifts a little further, forming a railing at about waist height.

I peer over the edge and see that, where we were before, there's now a slight dip to the floor, like it's one step down. Plus

I catch a motion out of the corner of my eye and turn in time to see the floor by the back wall lower back down, forming a set of black velvet stairs.

Okay, that's actually pretty cool. And Tall's couch-bed is here, along with his locker and bedside table, so this becomes a private bedroom whenever he needs it.

I just hope the nearest bathroom isn't a flight or two down.

"Better?" Heidi asks, floating up to our level—showoff! But I nod anyway.

"Yeah, much." Which it is. At least now we've got a bunch of us up here, and we can even sprawl on the stairs to get a little more room. "Thanks."

"No worries," he answers, dropping back down. "Okay, everybody comfy-cozy? If so, let's get this show on the road!"

He flickers through a series of colors—I found out that first time that most of the ship is controlled by those color-shifts, though I'm guessing they came up with some alternative for Tall because the only shades I've ever seen him do are an angry flush and a concerned pale—and the ships starts to hum around us, almost like a growl. The walls begin to shimmer, all the edges blurring slightly, which only adds to the effects of the dim lighting and all that velvet. I remember this from before—the sound and the blur will only build, then it'll all seem to shimmy to the side like you're trying to focus your eyes and can never quite manage it.

Only, that last part doesn't happen.

And then all the monitors start to flash red.

I remember that, too. And it wasn't a good sign.

"What's wrong?" I shout, leaning on the railing. Tall's leaning forward in his chair, flicking switches at the front console, and Heidi's practically strobing, he's cycling through colors so fast.

"Engines aren't responding," Tall replies over his shoulder. "Looking to figure out why."

"Maybe I can help," Ned offers. He was up front when the floor rose, so he's only a few paces from those panels and screens to begin with, but he waits for Tall's curt nod and Heidi's blue and green flicker before he moves to one of the displays and starts fiddling, then plugs in one of his doodads and begins scrolling through image after image at lightning speed.

"We're getting power," Tall reports, "but somehow it's not reaching the engines at all." He bangs a fist on the console. "It's like we're just spinning our wheels but can't get any purchase."

"That's pretty much exactly what's going on," Ned agrees, finishing whatever he was doing and removing the gadget, which he stashes back in a pocket on his overalls. "I'd need to go take a look directly, but judging from the readings I'd say you had a break in the motor linkage somewhere. Could be a frayed or loose wire, a shattered junction point, a gunked-up connector, but whatever's going on, there's a gap in the circuit, so your energy from the ignition can't reach the engines to actually fire them up fully."

"Damn." I put my head in my hands, though I'm careful not to lean too far forward when I do that. A noggin like mine, it's real easy to overbalance, and I don't much relish the idea of toppling ten feet, face first. "Talk about rotten timing."

Tall glances up at me, his eyes narrowed. "It is, isn't it?" For a second I feel like pleading innocent, but then I realize he's not glaring at me, just through me. "But excellent timing for Smith and his team."

"You think they sabotaged your ship?" Actually, now that I say that out loud it really does make total sense. Smith isn't stupid, not by a long shot—he'd have to know we were going to be going for the invaders ourselves, once we had everything worked out, and that he'd have to beat us to them. And, with the array on the fritz, he'd have to go the long way about, just like us. Best way to do that? Stack the odds in your favor. And how do you do that with a race? Make sure your opponent can't even leave the starting gate.

Heidi's been quiet through all this, but now he makes a sound like a growl himself, and flashes red and chartreuse as an image appears on one of the screens. It's the ship's exterior, timestamp puts it maybe an hour ago—and there's Smith, his MiBs, and the eggheads he talked into joining him. We watch as they approach the ship, disappearing from view as they step under the angle of whatever camera shot this, and then reappear a few minutes later, looking very pleased with themselves. Exactly like someone would if they'd just gotten to their biggest rival's racecar and yanked the spark plugs minutes before the starting gun.

"That weasel!" I burst out. "That's dirty pool right there!"

"He must've found a way past the security system," Tall is telling Heidi. "Either that or he figured out a way to disable us from the outside. We'll scan the whole ship top to bottom, find exactly what he did, and figure out how to reverse it." He grinds his teeth. "But every minute this takes is another minute's head-start for him."

"And for the invaders," Nathan points out. "Don't forget that we've got to beat them there, too."

He's right, of course. Three teams, one race. And we've just been hobbled before we could even take our first step!

"Can we help look?" Grant offers. He took the stairs back down while I was talking to Tall, with Andy right behind him, and now he shrugs. "Maybe we don't know spaceships but a fuel line's a fuel line and a linkage is a linkage. We can figure out the rest as we go."

"Yeah, that'd be great, actually," Heidi agrees. "Between the two of you, me, and Ned, we'll cover a lot more ground. Tall, you stay up here and keep an eye on the monitors. Whenever we find a likely spot you can let us know if the system's back online."

Tall nods, though I can tell from the way he's frowning that he hates being benched. Still, smart as he is, there's no way he knows this ship as well as Heidi, especially the inner workings. Ned's a genius at tech, so he'll have it all figured out in no time. And Grant's right, maybe he and Andy haven't even messed with starships before but an engine's an engine whether it's made of aluminum and steel or hard light or spinning crystals or bits of colored cloth. Once Heidi brings 'em up to speed they'll be an excellent extra two sets of eyes and hands.

Which leaves the rest of us sitting around twiddling our thumbs while we wait.

Well, not exactly. Mary straightens up and turns to the others. "We must finish our own preparations," she reminds them, gently but firmly. "Arriving first will avail us naught if we do not have our virus in hand and ready to be dispersed." The others nod and start spreading all the materials out on the floor. From where I sit it looks an awful lot like an old garage sale, the kind that's actually someone just emptying out their garage, with bottles and jars and cans and nozzles and bits of old tubing. But Mary clearly knows what she's doing, and she's got not only the Nerd Herd but half my relatives involved, which is great. The more she can keep 'em all busy, the better off we all are. Otherwise we'd be stopping Jimmy and Frank from cutting out sections of the floor to bring home and trying selling on eBay as "genuine alien ship floor covering" or some such.

Me, I traipse downstairs and plop onto the other pilot's chair—which I don't understand in the first place, since it's not like Heidi uses it, but maybe it came standard with the ship?—alongside Tall.

"Crazy couple a' days, huh?" I tell him.

He nods. "Yeah. But I'm hoping we're seeing the light at the end of the tunnel now." He sighs. "This whole invader thing, it's been going on way too long. We need to end it, once and for all."

He's right, of course. It was the invaders that first necessitated the Grays finding me and sending me to the Matrix. Then there was the first assault on Ned's world, now all this. It's exhausting, and sooner or later we're gonna get tired or sloppy and the invaders'll win. And then it's adios reality, hello other reality where we don't belong.

We can't let that happen, and we can't keep giving them chances to come back and try again.

It has to stop for good.

Just as soon as we can get ourselves moving again.

Chapter Thirty
Slingshots aren't just for rocks

An hour later, Ned and the others come traipsing back in. "Found it," Ned declares. "Clever little buggers managed to foul up the energy intake. That's why they were able to bypass the security systems, too—looks like you guys don't actually use that intake at all, it was part of the original engine configuration, but it was still connected so they were able to get in there."

I run that through my head a few times. "So what you're saying," I state slowly, "is that they basically poured sugar in the gas tank?"

Heidi flushes pink and even Ned looks a little embarrassed, but Grant and Andy both nod. "That's it in a nutshell," Grant agrees. "Heidi says it'll take a full flush of the entire system to get everything back up and running properly again." If he's at all flustered or surprised to be carrying on conversations with a floating, color-shifting bowling ball, he doesn't show it at all, but then Grant wouldn't. He's the King of Cool, and always has been.

I'm actually kind of impressed Smith would think of something like this, though maybe it was one of his agents instead. He always struck me as a little too highbrow for stuff like that, which is classic frat-level pranking. I could see him swapping someone's VIN for that of a stolen car, for example, or calling in a fake Amber alert on somebody, but sugar in the tank? I doubt any of Mary's old classmates would've thought of that, either, but I could totally see a random MiB saying, "hey, this is gonna sound crazy but we used to pull this on people back in school, I bet it'd work here." With the brainpower of Smith's half of the Nerd Herd they wouldn't have had too much trouble figuring out where the proverbial gas tank was, and then it was just a matter of getting the cap off and pouring in something appropriately vile. Well played, sir. Which means, of course, that I'm ready to punch through a wall, I'm so mad, but what good would that do?

"Can we get at least partial power up in the meantime?" Tall asks, drumming his fingers on the console. I can tell he's anxious to get moving as much as I am, and probably just as pissed—it's his and Heidi's ship, after all—but he's in full-on problem-solving mode, which means he's set his anger aside for the time being. Me, I'm multi-tasking.

Heidi flickers green and gray. "Maybe," he admits after a second. "We could wall off the main engines from the impellers, clean those out and at least get clear of this place, get a little momentum going. We wouldn't be able to get up to anything like full speed, strictly sub-light, but it'd be a start."

Grant grins and so does Ned. "If we can strip and clean the main engines safely while we're on the move, I say we do it," Grant suggests. "No sense wasting any more time than necessary." I can tell from his expression that he's enjoying the challenge here. How many auto mechanics can say they've done a full overhaul on a star cruiser, after all? I hope he takes a few selfies to bring back as proof!

Looks like we're all agreed, and Heidi shifts toward blue, both pale and bright. "Alright," he agrees. "I'll take care of closing off the chambers. Tall, you stand ready to hit the ignition once I give the go ahead." And his inner lightshow starts rotating and flickering and strobing much more rapidly. One of the screens comes to life and begins to match his color sequences, which looks like he's basically playing competitive Simon Says, until finally the screen goes full-on green and he settles into blue at the same time. "All set," he declares. "Hit it, bud!"

Tall grins and taps a command on the console, which splits open to produce an old-school handle like you see in those fighter-jet simulations. Once again I wonder if Tall got recruited by the MiBs out of the Air Force or the Navy—he acts enough like a flyboy at times. Now he grabs the controls like an old pro and hits a few more buttons, then tugs the stick back and rotates it slightly. There's a shudder as the ship starts up again, and then a definite sense of backward and sideways motion. I sure hope this thing has a backup warning so other drivers—and small planetoids—will know to get out of the way!

"Okay," he says after a minute, after toggling a switch. The sense of motion stops for a second, then resumes but now forward instead of back. Which means, I take it, that we're out of the driveway and actually on the road, even if we can only handle local streets for the time being. "We're on the move."

"Great." One of the screens is now showing a star map, and I try to find Artelusia IV on there. Or Betelgeuse, which Ned says is a lot easier, like getting directions to Kansas City instead of Ottowa or DeSoto. "So, at current speed, what's our estimate on reaching Ned's place?"

Tall frowns, tapping some keys, but Heidi beats him to the answer. I think he's got a calculator hidden in there. "Twenty-eight, twenty-nine hours," he says.

Damn. "And how long would it've been if we hadn't had this little snafu?"

"Two and a half, maybe three," is the reply.

Double damn. "So if we assume Smith's ship, whatever the hell he commandeered for this trip, is maybe, what, half as fast as yours, and the invaders, who aren't used to having to travel conventionally in our space, are maybe about the same—"

"They'll beat us by almost a full day, yeah," Ned pipes in. He shrugs. "Not much we can do about it right now, though. Once we get the main engines back online we can try to make up some of that time, but even so, they're gonna get there first by a pretty big margin."

I'd grind my teeth if I had any. "Crap. So the race just started and we're already dead in the water."

The sound of somebody clearing their throat gets our attention, and we all look around—then glance up. To where Mary is leaning on the balcony railing. "Perhaps not," she states. "There may be another way." She looks surprisingly uncertain about this proclamation, however, and all of us are left waiting as she turns and makes her way toward the stairs, then joins us by the controls. "I believe I may have an alternate method for us to get up to adequate speed," she says, though she doesn't meet any-one's eyes. "It is . . . unorthodox, however, and presents a high degree of both uncertainty and risk."

I look at the others, then back at her. "Eh, you gotta be in it to win it, right? What've you got, babe?"

She smiles and now she does look up, those bright blue eyes piercing me like they always do. "We have inertial dampeners onboard, I believe I noticed? And the way the ship oscillated at first, you are using an inertial system to separate from sur-rounding gravitational fields? Plus most likely a converter to translate that siphoned energy into propulsion?"

"Pretty much," Heidi agrees, shading to blue and purple and green. "Let's us slip right through orbits without getting snagged, like a greased eel." Not for the first time I wonder how some of these familiar Earth idioms made it out into space. Does Heidi even know what an eel is? Much less grease? But I've found it's best just to roll with it. Especially since it means that most of the people I meet can get at least some of my cultural references! Though the movie quotes still tend to go over most of their heads.

Now Mary turns to Ned. "You still have the invaders' energy signature on file, I assume?" He nods. "And by analyzing the data from around the Matrix an hour ago, we can determine what ship Smith and his allies used, and isolate that energy sig-nature as well."

She's got a definite glint in her eye now, one that I usually only see right before she whups my butt at Scrabble by pulling out some word I've never even heard of but that's legit according to all the Scrabble dictionaries and uses only vowels and some-how nets her a cool two hundred points. "How finely tuned could we make the dampening fields?" she asks. "If, for exam-ple, we had specific energy signatures—"

Ned is staring at her, eyes bright as twin high beams, and Heidi's gone a swirl of pale blue, white, soft gray, and warm yel-low. "We don't have that kind of range . . ." Ned mutters, but he doesn't look dejected—more like he's serving up a softball pitch he already knows she's gonna slam it out of the park.

Sure enough, Mary smiles wide enough to show her dim-ples. "We do," she counters, "if we tap into the array. Not for transport, but simply as an extension of our existing systems."

"That's . . ." Heidi's colors are swirling so fast I'm surprised he doesn't make himself sick. He looks like he's trapped inside a crazed blender while it's mixing some kind of fruit smoothie. "I don't even . . ."

"It could work," Ned cuts him off. "It could." He frowns. "It could tear this whole ship apart, too, though." Then he shrugs. "But what's life without a few risks?"

Tall glances at me, brow raised. "I don't suppose you know what they're talking about?"

I start to shake my head, but stop. "Actually, I think I do," I answer. Boy, the look on his face! "I think," I continue, eyeing Mary and Ned and even Heidi, "they're basically gonna steal the speed from Smith and the invaders' ships and use it to shoot us forward instead. Like tying a rubber band to both of 'em and turning them into a giant slingshot for us."

Mary beams at me, and so does Ned, in different ways.

"That is exactly correct, my love," she congratulates me. "If successful, we will stop both of them completely and catapult ourselves toward Ned's world at hitherto unthought-of speeds."

"If we don't snap into a billion pieces in the process," Heidi mutters. He's got some chartreuse in there now, but still mostly green and blue and yellow. "But yeah, I'm game. It's the whole universe at stake, right? That's worth the risk."

Tall nods. "I'm in," he agrees. Then he glances around. "Should we ask the others, too? It's all our lives if we screw this up."

"I believe my former classmates will agree that the science supports my theory," Mary declares, "and thus would be willing to risk themselves in this test of that hypothesis." In other words, they're all such nerds they'll trust their lives to the math. Well, whatever works.

I look at Grant, who shrugs. "Hey, we trust you," he tells me, slapping a hand on my shoulder. "If you're good with this, so're we."

I smile and give him a one-armed hug. "Then I say let's do this." I laugh and grab Mary with my other arm, pulling her into a quick embrace, too. "And here I thought I was the crazy one!"

She laughs at that, too. "Perhaps," she says, hugging me back, "our time together has simply caused me to better appreciate your approach to problem-solving, and enabled me in this instance to apply it myself."

Ha, so apparently being around me has rubbed off on her. Nice! Hey, what if I'm contagious like that? My own little version of Avian Flu—contract it and you start speaking without a filter and coming up with crazy ideas and spouting constant non sequiturs and odd quotes from little-known movies and TV shows.

There are worse things you could get. And it'd be a fun way to stymie all those doctors at UrgentCare centers—"No, really, I had tact and focus just the other day! I don't even know where this Hawaiian shirt came from!"

Chapter Thirty-one
Are trebuchets street-legal?

It takes twenty minutes of feverish preparation. Ned's basically drumming on the control console just below the main screen, which is flickering through different graphs and charts and pages of code like a hacker-turned-professor speedreading to cram for his next lecture. Heidi is strobing at almost the same speed beside him, the screen on that side matching his colors and pattern shifts. Tall is conducting a spot inspection emergency preparedness drill, making sure all the hatches are locked down tight and everyone's got their seatbelts on and there's no loose objects like plates or old family photos to go flying at the last second. Mary looks like she's in a trance, standing right behind Ned, straight and stiff as a statue, eyes staring straight ahead but unfocused, as a string of numbers drops from her lips. She's running calculations, creating a formula that, when piped through the array, will latch onto Smith's and the invaders' ships like Ma grabbing our collars as we try to skedaddle, and will then drain the energy from those two and transfer it all to us.

Hopefully without tearing us into little, bitty pieces.

Jerome, Nathan, and Theresa are clustered around Mary,

typing furiously on pads Ned produced for them. They're double-checking Mary's math. She insisted, no doubt still thinking about that bit in the hallway, and they were only to happy to agree, but I can see from the sweat on their brows and the way they're grimacing while also staring in awe that they're only now realizing what they got themselves into. Meaning, trying to keep up with her. Not so much of a doormat now, huh?

Me, there isn't much I can do to help right now, so I'm just standing behind Tall's chair, hands gripping the back of it tightly, ready to provide moral support. Or strangle the furniture if it misbehaves. Hey, in this line of work you've gotta be ready for anything!

My family doesn't have anything to do either, so they just assume crash positions and grab on tight and wait. This is either gonna be amazing or it won't, but no matter what I'm expecting one seriously bumpy ride.

Finally, Mary stops spewing numbers and closes her eyes. She sways a little on her feet, and I'm quick to release my death-grip on the chair in order to catch her before she can topple. "I will recover in a moment," she assures me, patting my hand. "I simply overtaxed myself." In other words, "I was pretending I was a supercomputer and forgot I didn't come with a built-in fan."

Though she does have me, so close enough?

Our Nerd Herd nod, though they look just as wiped as she does. "Everything looks right," Jerome agrees, his voice strained. Even his mustache looks beat. "At least, as far as we could tell." That's probably as close as he'll ever get to admitting "I could only follow half of that."

"Okay, everything's loaded into the system," Ned reports, giving one finally tap before tucking his little toys back away. "Hit the ignition and the whole program'll launch along with the engines."

Tall's back now, and slides into his chair like a racecar driver slipping into his car just before the starter's gun. "Right," he says, gripping the wheel. "Everybody ready?" There's a chorus of assents to various degrees of enthusiasm, but he nods like it's a whole arena full of cheers. "Here we go, then."

And he hits the button.

The whole room starts to shimmer again, but this time it doesn't stop. Instead, the edges of everything and everyone begin to blur, and then it feels like we're being stretched back—and fired forward with a resounding crack.

I will never look at rubber bands the same way again.

"It's working!" Heidi shouts, chartreuse and white giving way to brighter and brighter blue mixed with streaks of purple. He is absolutely loving this! I guess it helps to have your own internal stabilizers. The rest of us are trying to hold on to something and to keep our teeth from being shaken right out of our heads. If this is what happens every time they take off, I can see why Tall is always grinding his teeth. He's just pushing them back into place!

None of that matters at the moment, though. What does is the star map that's returned to the main screen, and which shows the Matrix, Artelusia IX—and the little blue dot that is now leaping from one toward the other like an ambitious flea that's already filled up on a small dog but just spotted a pony nearby and figures, "Why the hell not?"

There's no speedometer, but I'd guess we're going at a pretty good clip. Like, say, as fast as two racing ships put together?

"Where are they?" I ask, having to shout to be heard over the shuddering and shimmying. Heidi flares a quick pattern and two new dots appear on the map, both of them an angry red. They're both about halfway from Point A to Point B, but they aren't getting any farther and we're rapidly catching up to them.

Which is when one of them blinks out and reappears a little closer to the second dot. That's cheating!

What's worse, when it does that our shuddering turns to actual shaking, enough to knock some of the others off their feet—though not me, since mine are the size of entire life rafts. And on the map our dot suddenly skews to the side.

"The invaders figured out what we were up to!" Ned hollers. "They're warping reality to break the lock and punch forward, and it's screwing with us because we're still linked to them!"

"We need to cut that link before we get shoved all the way the edge of the galaxy!" I yell back. I get an idea. "Keep stealing from 'em, but don't absorb it here—just let it bleed out!"

Ned nods and draws those same two gadgets, or maybe these are different ones, I can't tell 'em apart. Then he sets to twisting and tapping and swirling and flicking like he's either conducting a symphony, practicing a new drum major routine, or preparing a five-course meal using nothing but rice noodles, limes, and fresh ginger. Maybe all three at once.

Whatever he's doing, it seems to work. There's a *sproing* sound like someone flicking the taut rubber band, and suddenly the shaking stops.

"Good call," Heidi agrees as everyone catches their breath. "We were tied in too tight—they were dragging us around behind them, and that wasn't going to work for anybody." He turns pink and brown and chartreuse. "We've only got Smith's ship to pull from now, though."

I know what he's thinking. We may still wind up being too late to stop him. Or the invaders. Or both.

But we're still gonna give it our best shot.

A small blonde head bobs up on one side of me, and an equally tiny dark head on the other. Oh boy. With Lizzy and Lila here I feel like I've got an angel and a devil on my shoulder—only the devil's less evil than just sharp-tongued and the angel's not so much good as mischievous. "Lost the slingshot arm, huh?" Lila comments as the three of us stare at the huge display.

"Yeah," I agree.

"Too bad," she offers. "That was pretty clever."

"It was." I'm clearly contributing a lot to this conversation.

Lizzy's got her head cocked sideways, staring at the map and its little glowing figures. "You know what it looks like now?" she asks, gesturing toward the dots marking us and Smith's ship. "Those old whips, the kind coachmen carried, with a long stick and then the braided cord above that. So they could strike down anybody who got too close."

I turn and look at her. Then over at Lila, who shrugs. It's

very, "How should I know? I just throw literally killer fastballs." Great, glad you could come out for this.

But Heidi's overheard at least a few words, and comes drifting over. "What's all this about, now?"

Lizzy repeats herself, and Heidi—who was shading to brown and yellow again, brightens back up like a mood ring somebody just hooked over a teakettle. "Hey, that might do the trick!" he agrees. "Yo, Mary!"

Mary'd sat herself down at the edge of what's nominally Heidi's chair, and she glances up at hearing her name. Man, she looks wiped, though! I guess mental gymnastics are as exhausting as the normal kind, which explains why I'm always sweaty and out of breath after I've been rationalizing. Who knew? "Yes?" she asks.

"Never mind a full slingshot," Heidi tells her, "can we get a sling effect going instead? Or a whip?"

Mary glances up at the screen. I can see the instant her eyes focus and her brain kicks back in. "Possibly," she agrees slowly. "It would be even more difficult to control, more difficult to target, but could potentially generate an even greater speed." A furrow appears in her brow, adorable but troubling. "The difficulty," she continues, "lies in the number of calculations necessary to determine our course from present location to destination, considering the number of variables involved. I can manage the energy conversion but we must have pinpoint accuracy or, given the speeds involved, we will completely overshoot."

Beside me, Lila smirks. "You want pinpoint accuracy? Talk to a pitcher." She produces a baseball from her messenger bag and tosses it gently but ominously. Like when the big monster approaches but its footsteps don't make any noise.

I think she's as surprised as I am when a greenish hand snatches the ball out of the air. "That's genius!" Ned mutters. He pulls out one of his gizmos and sticks it onto the console, where it stays like someone took one of those little hula dancers and got halfway through the process of making her into a cyborg. Then he waves another one over the ball, tapping it in a few spots and leaving what looks like circuitry staining the surface where he does. After a few seconds of this the ball starts to glow, and little readouts rise from its surface, looking suspiciously like the same ones displayed up on the screens. "Okay, all synched up," he declares, offering the ball back to Lila, who nearly takes his fingers with it. Ned backs up a pace—always a wise move, as long as he stays too close for her to get a proper wind-up—and then indicates the star map, which has somehow lifted off the display to become a holographic image instead. "You see where we're going?" he asks, indicating the dot that's his homeworld.

Lila's glare is answer enough.

"Great." Ned takes another step out of her firing path. "Mary's gonna set up the energy pull. When I give the word, I want you to nail my planet with that ball."

"I beg your pardon?" That comes from Jerome, who had just sprawled on one of the couches but now clambers to his feet. "Have you all become delirious? We're in a spaceship hurtling across the cosmos at hundreds of light-years a second and you want to trust our navigation to—what? A girl and her toy baseball?"

Wow, dude. You do not even know how many triggers you just pulled all at once. I start to reach out for Lila's pitching arm—wincing at the pain I know this is gonna bring me—and on her other side Lizzy goes for that arm, but Lila bristles and we both stop mid-motion. When the cobra flares its hood, you don't keep moving toward it. You just don't.

I'm completely unprepared for Tall to cut in, but that's exactly what he does, with the kind of contempt in his voice that can only come from a lifelong government employee. Or a trust-fund baby. "Do you have any idea how many calculations a pitcher does instinctively every time she winds up?" he demands, half rising from his seat and twisting around to tower behind me and Lila and Lizzy. I can practically see the heat trails from his glare burning their way toward Jerome, who quails a bit but manages to stand his ground. "Distance to target. Height of both target and pitcher. Optimal angle. Wind. Sun. Spin. And they do all that in their head without even realizing it." Tall clamps a ham-sized hand down on Lila's shoulder. "I'll trust an ace pitcher to pilot me home any day."

Nice one, man. I definitely owe you one.

"Very well, perhaps that is true," Jerome concedes, doing his best to keep his voice level. "But that does not mean we should trust *her*." He puts on his best scoff-face. "She's not exactly one of the Yankees."

I swear, the air goes so taut if you walked through the room right now you'd slice yourself to a billion pieces. And probably still manage a few more steps before you realized.

I start to say something, but Lila holds up her hand. "Hold

this." And she tosses me the ball Ned just souped up for her. I fumble it a bit but manage to hold onto it.

Meanwhile, Lila faces off with Jerome like a pair of Old West gunslingers, one armed with a messenger bag, the other with only his mustache and his smirk.

Wham! I barely see her pull out the ball and go through the windup, but the next second one of those pink baseballs is skipping across Jerome's left hip, just enough to bump him off his stance and send him stumbling to the side.

Wham! A second ball grazes his left elbow, and he yelps as he tries to dodge, twisting and taking a second step.

Whap! A third ball just barely taps the tip of his nose, but he falls back anyway.

Zip! A fourth one tags the bottom edge of his right ear and he takes another shuddering step to the side, his face red, sweat streaming down—and now standing back in the exact same spot as before.

Lila controlled his movements as precisely as if he'd been a marionette and she was a master puppeteer. Which is a horrifying image, especially for those of us who remember her "I study comic-book supervillains with disturbing intensity" phase.

I smirk at Jerome, who's quivering on the spot, too terrified to move. "Looks good to me."

He stares down at his feet, and at the baseballs gathered there. Then, slowly, he bends down and picks one up. Hefts it. Studies Lila.

"Go for it," she challenges, standing as straight and tall as someone five-foot-nothing can manage.

His pitch barely covers the distance between them—and is about three feet to the right. Tall catches it easily and hands it back to her with a short bow.

"Anybody else got a problem with Lila piloting us?" I ask the room.

Even the crickets are biting their tongues on this one.

Ned grins at Lila, taps his cap in salute, and turns to Mary. "All yours," he tells her.

Mary is already back on her feet and standing at a keyboard that seems to have grown out of the console. Her fingers are flying faster than Clark Kent trying to hit the early edition deadline, and numbers are scrolling across the side screen quicker than I can follow. Finally she hits "Enter" and pushes away. "It is done," she declares. Then she directs her gaze toward Lila. "We rely upon your aim now," she tells my little sister.

For once, Lila doesn't snark back. I guess she realizes how important this is. Instead she just squints, takes a deep breath, winds up, and throws.

It's a perfect pitch. Lightning fast, arrow straight, and dead on target.

And, with a mighty shudder and a sudden wrench to the side followed by a leap forward that I'm pretty sure leaves my heart about three star systems back, the ship follows that course, linked to her trajectory by Ned's technowizardry and powered by the momentum stolen from Smith's ship through Mary's genius number-crunching.

It really does feel like we just played Crack the Whip again—only this time, the entire ship was the tip of the whip, and we broke loose right at the crack, to be propelled forward at the speed of sound. Times the speed of light. Or something like that.

All I know is, everything goes from a shudder and a blur to a complete whiteout, all my senses dropped in a blender and placed on "Scramble." I can't even tell if I'm still standing up because I can't feel my feet, the floor, or anything else besides a vague sense of nausea and rapid acceleration.

The good news is, if this doesn't work, we've probably just punched a hole through to a whole other reality.

That one had better have decent margaritas, though, because otherwise I'm coming straight back.

Chapter Thirty-two
Careful with the salad

I like Ned's world.

No, I really do. It's got just the right mix of nostalgia, familiarity, and weird to appeal to me.

Plus, they make killer egg creams. And I'm not being literal, unlike Garsacon Veruna, where the fountain drinks might be the ones consuming you if you're not careful! No, on Ned's world it's just that the egg creams're insanely good. In large part because they're made the proper way, right down to the Fox's U-Bet chocolate syrup. That's because Ned's whole world is basically like Brooklyn, New York, as it was in the Sixties.

Except, of course, for the fact that everybody on his planet apparently sprouted from a vegetable patch.

I've kinda gotten used to it by now, which is why I'm not all that surprised when we land—fortunately Ned's world has supra-orbital docking stations, since Heidi's ship is a bit on the monolithic side to be parking on the side street next to Granny's old wood-paneled Winnebago, so we dock and then take a shuttle down to the surface—and find a handful of veggies in sharp suits and sunglasses waiting for us. They're polite enough as they invite us back to the trattoria for a quick nosh, but it's clear it's not really an invitation we can refuse. That's fine too, though, 'cause we really need to speak with the Big Boss anyway, and better sooner than later.

He's waiting at his usual table, right in the middle of the courtyard, and several of the seats beside him are filled but the guys in those quickly vacate at a wave of his hand. "You, you, you, you, and you," one of our escorts, a full-figured lettuce type with floppy hair, says, pointing at me, Mary, Tall, Ned, and finally Heidi. "You he wants to speak to. The rest of you can wait with us."

I can feel my family tensing, prepared to go into full attack mode, and pause to reassure them. "It's all good," I promise. "We need to let him know what's going on. We'll be right back." Then I add, "Order something to eat while you're waiting. The food here's amazing." That gets their attention. My family definitely gives props for good grub.

The five of us cross the courtyard, stopping at the Big Boss's table. He's still seated, though even then he's nearly as tall as I am, and gestures for us to join him. "So, we meet again," he rumbles. He looks the same as before: weathered orange skin, long thin face, strong brow, bright green eyes that match the ruff lining his chin and jaw and the small, neatly trimmed patch centered atop his head.

Trust me, you've never seen a carrot this snazzy before.

"Good to see you again too, sir," Tall tells him as we sit. There's a veritable feast on the table, and at a nod from the big guy I grab the nearest dish—lasagna, yum!—and serve some onto my plate. I'm starving! This does keep happening to me, too, where we'll get caught up in something and have to save the universe and wind up missing several meals. I should start carrying food with me, just in case. Like a go-bag, but with food. But not a go-meal, 'cause that sounds too much like a To-Go Meal, which makes me think of TV dinners. "We were actually on our way here. There are some new developments you should know about."

I eat while Tall fills the Big Boss in on the whole "invaders coming back, trying to uncork the wormhole, but we're here to stop 'em" deal. Ned took some food as well—I've seen this guy out-eat most football teams—and even Mary selects a breadstick and sits nibbling on it. When Tall finishes the Big Boss leans back in his chair, brow crinkling, and considers.

"What is it you would have me do?" he asks finally.

Tall's already got an answer for that. "Clear the area," he replies at once. "We don't want to risk anyone getting hurt if the invaders decide to put up a fight. That includes you and your men," he adds as respectfully as one can say "get the hell behind the yellow tape. Now."

Our host doesn't seem to take offense, which is good because when his kind does get irked the irker tends to wind up at the bottom of the nearest ocean. "I appreciate your concern, and will instruct the residents to retreat to a safe distance," he says slowly, "but I believe my boys can be of some assistance to you in this matter. We take care of our own, after all."

I can see Tall weighing his odds. He could try to convince the Big Boss to change his mind, but that doesn't look likely and could wind up pissing the guy off. Or he could just accept the inevitable, and stay on our host's good side. Tall's smart, especially about stuff like strategy and alliances, so finally he nods. "We would certainly appreciate the help, sir."

The carrot beams. "Excellent! Eat up while I order the area cleared," he says, motioning one of his guys to come over.

So we do. No sense letting good food go to waste!

After lunch or dinner or second breakfast or whatever that was, we drag our stuffed selves over to the side of the courtyard. This is where the first wormhole sits, the one that leads back to Earth. It's locked down tight, though, and Ned checks to make sure that's still the case. We don't want to risk any fighting spilling over onto my world. Better to keep the fight local, contain the violence and all that.

Then we move on, at least our group. The Big Boss has most of his guys completing the evacuation, then he says they'll join us over there. The second wormhole is only about eight blocks away, but its other end is a whole lot farther.

Like, in another reality altogether.

Tall's in the lead, and he slows when we're still a block or two from it, holding up a hand like we're in one of those "elite military unit" movies. Which is funny, 'cause Ned and I aren't exactly Army material—the only pull-up I can do is my pants, and even that's a little tough sometimes after a big meal and a long nap. But Tall is determined to play Scout Leader or Top Dog or whatever it is, and the rest of us don't mind humoring him, especially since he does know about this stuff. "We need to be careful from here on out," he warns. "If the invaders did leave anyone here to try cracking the wormhole open again, they'll be waiting for us there."

"And possibly coming up behind us," Heidi adds, "if the rest of 'em are getting here right about now." Um, okay, now everybody looks suitably scared spitless. Yay for not having to worry about anyone falling asleep from boredom?

We sneak the rest of the way—if you can call it sneaking when there's a dozen of you and you're a mix of clueless nerds and equally clueless relatives plus a techie and, oh yeah, a guy whose feet practically have their own zip codes. Only Tall, Mary, Theresa, Lila, Lizzy, and Heidi are really any good at keeping quiet. The rest of us sound like the world's most awkward and poorly organized parade.

When we're up to the corner before the wormhole, Tall stops us again. Then he peeks around the edge of the building there. He pulls back a second later. "I don't see anything," he admits.

Um, yeah, because the invaders are mostly invisible, brainiac, and so is the wormhole. At least, to normal eyes. "Hey Heidi," I say, "any chance you can take a gander and somehow show it to us?" I suspect Ned could too, but Heidi's equipment is all built in, and he can fly.

"Sure thing," he answers, and floats up over Tall's head, then edges just around the corner. After a few beats he pulls back, drifts down to my head level, and says, "here you go." Then a beam of light emerges from his center and projects an image against the wall beside us.

We're looking at a normal street corner, nothing too exciting, with a shop of some sort just behind it. Then Heidi does something and suddenly all the colors go wonky, like he's just applied some sort of weird filter. "Different wavelengths," he explains with a touch of pride. "I'm tweaking it to so you can see 'em too, more or less." Now there's a big swirling mass floating just above the sidewalk, and three smaller shapes hovering in front of it. The wormhole and three of the invaders.

"Nice. Thanks, man," I tell Heidi, and he flushes pink with splashes of blue. "Okay, we've got three of 'em, that looks like a decent guard to me, which means we probably did beat the others back here, and they haven't managed to get the wormhole all the way open yet." I can tell that the others agree with my assessment. "Ned, Heidi, how does it look compared to last time?"

"Bigger," Ned replies, and Heidi strobes confirmation. "They've definitely been working on getting it open and equalized again."

"But you don't think they've managed it yet?" Tall asks.

Ned frowns, studying the image. "Not completely," he says after a minute. "I think they're going slow—they don't wanna risk screwing up and jamming it up for good, not when it's the only way they've got to get back here." That makes sense—it's like when your sink's mostly clogged but not completely, and you wanna get it working properly again but know if you muck with it too much you could wind up making it worse.

Where's a wormhole plumber when you need one?

"So they're still working at it," I muse. "The question is, do we go for them now, or wait until they've cracked it fully?"

"They'd be a lot easier to take now, with only three," Tall

points out. He rubs his chin. "But if we're looking for maximum dispersal, better to wait."

"Yeah." I glance at the Nerd Herd, who're lugging bags filled with the spray cans they whipped up. They said the stuff'd be contagious, but it isn't clear for how long—if it can only spread for a minute, we need to make sure all the invaders are present when we start coating 'em with the stuff. "So we wait." I turn to my family, sigh, and ask the inevitable question:

"Anybody got a deck of cards?"

Chapter Thirty-three
Spray tans save lives!

Not surprisingly, the first warning we have is when night falls. Literally. One minute it's a pleasant evening, still plenty of light to see the cards by, and then—whammo! Total darkness. I mean, we're talking pitch-black, like somebody just took a Sharpie to your eyeballs.

"Okay, that can't be good," I mutter, setting my cards down and getting to my feet. I don't move from where I was sitting, though—both because I don't wanna accidentally kick somebody in the face and because I don't want to lose that hand. Hey, I had a boat there!

A pair of small lights appears somewhere nearby, starting at about knee height but then lifting to just below my bill. They bob about a bit, twisting this way and that—and then they blink. "Looks like an invaders trick to me," Ned says.

I'm a little taken aback when the moon rises, mainly because it seems to come from the ground a few feet ahead of us rather than over the horizon, and it only gets maybe eight feet off the ground before it stops, but then I see the faint blotches of color behind the glow and adjust my sense of scale and distance. "Nasty," Heidi agrees. "You guys need a little more light?" He brightens enough that I can now see Tall, Mary, the eggheads, and my relatives. The whole side of the street is lit up, in fact.

Which is great for us being able to see, but not so great for having other people not see us.

Whoops.

Rustling fills the air, like somebody just stuck us in a big box of Styrofoam and is now shaking it all around us. Ick. Then, in Heidi's light, I see a patch of shimmering air drift around the corner and head straight for us.

Gotcha.

"Okay, showtime," I whisper, and step forward. "Hey there!" I call out, nice and loud. "How's it going? Looks like that wormhole's coming along nicely, huh?"

The patch stops dead, like it's hoping maybe I didn't actually see it and I'm just talking to myself. Which, let's face it, nobody who knows me would discount as a possibility. Not even me. I was named "Most likely to monologue" in my graduating class, after all.

"Yeah, I see you," I tell it. "And yes, I know what you're up to, you and your buddies. So, how is it going? Seriously, I'd love a quick tour. Show it off, brag a bit, posture and threaten, twirl your proverbial mustaches—you know, the whole shmear?"

It creeps forward again, but more cautiously now. "You are attempting to trick us," it whispers, its voice the same eerie echo they always have. "You hope to get close enough to shut down the wormhole completely."

But I hold up my hands. "Hey, you've got me all wrong," I insist. "I'm just curious, is all. Come on, you know you wanna let me see it so I can despair and all that, right?"

It seems to consider this a moment. Then it rustles again in what I swear is a shrug. "Very well," it agrees. "You may tremble at our progress and shudder as witness to our final success." Good thing it said yes, otherwise I'd have to go to Plan B. Which involves tapioca and a stuffed wombat and . . . you really don't wanna know.

"Cool, trembling and shuddering, you got it." I march toward the corner, and the invader has no choice but to turn around and follow me. I know what it's thinking—"How did I lose control of this situation so quickly?" All I can say is, better men than you've tried to keep me in line—hell, an entire pro football team once did their best to get me to do what they said. By the end of the day I had half of 'em doing karaoke in the manner of Yosemite Sam and half of 'em putting on tuxes and delivering fancy drinks on little silver trays. Ma always says I could talk the ear off a horse and then convince it the darn thing is hay, just by talking so much I eventually make its brain melt. I prefer to think of it as my own little superpower, baffling people with so much bullshit they start agreeing with me just to give themselves an anchor point from which they can make their way back to reality.

Assuming they survive that long.

We round the corner and head straight toward the wormhole. From here, with the lights still all out, the tear in space and time has a faint glow about it, but it's a deep, almost angry violet hue. Not exactly something I'd want to leap through!

The other faint patches in the area drift over as I approach.

"What is he doing here?" one of them demands. "This must be a trick!" Ah, it's nice when your reputation precedes you. Except when it comes to dating. Or checking out books. Or going for your driving test. Look, I know I was underage at the time, but I was the only sober one in the car!

"No trick," I assure it. "Just wanted to pop by, say hi, hear the wormhole sizzle and pop, and then off I go again." I've got my hands up again, and even do a slow twirl to show that I'm not hiding anything behind my back. Nothing here but good ol' DuckBob.

I think they confer for a second, because the rustling increases but also sounds distant, like they're talking but on the other side of the street or in hushed voices or behind an artfully shaped bush or something. Then one of them says, "Very well. Behold, o honored enemy, and know that your time in this reality is nearing an end, and ours is only just beginning!" If it could do a triumphant flourish it totally would, but that requires some things it lacks, like a full orchestra and some lovely satin curtains.

And, y'know, arms. And a head.

Still, for a spot of air that just ripples a little, it does a pretty solid job.

The only problem is—nothing happens.

"So, uh, not to spoil your big moment and all," I say slowly, "but that was basically a 'ta-da!' And usually you don't go 'ta-da!' unless there's something to ta-da about. Something big and impressive. Like a volcano erupting. Or a helicopter landing on your rival. Stuff like that. This?" I scratch my bill. "It's just a weird glow in the air. Big deal."

"That would indeed be unimpressive," one of the shapes agrees. "But what about now?"

Which is when I realize the shape in question? Isn't over to the side. It's right in front of me.

As it slowly emerges from the wormhole.

"Or now?" Another one asks, popping out right behind the first one.

"Or perhaps now?" The third one in line asks as it follows the other two through.

They're coming through faster and faster now, so fast I lose count. Though, admittedly, that isn't always because the math is super-hard. Sometimes I just get bored. Or distracted. Or sleepy.

I'd definitely say, though, that whatever lock we had on the wormhole before, it's been broken wide open now.

Of course, the funny part is, that's exactly what I've been waiting for, and I can't help the grin that start spreading over my face. "Oh, yeah, that is impressive," I agree. "So, just how many of you are there, anyway? You guys ever do a census? A lineup? A karaoke night? I'm just curious how many cups we need to put out."

"We are legion," one of the newcomers replies, but I'm not buying that. Though I do wonder when they found the time to read the Bible. Maybe one of 'em who came through first to scout had the chance to stay at a Best Western?

"Right, okay, sure," I tell it, "but how many is a legion, exactly? A hundred? Forty? Seventeen? Come on, you can't tell me you don't even know how many you've got in the queue!"

"One hundred and seventeen," one of them admits sulkily, and the others quickly shush it but too late. Damage done.

"Hey, that's nothing to feel bad about," I tell them. "A hundred and seventeen? That's a respectable number. You guys could fill a small ballroom. Pack at least two McDonalds. Put on a couple of full-cast-and-crew plays—simultaneously. And still have a bigger audience than most high school musicals." I squint, trying to see the shimmers better. "So you're, what, maybe half here now?" That's just a guess, but I've already picked up on the fact that these guys hate to be underestimated.

Sure enough, one of 'em can't help snapping, "No, you fool, we are all here now! Every last one of us!"

"Oh, yeah? Groovy." I raise my voice. "So it's go time!"

That's the signal for everybody else—Tall, Mary, Ned, the eggheads, my family, the Big Boss's goons—to swamp these guys, filling in from all sides with spray cans out and spraying, to make sure we get 'em all.

Unfortunately, that's not what happens.

Instead there's what looks like a small lightning storm.

Directly over us—and all around me, the invaders, and the wormhole. It's like somebody tossed a crackling, spitting, sparkling blue net over us, or a big dome made of electricity.

And I have a sneaking suspicion who.

Right on cue, an immaculately dark-suited figure steps from a nearby shadow and glides toward us with all the menace of a classic comic book villain. "Got you now!" Agent Smith gloats as his MiBs emerge after him—just how big was that shadow? Did they bring it with them?—with his pet eggheads right behind.

"Uh, hey, Smith," I call out as he approaches. "Good to see you again, buddy. Little busy here, though—maybe you could drop the dome and we'll catch up in a bit?" Over on the other side I think I can make out Tall and Mary and a few of the others, but obviously they can't exactly get to us right now. Which kind of kills our whole plan.

Thanks, Smith.

"Not a chance," he replies. "You may have beaten us here—only because there was some unexpected trouble with our ship—but I will take it from here, thank you." He grins at me, that same "I am a shark and you are dinner" expression I saw on him the first time we met, right before he shoved me into a room with one of the Grays. "And afterward, I will discuss new Matrix arrangements with the Grays."

Ah, I guess that answers the question of how he plans to extract me from his net before he tosses the invaders into a semi-reality bubble—

He isn't.

I hope Mary doesn't have a problem with long-distance, out-of-phase relationships.

For a second I have this crazy notion that she and Tall are gonna teleport in and save the day. Then I remember, the array isn't working here right now because of what the invaders are doing to crack open the wormhole.

Except that they're done, aren't they?

"Shut it off," I whisper to the nearest shimmer.

"Shut what off?" it replies, its voice already that muttery. "The force shield? We are trying, but it keeps changing frequencies. We cannot pin it down long enough to alter it." Huh. Clever.

"No, whatever you were doing to the wormhole," I tell it. "You're done, right? You're all here? So stop whatever you had going on with it. Now!"

"Why?" It asks. Okay, that's fair enough.

"Because I can save us," I hiss at it. "But only if you do it right now!"

It flutters and shimmers and hovers for a second. I can't tell if it's thinking, conferring, or just rustling in the breeze. But finally it says, "done."

"Mary!" I call out. "Array's back up!"

I see her straighten, look right at me, and smile.

Then she disappears.

She's still fading over there when a blue glow appears at my side. A second later she's here instead of there, and wastes no time throwing her arms around me.

Which is a little awkward, given the bulky canvas shopping bag she's got slung over her shoulder, but we manage.

Ned and Lizzy appear too, and Heidi. Ned and Lizzy both have bags. Heidi doesn't, since that would require something like a halter-fanny pack, and that would just be ridiculous. Or maybe one of those beer caps? Regardless, Mary passes me two cans from her bag. Ned and Lizzy have some out as well.

"Now," the nearest invader is saying to me, "we have done as you requested. You claim you can save us. Please do so." I swear, it manages to rustle anxiously. "We suspect our fate is now in your hands."

"Yeah," I agree, glancing at the cans I'm holding. "You have no idea how right you are."

And I spray it full in the face.

"What?" Ever heard a floating piece of cellophane sputter indignantly. It's actually pretty hilarious. I should be looking at the others, spraying more of 'em, but I just stand there, watching. This guy's the test case. Patient Zero. Typhoid Mary. The ultimate Nielsen family. It's do or die time, here.

Which is why I wanna cheer as the rustling stops and he slowly fades into view.

I don't know what I was expecting, really. Guys who looked like Mr. Myxzptlk, little impish types with pointy noses and jaunty derbies? Classic fairies with great big butterfly wings? That's what Tansy looked like, after all—all of three feet tall, cute, blond, blue-eyed, golden-skinned, with butterfly wings and antennae—and she was half-invader. Or maybe they'd just look like tiny clouds, all fluffy and white.

Instead we get—space squid.

The invader looks like tiny octopi, sort of a pale blue-white color, with big shiny dark eyes and short, stubby tentacles that almost form a ruff around him and two little rounded bumps on his head like a bear's ears.

He's kind of adorable. I wonder if Mary'll let me keep him?

"What have you done to me?" this one demands. "I feel . . . odd." It flutters its tentacles at me. "I will . . ." Then it pauses. Its eyes flash different colors, almost like little mini-Heidis, which is a thought and a mental picture I quickly shy away from. "Why does the world no longer conform to my wishes?" it demands. "Change me back at once!"

"Nope, not gonna happen," I tell him. "But don't worry— you're about to have company." Because, even as we speak, the next shimmer over is starting to change into a matching shape.

I guess the virus thing really does work.

We don't have time to wait around and let them all infect each other, though. Mary, Lizzy, Ned, and I raise our cans pretty much in unison and just start spraying all around us. Good thing Smith put up a dome to keep all the invaders trapped in one place.

Thanks, Smith!

In less than a minute, the energy-dome is filled with cute floating octopi. "Okay," I call out to Smith, lowering my can after I check to make sure I didn't miss any shimmering squares. "We're all set. You can drop your little electric fence, now."

Smith frowns. "Why are they still here?" he demands. He isn't talking to me, though. He's looking at Kimura, Taki, and Cab. The Dark Nerd Herd is standing beside him holding some kind of device like an old-school metal vacuum cleaner canister that mated with a bazooka.

"It isn't working," Kimura mutters. "There's some sort of energy drain."

"Whyever could that be?" A familiar villain-ish voice calls out. "I wonder?" Jerome is gloating at the evil egghead trio, with Theresa and Nathan smirking beside him. In their hands they've got that analyzer Ned loaned them before, only now it's aimed at Kimura's vac-cannon. Aha, saved by the One True Nerd Herd! Thanks, guys!

Of course, that means that Smith didn't even wait to talk or see if our plan worked or anything—he'd already given the go-ahead to shunt us all into semi-space. What a swell guy.

"Just drop it," I urge him. "You don't need your plan now, anyway."

In response he gives me that same smile, but slower and even more menacing. "And why not, exactly?"

"Because they're not a threat anymore," I point out, waving at the cute little aquarium bobbing all around me. "They're part of our reality now. They don't need to change anything to survive here."

Beside me, the first invader turns pale blue. "Wait, what?" it asks. "Is this true?" It goes through several more colors before brightening. "It is! We are no longer at odds with this reality!"

"Yep," I tell it. "You're just one—or a hundred and seventeen—of us, now. You can go anywhere in the cosmos. Enjoy."

"No!" one of the invaders cries out. "It is us or them! That is the way it must be!"

"Dude, stop being so binary," Ned tells it. "Welcome to Option C, All of the Above." I really am rubbing off on people—he's starting to sound like me!

The invaders are all milling about looking confused. I guess that happens when you're forced to confront the fact that your previous stance on, well, everything now needs some major readjusting.

"Look at it this way," I tell them. "You said it was 'us or

them,' right? Well, now you're part of 'them,' or we're part of 'us.' Either way, there isn't any reason for two sides anymore. We're all one big happy reality here."

Slowly they start to brighten, until it's like somebody planted me in the middle of a rock concert during the big finale. "We are not at war anymore?" one asks.

"Nope, no more fighting," I tell it. "No need."

"And we can stay?" says another.

"You betcha. Welcome to our reality, try not to scuff the floors too much."

"You did save us," the first invader—I guess we'll have to rename them now—whispers. "Just as you said."

See, told you I don't lie.

I shrug. "Eh, it was a team effort. But you're welcome." Then back to Smith: "See? Not a threat. No need for the corral." And there'd better not be any branding irons.

He doesn't move. "I'd prefer to play it safe," he answers instead, folding his arms over his chest. "Just in case the change is temporary." He waves at his pet brainiacs, and Kimura nods. He and his two pupils have been fiddling with the controls on their weapon. Meanwhile, on the far side of the dome, Jerome curses. Taki smirks at him.

This does not look good.

"Oh, come on!" Lizzy shouts. "You're seriously going to, what, blast us into a side reality for no reason? When we've already fixed the problem?" She pouts. "You're a jerk!"

Okay, I've now met the one person Lizzy's pouts don't effect. "Perhaps I am," Smith agrees, "but this reality is too important to risk. I'm sure you understand." Another nod and the Dark Nerd Herd fires up their gizmo, which begins to hum and rattle ominously. The two of them are having a hard time holding onto it, it's vibrating so much.

Wait. Two?

It's difficult to see through the glow, but I do a quick head count. Professor Kimura is holding the front, the blaster portion. Taki is struggling with the body.

But there were three of them before. What happened to Cab?

I get my answer when I see a pink blur nail Taki right in the temple. He lets out a grunt and drops like a sack of potatoes if it'd first been dipped in lead and then flung from a three-story window. The canister hits the ground with a loud clank, almost dragging Kimura off his feet as the nozzle gets yanked from his hands, and then a tall, muscle-bound figure appears behind him and puts him in a headlock. A second later the prof's eyes roll back and he slumps to the floor as well.

Tall gives me a big grin and a thumbs-up, and I return the gesture. Glad you've got my back, buddy.

Smith turned around at the noise, and is now glaring daggers at Tall. Poison-tipped ones. "Get him!" he orders, and his MiBs tense—

—and then lift their hands. Slowly. So as not to anger the Big Boss's goons, who have surrounded them and have guns pressed into their sides, backs, and heads. It's like every MiB over there just sprouted a half dozen nozzles of their own.

"Looks to me like you're done," I tell Smith. "So turn it off. Now."

He glowers at me, but Tall steps over to him and holds out a hand and after a second more Smith pulls what looks like a remote from his pocket and slaps it into Tall's palm. There's a flash of light to my left as Ned teleports back out and takes the device. Carefully.

"Ah ah," he says after examining it, tutting at Smith. "A booby-trap? Really? Not nice." He pushes something on the back, slides something else, then presses a switch, and the glowing dome disappears, leaving only after-images and the smell of burnt rubber. And a whole bunch of former-invaders standing with me and Mary and Lizzy in a ring of cheering family, half proud and half disgruntled eggheads, and sullen MiBs.

I'd say that's a definite win for Team Way Beyond Awesome.

Chapter Thirty-four
Won't you be good neighbors?

First things first. I turn to the nearest invader—I've got to stop thinking of them like that! "This really is all of you, right?" I ask him.

He nods. Okay, I have no idea if he's a "he" or a "she" or an "it" or a "they" or whatever. I'm just saying "he" because it's easier for me. "All of our race who survived," he agrees.

"Survived?" That's Tall, who's shoved through to stand beside me and Mary now. "What happened to the rest of you?"

"Our reality began to collapse," says another one. I'm gonna say this is a "she," just to be even-handed. "Its basic structure began to unweave. Many of us were lost trying to slow the dissolution long enough for the remainder to escape."

So these guys really are refugees! And they were just trying to escape before their whole universe came crashing down around them. I shoot Smith a "see?" look, but he just glares back. I notice Kimura and Cab and even Taki all awake again and looking appropriately chastened, though.

"Okay, we get why you were so desperate to come here, then," I tell the two refugees. See, better already! "But why try to remake our whole reality? Couldn't you just share? We'd have set aside some space for you." Like Minnesota. Most of that is just snow and rock anyway. Or Arizona, if they like heat and sand and rock better. Or somewhere in the ocean, if they're as aquatic as they look.

Or maybe just a nice quiet office park.

The two of them both flash different colors. They're not operating on the same pattern scheme as Heidi, I think, but I'm guessing the sequence is shame, embarrassment, guilt, stuff like that. Or it could just be them radioing for a cab. "It did not occur to us that you might be amenable to such a suggestion," one of them admits. "We are, as the other pointed out, accustomed to binary equations. Yes or no, life or death, us or them. We are sorry."

I glance at Mary and then at Tall. Both shrug. Lizzy beams. Guess we're all about forgiveness here on Team So Far Beyond Just Plain Awesome.

"Well, what's done is done," I tell our new friends. "So talk to me about this wormhole. Your reality's collapsing, and this thing is still tied in there and open. That doesn't sound like a good thing. Any chance you know how to shut it down for good?"

They both brighten. "Yes," the second one says. "Our powers are severely diminished now, but I believe if we all act in concert we can close the wormhole, severing the connection."

The four of us step back as the newcomers all group around the wormhole. They all start glowing in unison, cycling through colors like the world's biggest string of Christmas lights.

But nothing happens.

"We . . . may have a problem," the first one reports. "In anchoring it so securely, we appear to have made the wormhole too solid for us to close with our newly reduced abilities."

Great. So we're stuck with an open door to a collapsing reality. That's bound to go well.

"Guys?" I call out to Mary, Ned, anyone. "A little help over here?" Suddenly I've got the whole party packed in around me. "We've gotta shut this thing down," I tell them. "These guys are trying, but it's tied in too tight. Any ideas?"

Surprisingly, it's Cab who answers—by laughing. Okay, not sure what the joke is here, man. But then he glances over at the vac-cannon he and Taki and Kimura dropped. The thing that was supposed to shift us out of synch with normal reality.

Oh.

The others all looked as well, and now the whole Nerd Herd is nodding, as are Mary and Ned. "That could work," Ned agrees. "Basically shake it loose at this end, so they can cut the cord and slam the door to there."

"We can adjust the focus," Kimura offers. "Narrow it to just the wormhole itself."

"The second this end's loose, shut that thing off," Ned warns. "We can't risk it interfering with their ability to close it."

"Understood." The Formerly Dark Nerd Herd hefts their weapon again, but this time we're all safely out of the way. They hit the switch, and I can practically see the hum in the air as it gushes forth from the nozzle and strikes the wormhole head on.

The whole thing starts to shudder and shake like it's doing an angry jig, and after a second the lead invader calls out, "It is working! The moorings are coming undone!"

The geek trio continues to fire, until the second invader says, "It is severed!" Then they shut it down fast. Meanwhile, all the invaders surround the wormhole and start flickering again.

And, after a second or two, the glow of the wormhole fades.

"It's shrinking," Heidi reports, floating over to join us. "It's maybe half its size now. A third. A fourth." He pauses, then flares bright blue. "And—it's gone!"

Nice! One more threat to the universe, gone. Go, team!

On to problem number two. Mary's way ahead of me on this one, and marches straight over to Agent Smith. "The wormhole is sealed," she states. "The invaders have ceased to be a danger to our reality—their powers have been reduced and their very nature altered to be at one with our existence rather than opposed to it. Do you concede that they are no longer a threat?"

Smith shifts from foot to foot, staring at his feet, exactly like a little boy caught screwing up and being forced to admit it. "Yes," he says finally. "They are no longer a threat."

"Then you no longer have any reason to threaten them or to work against them or in fact to have anything to do with them unless they visit Earth and its solar system," Mary presses. Damn, you go, girl!

Smith nods. "Yes. They are no longer our problem or our jurisdiction." Come on, man, you should be relieved! It's not every day you can cross "keep an eye out for extra-dimensional beings intent on corrupting our entire reality!" off your to-do list!

"Very well." Next Mary turns on her old professor and his

other students, the ones who stood against us. Though they did just help us shut the wormhole down, so that's something. "Are you also satisfied that the threat is ended, and does not require any additional interference on your part?"

The three of them nod, all visibly cowed. As well they should be—when Mary gets like this, it's a bad idea to get in her way!

Me, I just stand back watching her take charge and thinking yet again how awesome she is and how lucky I am.

Next Mary steps away from everyone, leaving a little room around her, and closes her eyes. A second later, there's a familiar blur to her right, and then three also-familiar figures materialize.

This time the one in front's footies have a pattern of tiny penguins in space, complete with little space helmets and rocket packs. I have got to find out the name of his supplier! And whether they can do the foot portion in "extra-super-crazy-huge-ginormous."

"Well done, MR3971XJKA," it declares after glancing around, though I'm positive it already knew everything that took place long before they teleported in. "Well done, DuckBob Spinowitz. The two of you and your friends have once again saved our reality, and this time it appears you have eliminated the threat completely." It focuses on Mary. "We are particularly impressed that you succeeded in finding a way to coexist with these beings rather than accepting the 'us-or-them' paradigm they encouraged—and that we, along with many others, were foolish enough to accept as the only option."

Mary practically glows herself. I know how she feels. The

Grays are a bit sparing with their praise, so this is a big deal.

They're right, though. She was the one who stood up to Smith and the others and said no, we weren't going to destroy or exile the invaders. A whole bunch of us agreed with her, but she was the one who took the initiative to speak up for what was right.

"Thank you," she tells them. "Please note, however, that I no longer go by the designation MR3971XJKA." She glances over at me, and smiles bright enough to shame the sun. "I prefer the name Mary."

If they're at all offended that she's ditching the name they gave her, they don't show it. Instead they just nod. "So noted," Mr. Footie states.

"They're gonna need a home," I call out to the Grays. "Maybe you've got some place that'll do, at least to start?"

The three of them approach, Mary with them, and stop by the refugees. "We would be happy to assist," Captain Pajama agrees.

The two who'd been talking to us—I've started thinking of them as the leaders—pulse several bright colors. "Thank you," they state together. "We appreciate your assistance, and apologize for all earlier mishaps."

The Grays nod. Then they hold up their hands, and all of them—Grays and refugees together—disappear in a flash like a sideways flare.

Now it's just Ned, Heidi, me, and a whole bunch of regular Earth folk.

Kimura speaks first. "I'm sorry," he tells Mary. "Agent Smith's fear infected me, and I let that influence my judgment. You were right to help instead of hurt." He smiles. "For what it's worth, I'm proud of you."

Cab nods. "Yeah, I should've listened to you," he agrees. "Even back in school, most of us only cared about results. You cared about doing what was right."

Mary studies him a second, then shakes her head. "I should have cared more," she replies. She sighs heavily. "If I had, I might have spoken up about Andrew."

Andrew? I wrack my brain. Wait, he's one of the classmates who couldn't make it. I can't remember why, though.

Theresa joins us. "You mean the fact that he used to cheat off you?" she says. She's not as snide as before, though. And is that—gasp!—sympathy I see in her eyes?

The others all look shocked. "What do you mean?" Kimura demands. "Andrew was one of our best and brightest."

But Mary shakes her head. "He frequently copied off my work," she admits. "And, because I thought he was interested in me romantically, I allowed it." She eyes Theresa. "You knew of this?"

The Wasp Woman shrugs but looks at least a little contrite. "Yeah," she says after a second, glancing away. "But I was jealous of you—smart *and* pretty, totally not fair—so when I saw he was just using you to get good grades I figured it served you right." Now she does meet Mary's eyes. "Sorry. That was rotten of me."

For a second, nobody moves. I'm wondering if I need to get Tall to switch that electric fence back on, but then Mary manages a small, slightly bitter smile.

"I forgive you," she says. "It was not your choice to let him behave that way. It was mine." She straightens. "But I am done pretending, or letting others pretend through me."

All the other Fartcaps have gathered around now, and I can see from the way they're staring that they're finally seeing Mary the way I always have. Super-smart, crazy-hot, but also amazingly strong. Maybe they ignored her or belittled her or fantasied about her back in school, but now they know she's a whole lot more than that, and that it's not up to them who or what she is. It's up to her.

Still, I'd say this awkward moment's gone on long enough. So of course I stomp all over it—with feet as big as mine, I'm really good at that. "Right," I state, stepping over and rubbing my hands together. "Job well done, all. Universe saved and all in time for tea. Or something like that. Now we just need to get everybody home and we can all go back to our regularly scheduled program."

Mary laughs and wraps an arm around me. The eggheads look a little bemused again, but I can live with that. My family cheers again. Even the MiBs perk up a little, no doubt looking forward to going back home where they can once again be big cheeses and give parking tickets to loitering Venusians or something. Meanwhile, one of the goons—a big rutabaga-looking fellow—catches my eye. He gives me a manly nod, the whole "yeah, we're cool, but don't expect us to hug or anything" move, and then he and his pals stomp off, no doubt to report back to the Big Boss that their world is safe once more and that all those annoying flesh-colored people are finally going back where they belong.

Which is when Tall taps me on the shoulder.

"What do you want to do about them?" he asks, gesturing toward Lizzy, Grant, Bonnie, and the rest. "And, for that matter, them?" This time his hand waves toward the eggheads.

I shrug. "The Grays didn't say we had to wipe 'em," I point out. "And I'm getting tired of lying to my family about what I really do for a living." I walk over to them. "So, listen up," I declare, raising my voice so they can all hear me. "All this, the Matrix and the aliens and the other worlds? Yeah, it's all real, and it's what I do. But, I'm gonna need you to not tell anybody about it. Mentioning this to anyone—including Ma or Eddie—could put all of us in danger." I glare at Frank and Jimmy in particular. "Clear?"

Somebody small and dark steps up beside me, and a pink sphere rises and falls in my peripheral vision. "And if you do open your traps," Lila warns, "you're gonna answer to me."

Frank and Jimmy both lose a few shades as I try not to grin. Lila's always been way scarier than me, but it's nice to have that back on my side after all this time.

"No worries, little bro," Grant states for everyone. "You know we've got your back." There's nods and agreements all around, and I blink back a tear or two. My family may be weird, and a little nuts, and wanted in several counties, but they're still mine, and I do know they're behind me. And that means an awful lot.

Then Lizzy wraps her arms around me. "Can I come visit again sometime?" she asks. "I wanna see the whole place properly!"

I laugh and squeeze her back. "Yeah, 'course you can." I turn to Lila. "You too."

Was that a smile for just a second there? Then she punches me in the arm. "I just might." She makes it sound like a threat, but that's the way Lila says everything. Even "Happy Birthday," which is just creepy. You do *not* want to hear her shout "Surprise!" But the fact that she's saying it at all almost overwhelms me, and I do my best to keep those emotions locked down. Damn it, nobody needs a big man-duck getting all weepy in the middle of the street!

Completely unexpectedly, it's Jerome who saves the day, at least as far as my composure is concerned. "Now that all of the congratulations have been made," he drawls, arrogant smirk fully in place once more, "would it be too much trouble to be returned to our old alma mater? I believe some of us still have a reunion to attend."

I grin at him. "Heck, yeah! Universe saved, check. Time to get our party on!"

He looks like he's gonna swallow that mustache when he realizes I'm serious about accompanying him back, which puts another smile on my face and makes Mary giggle.

Sorry, pal. You may have five PhDs, but I've got an honorary Doctorate in Life of the Party. Chew on that along with that mustache!

Epilogue
Suckered by a punchbowl

"Okay, we're back!" I shout as we shove open the doors and enter the auditorium. "Did y'all miss us?"

The dead silence that follows, and the cold, disbelieving looks that go with it, couldn't be more dismissive if I'd just farted in the middle of a funeral.

Cab and Jerome and the others are right behind us, though, and once they also file in the temperature in the room rises back up to something approaching normal. Conversation starts back up again here and there, though it still resembles a book club meeting or maybe an actuarials conference. Whee.

It does make me wish I'd actually brought my kin with us. I'd wanted to, but didn't feel it was entirely appropriate—after all, it isn't my reunion! So instead, after a whole bunch of hugs and fist-bumps and all the rest, I left Ned and Tall to shepherd both Smith and his MiBs and my family back to New York while Mary and I took the Nerd Herd back here to good ol' Fartcap. Where, clearly, things have been rocking and rolling just as much without us as they were before.

"Ah, Mirabella!" I look over and there's the Doggie Dean, making his way toward us. "We had wondered where you had run off to!" He glances about. "And with Jerome and several of the others as well! I trust everything is all right?" He glances at me from under those hairy brows like he's wondering if I'm somehow bothering her and need to be removed. Um, no, Professor Pekingese, We're all good here, thanks.

"Thank you, Dean Pickens," Mary replies. "It is lovely to see you again. I apologize for our disappearance earlier—Jerome and the others and I wished to revisit some of our old haunts, such as the astrophysics wing of the library, and prevailed upon Professor Kimura to take us." Oh, wow, a section of the library? Hold me back! No wonder this place is so hopping!

But the Terrier Teacher buys it. "Oh, of course," he says, clasping one of her hands in his. "How delightful! You look well, my dear. I hope you have been leading a rich and fulfilling life. Such a shame Andrew could not attend—I know how close you two were."

I see her lips tighten and her eyes flash, and for just a second I think Mary's gonna blow her top. Maybe expose ol' Andrew's secret right then and there. And if she does, I'm totally with her. But, instead, she composes herself and just smiles. "Yes, I had hoped to see him," she agrees, sweet as apple pie. "We have some reminiscences to exchange." That last part comes with a bit of a bite, and I try not to laugh. Maybe she'll just 'port over to the Space Station and set Andy straight on a few things. Wouldn't that be a hoot!

The Labrador Lecturer nods, mutters a few more platitudes, gives me a vague "I'm not sure who you are but I'm not going to say anything in case you were a student and I'm just going senile" look, and then wanders off. Whew!

Once he's gone, Mary turns to me. "I fear the atmosphere here is not entirely to my liking," she states softly, and there's a twinkle to her eye. "Perhaps my former classmates would appreciate it if we were to increase the volume."

I've gotten pretty good at translating Mary-speak into normal English. "You mean crank it up a notch?" I ask, rubbing my hands together. "I'm all for it!" I pull out a little metal canister about the size of my index finger and uncork it. "Come forth, my pets!" I shout as the nanites inside burst out, rising like a small, glittering metal cloud. "Rise and be free!" We watch as they scatter themselves across the ceiling.

"Are those . . . ?" Mary asks, raising an eyebrow.

"Ned's phone? Yeah. I asked him if I could borrow it." I shrug. "Thought we might need a little added entertainment." I tap the canister, which remains linked to the cloud. "Hit it, boys!" Good thing I asked Ned to program this in for me, just in case.

The phone switches on. But of course its components are now spread out all over the room. But that's fine, because I didn't have him set it up to work as a normal screen.

Instead, each of the nanites emits a beam of light to one of its fellows. Now there's a grid of thin, glowing beams laced back and forth on the ceiling.

Then the music kicks in. Each nanite has a speaker inside it, and those mini-machines pack a lot of power! As the beat picks up, the lights start to pulse in time, then change color, then shift, sweeping down over the crowd.

Instant laser-light concert. Also known as college reunion, DuckBob style!

"Everybody, dance!" I shout, grabbing Mary's hand. Out of the corner of my eye I see Kimura thrashing his heart out, and Nathan getting jiggy with it. Jerome and Taki are doing their best, though they're all pretty stiff. Cab actually launches into some old-school breakdancing, and he's surprisingly good. But Theresa is the one who shocks me. She grabs a passing nerd by the hand and, I kid you not, launches into a tarantella.

Maybe she figures arachnids aren't that far from wasps?

Anyway, before too long about a third of the people are dancing to some degree, and this place is feeling more like a party and less like a morticians' final exam. Mary and I are definitely into it, and she's got her arms draped over my shoulders, so I'm feeling no pain.

"Thank you," she tells me, leaning in a little so I can hear her over the music.

"Hey, any time," I reply. "Uh, for what, exactly? Just so I remember to do it again."

"For accompanying me," she answers. "And for always believing in me." She plants a sweet little kiss on my cheek.

"Oh, pshaw," I tell her. "Happy to. You know I'd go anywhere with you. Besides, who'd want to miss all this excitement?"

We both laugh at that, but to be honest, I am having a good time. And it's cool to get to see some of where Mary came from, and meet some of the folks she knew back then.

Still, they knew her then. I'm the one who gets to know her now. A few of them got a glimpse of how awesome she is, and

I'm glad. But I'm the one who gets to see her all the time, and who really knows how amazing she can be.

Which makes me the luckiest duck-guy in the world.

Especially if we can make our way over to that punchbowl—and I can manage to doctor it with the Sonalian fire-rum Tall slipped me.

Then we've got a party!

The End

About the Author

Aaron Rosenberg has not been altered by aliens, as far as he's aware. He is, however, very silly, and he and DuckBob have similar taste in shirts.

When Aaron isn't busy taste-testing fried chicken and barbeque or watching movies or sleeping, he's writing. So far he's written roleplaying games (including the award-winning *Gamemastering Secrets* plus work for *Warhammer, Dungeons & Dragons, Deadlands, Vampire: The Masquerade*, and many others), children's books (such as the middle-grade series Pete and Penny's Pizza Puzzles, the #1 bestselling *42: Jackie Robinson Story*, and books for *iCarly, Ben10, Chaotic*, and *Transformers Animated*), educational books (including books about cryptology, history, and the Bermuda Triangle), and of course novels (like his two WarCraft novels, his Daemon Gates Warhammer trilogy, *Stargate: Atlantis: Hunt & Run*, and the Eureka novels *Substitution Method* and *Road Less Traveled*). He is also the author of the *Dread Remora* space-opera series, the O.C.L.T. paranormal thriller series with David Niall Wilson, the Relicant Chronicles epic fantasy series with Steven Savile, and the *ReDeus* urban fantasy series with Robert Greenberger and Paul Kupperberg. If he did meet Grays, he'd probably ask them to increase his typing speed.

Aaron lives in New York City with his family, and makes sure to always have a MetroCard and a finger puppet handy. You can read more about his life and his books at gryphonrose.com or follow him on Twitter @gryphonrose.

Missed out on DuckBob's first adventure?
No problem!
Here's the opening chapter of

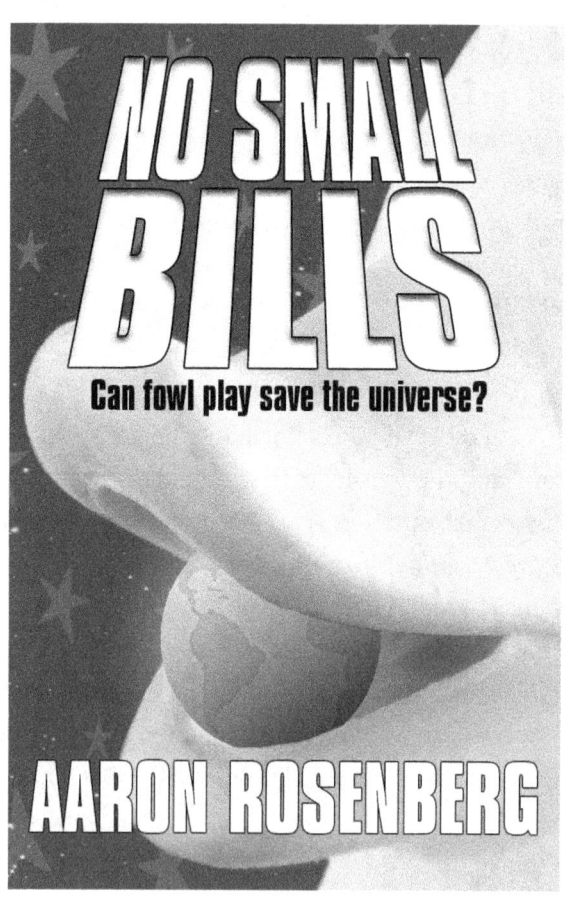

Chapter One
DuckBob, meet the Universe.
Universe, meet DuckBob.

Ever have one of those days where nothing ever seems to go quite right? Where you miss the train by seconds each time, fumble your change at the snack machine, click away from the porn site too slow to fool your supervisor, kick yourself in the head when you're trying to tie your shoe, take a swig of your beer only to realize it's a canister of baking soda instead?

That's pretty much every day for me.

The name's DuckBob. DuckBob Spinowitz. No, that's not a nickname or a pet name or any of that other funny stuff. It's my name. I had it legally changed. Figured it was easier to join 'em than try to stop 'em, and when you beat 'em to the punch, it stops being funny. A little. Sometimes. Why "DuckBob"? Well, okay, here's the thing—

—I've got the head of a duck.

I know, right now you're thinking, "oh, he's got a flat nose" or "he's got a weak chin and a high forehead" or "he must have feathery blond hair." No. That's not it at all.

I.

Have.

The head of.

A duck.

Really. My head? It's that of a mallard—a Wood Duck, to be precise. Complete with black-tipped red-and-white bill, white below the bill and down the front of the neck, a touch of yellow rising up from the bill and leading to a white streaks above red eyes, and emerald green feathers covering the rest, with a few white streaks mixed in.

A duck.

Only, y'know, man-sized.

I've also got webbed feet. And feathers instead of hair. All over. Soft downy feathers, looks just like fine hair until you feel it. Speckled brown down the chest and on the feet, tan across the arms and hands, emerald green on the back (yes, all the way down!), and white on the belly, groin, and legs.

It's pretty slick-looking, actually. If I were a crazed xenobiologist with leanings toward ornithology, I'd say I was an impressive specimen. I even won a few awards at bird shows, before I was disqualified—seems the entry and the owner can't be the same person. Purists.

Plus there was that whole "disrobing in public" thing. But hey, is it my fault they wouldn't take my word for it about the feathers, y'know, Down Below?

On the plus side, I can walk in the rain and not get wet. And swimming? Fuggedaboutit.

No, I wasn't born this way. And no, I don't want to talk about it. Just another example of the colossal bad luck that routinely plagues my life. Because that's what it was—bad luck. I mean, was it my fault I was hiking through a restricted area in the Catskills in the dead of night, waving a lighter in one hand and a neon-orange fishing pole in the other? While naked?

Long story. There was a girl involved. At least I certainly hope so, because otherwise I've got no excuse.

Beyond that—let's just say that, all those stories about alien abductions and crazy experiments? They don't know the half of it. Those little gray buggers are downright cruel.

So you're probably thinking, "Okay, this guy's half man, half duck. That's weird. I'll bet he's a superhero, with a face like that—DuckBob the Aquatic Avenger. Or a mad scientist. Or a professional deep-sea diver. Or at least a sunglasses model."

Nope. Sorry. I'm just your ordinary average guy, and when I'm dressed I look completely normal, 'cept for the whole duck-head thing. I'm no superhero. I work at—aw hell, does it even matter what the name is, really? It's an office job, okay? I'm a pencil pusher, and not even a glorified one. I shuffle papers and push buttons in a little cubicle all day. Then I leave.

Whee.

Some life, huh? Well, it beats the alternatives. At least that's what I like to tell myself. Hey, whatever it takes to get through the day. For me that usually includes watching a few minutes from old Donald Duck cartoons at some point. It's about the only way I can convince myself things could be worse. Look like this, not be able to talk straight, and be forced to walk around with my butt and my business hanging out all the time? Yeah, that would pretty much be the last straw.

Anyway, I'm used to being the butt of some cosmic joke. That being said, I was still surprised when I walked into work one Tuesday and two guys suddenly showed up alongside me and grabbed me by the arms. Big guys, too—they lifted me right off my feet, and I'm not small myself. Plus the bill weighs a lot— I've got amazing neck muscles.

"Hey, what's the big idea?" I demanded as they turned and carried me back out the door. "I've gotta punch in!"

"Mr. Spinowitz?" One of them asked. He had a face like a microwaved potato—squishy and overflowing—and a voice like a hoarse bulldog. He was wearing a suit, a dark one, and I was pretty sure I heard fabric tear each time he shifted.

"Yeah. Who the hell are you guys?"

"We need to speak with you about an urgent matter of national security," the other guy said. He was taller than his buddy, athletic where Mr. Potato Head was just squat. (I'm big-boned and slightly rotund, by the way. It's the slacker lifestyle that does it.) Matching suit, though. I thought that was sweet. Like jewelry but washable.

"National security? I was just curious what sort of brownie recipes it had," I said quickly. "I didn't try any of the other stuff, and even if I did Missus Gries down the hall had it coming! I'm sure the twitching will stop soon!"

The shorter guy raised an eyebrow but shook his head. "That's not why we're here."

"What, then?" I thought for a second, then gasped. "Oh, come on! I know the porn was from Yugoslavia but I only traded an old Steve McQueen movie for it! It's not like I was selling state secrets! It's not even a clean copy!"

By this time we'd reached the curb, and a big black sedan idling there. Mr. Potato Head opened the passenger door and slid in, then Mr. Tall shoved me in after him. I've never understood the whole "dark sedan with government plates" thing, actually. Why that kind of car? Why not those crazy monster SUVs, so the agents can drive over anyone who gets in their way? And nobody'd escape custody—it's not like you can get out of one of those without a ladder and some pitons. Or go for sports cars, classy and great in a car chase. Or the old kidnapper classic, the white Econoline van—cheap, ubiquitous, and now with faster sliding doors! Or maybe something to counteract their whole "we're not really on your side after all" image. I bet government agencies wouldn't seem half as scary if they all drove brightly colored compact cars or minivans with "My Kid's an Honors Student" bumper stickers.

Instead, there I was in the back of a dark sedan. The windows were tinted—I could have made faces at my co-workers and they'd never have known. Not that I can do many faces anymore—duckbills are not very versatile. I'm great at Charades, though. As long as it involves water fowl.

"Where're we going?" I asked as the car pulled away—there must have been a third guy driving but I couldn't see him. "Who are you? What do you want from me? Say, what's that?" That last one I asked while pointing at the Empire State Building, just to get a reaction. I did. They looked at me like I was a moron. I know that look all too well.

With a head like mine, it's hard getting people to take you seriously.

"Our superiors want to speak with you," the taller guy answered.

"They never heard of the phone?"

He glared at me. "It's a matter of national security."

"Yeah, you said that already. Couldn't they have used a nationally secure phone?"

That got snorts from both of them, and I think from the driver as well. "No such thing," Mr. Potato Head said. "You have any idea how easy it is to tap into a cell phone conversation?"

"No. Could you show me? I'd love to know what my boss says about me." Though actually I think I have a pretty good idea. "Quack, quack" is surprisingly easy to lip read.

They didn't answer, and we spent the rest of the ride in silence. I hate silence. It gives me time to think.

Finally we pulled into a building down near the south piers. A warehouse, it looked like, on a narrow street full of warehouses. I didn't see a sign or a street number or anything. Which I guess was the point.

"Out," Mr. Tall demanded once we'd stopped and the garage door clanked shut again. He got out first and Mr. Potato Head shoved me from behind to make me move, then clambered out after me. Maybe his door was broken. I looked around as I got out but it just looked like a warehouse. There was a guy standing there watching us, though. Average height, skinny as a razor blade, with features to match and glossy black hair that looked painted on. Same suit as my escorts but his looked better on him.

"Mr. Spinowitz? I'm Mr. Smith," he said, offering his hand. "Thank you for joining us."

"I didn't really have a choice," I pointed out, but I shook hands with him anyway. Hell, I was in a nondescript warehouse somewhere in Manhattan with at least four guys, all of them probably armed. Being rude didn't sound like a good idea.

"I apologize for our insistence," Smith explained. "But this is an urgent matter and we couldn't risk you refusing our invitation."

"Okay, so I'm here." I glanced around again. Nothing to see but rusty walls and stairs and railings, concrete floor, the car we'd pulled up in, and us. "What's this all about?"

Smith started to say something, stopped, and started again. "We have a situation, and we think you may be uniquely qualified to handle it for us," he said finally.

"Qualified? Me? You haven't read my performance reviews. What makes me so qualified?"

Smith pointed at my head. "That."

"Oh."

"Yes. You see, we've been approached by extraterrestrials. We have no idea what they want, and none of our attempts to communicate have worked. But you've encountered them before—we hoped that might have granted you some rapport with them."

I stared at him, at the guys behind me, and then back at him again. "Let me get this straight—you've got some aliens you want to talk to, and you want me to do the talking because I got abducted and given a duck head so you figure I can relate to them better? Are you mental?" Okay, I might have forgot about the whole not-pissing-off-the-men-with-guns thing.

"You may be correct," Smith admitted. He actually didn't look pissed-off at all, which was unusual for anyone I talk to. "But we have little to lose at this point, and it seemed an avenue worth exploring. Would you be willing to make the attempt? For the good of your country?" Man, this guy was good! Those callers from the Fraternal Order of Police had nothing on him!

I took time to think about it, though. I didn't want to just jump into anything. "Yeah, okay, sure."

"Excellent!" He actually rubbed his hands together. I thought they only did that in cheesy movies. "Come along, it's right this way." I followed him to the back of the warehouse, which had several doors. The floor above continued back past this point so I was looking at the doors to several rooms rather than a whole set of back doors. Which makes sense because why would anyone need more than one back door, especially all in a row? Why not just have one great big giant door? Smith gestured toward the door to the left. "After you."

"Oh, the alien's in there?" He nodded. "And you want me to talk to it?" Another nod. "Alone?" Nod number three—one more and I walked. "But you just said 'after you'—doesn't that mean you're going in with me?"

Smith smiled then, which looked like something you'd see on a buzzard that suddenly found itself at a breakfast buffet. "I lied." He indicated the door again, and rested one hand on his side. Right below the bulge I suspected was his gun—either that or he had a hideous growth under his left arm. Either way I figured I'd better do what he wanted.

"Okay, okay, I'm going." I turned the knob and pulled the

door halfway open. At least it looked dark on the other side, no blinding lights and sets of examining tables and rows of glistening tools. Not that I think about such things. Much. Ever.

"Right." I took a deep breath. "Here goes." And I stepped inside.

And promptly screamed as the door slammed shut behind me. Then the lights came on, showing me four plain metal chairs and a small folding table—and the little figure sitting in one of the chairs facing the table.

Short, skinny, gray skin, huge head, huge eyes, no hair. An alien. Just like the ones who . . . anyway, an alien.

Though I wondered where he'd gotten the Halloween-themed footy pajamas. Those didn't seem like standard issue. At least the black-bat pattern went with his skin tone and his eyes.

I was trying hard not to panic. I figured I could always do that later, in a pinch. I'm good at spontaneous panic. Also, shooting spitballs. I've got wicked velocity.

Right now, though, I figured the best thing was just to get this over with. Face my fear. All that.

"Uh, hi." I like to think my voice didn't shake much at all. I walked over to the table and leaned over it so we were roughly face-to-face. "I'm Bob. DuckBob. Um, have we met?"